T0149280

TASTE THE DARKNESS

"If I take your blood, I'll be bound to you," she warned in a husky voice.

Ryshi shrugged. He didn't know the intimate details of a mating, but he did know that once they shared blood their union would be indestructible.

"We're already bound together. The blood merely makes it official."

"You're sure?" she pressed.

"It's the one thing that I have ever been sure of," he assured her, once again offering his neck.

This time, Sofie didn't hesitate. Like a snake, she struck with blinding speed, sinking her fully extended fangs deep into his throat.

Ryshi jerked, his hands grasping her hips as the pain that was on the right side of bliss seared him.

Who knew the feel of her fangs could create an erotic tidal wave that threatened to overwhelm him? Or that each suck of his blood could make his erection twitch in response?

It was glorious.

Moaning in approval, Ryshi positioned himself between her legs and with one steady thrust buried himself in her body. They moaned in unison, both savoring the intense satisfaction as they at last surrendered to their desire...

Also by Alexandra Ivy

Sate the Darkness

Alexandra Ivy

LYRICAL PRESS
Kensington Publishing Corp.
www.kensingtonbooks.com

LYRICAL PRESS BOOKS are published by

Kensington Publishing Corp.
119 West 40th Street
New York, NY 10018

All Kensington titles, imprints, and distributed lines are available at special quantity discounts for bulk purchases for sales promotion, premiums, fund-raising, educational, or institutional use.

Special book excerpts or customized printings can also be created to fit specific needs. For details, write or phone the office of the Kensington Sales Manager: Kensington Publishing Corp., 119 West 40th Street, New York, NY 10018. Attn. Sales Department. Phone: 1-800-221-2647.

First Electronic Edition: February 2023
ISBN: 978-1-5161-1136-7 (ebook)

First Print Edition: February 2023
ISBN: 978-1-5161-1137-4

Printed in the United States of America

Chapter 1

Levet tried to ignore the whispers of the fairies as he pushed his way through the thick underbrush. They were no doubt admiring his large, gossamer wings that sparkled in the moonlight, he told himself. Or perhaps the rigid bulges of his stout body. He might be small for a gargoyle—okay, maybe more than small. He was only three feet tall; still, he was hard in all the right places. Plus, his gray, lumpy features were sheer perfection.

No, wait. He snapped his fingers. They'd no doubt heard the rumors of his most recent battle against evil. As a knight in shining armor, he was often called upon to save the world. Being a hero meant he was constantly recognized by the lesser creatures.

Never slowing, Levet continued to ignore the whispers. At the moment, he didn't have time for his flock of admirers. He'd spent the past week attempting to track down Troy, the Prince of Imps, who'd mysteriously disappeared. Thankfully, tonight he'd decided to check out the Hunting Grounds, the exclusive demon club outside of Chicago that belonged to Marco, a pureblooded Were. That's where he'd finally caught the scent of the imp.

Reaching the front door of the cabin that was built on the outskirts of the private club, he banged his fist against the smooth wood.

"'Allo? Troy?"

Levet could hear muffled sound from inside. It sounded like curses. Then a voice called out.

"Troy isn't here."

Levet scowled, sniffing the night air. The rich scent of exotic fruit swirled through the breeze. "I can smell you."

There was more cursing before the door was wrenched open to reveal Troy. The flamboyant imp was absurdly large with the sort of muscles only an orc should possess. He had long hair that shimmered like a river of fire as it tumbled down his back and brilliant green eyes. Currently he was attired in a black lace shirt that clung to his broad chest and white satin pants with fringes down the sides.

He was like a rare, glamorous flower who could lure others into his sensual snare.

Tonight, he didn't appear to be in the mood to ensnare anyone or anything. There was a peevish expression on his pale face and a sharp-edged impatience in his voice.

"Go away," he snapped.

Levet pursed his lips, valiantly pretending he didn't notice the rude greeting. "I need a favor."

The green eyes widened, as if the imp was shocked by his words. "A favor? Are you kidding me?"

"I do not think so." Levet considered for a moment before giving a firm nod of his head. "Nope. I am quite certain I need a favor."

"You trapped me in the netherworld, where I was forced to listen to your endless babbling for what felt like an eternity. And as if that's not bad enough—and trust me, it was bad enough—you led me straight into the lair of an ifrit who tried to turn me into a crispy critter." Troy turned to reveal the seat of his pants, which had been cut out to reveal the male's derrière, red with several blisters. "My ass is still healing, and I had to have a new weave put in my hair."

Levet clicked his tongue. It wasn't his fault they'd nearly been fried by the demon from hell. Okay, maybe being sucked into the netherworld might have been a teensy tiny bit his fault, but in the end they'd saved the world, hadn't they? The stupid creature should be proud to have been included in the daring adventure, not whining like a dew fairy.

"You are such a drama drag," Levet muttered.

"Queen. I'm a drama queen, you..." Troy shook his head, struggling for the proper word. "Pest."

"Pest?" Levet blinked. "That is the best you can do?"

The sour scent of citrus blasted through the air. "I'm tired, charred, and in dire need of a vacation that is gargoyle-free. Go away."

"You have not performed my favor."

"You want a favor? I'm not going to stab you in the heart with a cursed dagger. That's your favor. Now go away."

Levet's wings fluttered. The male was in a *mood*. It was inexcusable.

"Party pisser."

"Pooper. Party pooper. Argh." Troy grabbed the edge of the door, as if he intended to slam it closed.

"Wait." Levet took a hasty step forward. "I need you to open a portal."

"Tough."

"This is important."

Troy rolled his eyes. "Let me guess. You have to save the world from some new disaster?"

Levet sent the male a confused glance. "I just saved the world, remember? I am on vacation. I wish to return to the merfolk castle."

"Then have Inga open a portal."

Levet cleared his throat at the mention of the Queen of the Merfolk. It'd been far too long since he'd been with Inga, and the desire to be reunited had become a ruthless ache in the center of his being.

Others might see a towering ogress with patches of red hair and pointed teeth who had the temper of a rabid hellhound and run screaming in terror, but to Levet she was sheer perfection.

"*Non*. I desire my return to be a surprise," he insisted.

Troy stilled, studying Levet as if he'd been struck by a sudden thought. "She won't open a portal," he said abruptly.

Levet's brows snapped together. "Do not be ridiculous. Inga adores *moi*."

"Are you sure?" Troy pressed. "You keep running off when she needs you the most. It's possible she's done waiting for you."

The words drilled into Levet with painful force, each one finding a vulnerable spot. It was true he was worried that Inga had become weary of his constant absences. And that perhaps she had decided he was not worth the effort. And Troy was right. When he'd attempted to contact her telepathically, she'd refused to answer.

He wagged a claw in Troy's direction. "You are a very mean creature."

Troy shrugged. "Hey, I'm not the one who abandoned the female I supposedly care about. That's on you."

"I did not abandon—"

Bam. The door slammed in his face. Levet stomped his foot before he turned and marched away. Obviously, the selfish imp wasn't going to help. He would have to find assistance somewhere else.

"I did not abandon Inga. I was busy saving the world. Again," he muttered as he left the Hunting Grounds and headed back toward Chicago. He was not technically supposed to be at the demon club after a certain incident that included his fireballs landing in the middle of a werewolf wedding and setting the groom on fire. "And once I can explain why I have been absent from the castle I am certain she will understand," he continued to try to reassure himself. *"Oui.* Of course she will." He heaved a sigh. "But only if she will speak to me."

He was wandering aimlessly through a flat field that had recently been plowed by a local farmer when he caught a strange scent. It was definitely demon. But he couldn't recognize the species. Odd. He possessed the best sniffer in the world.

"Who is there?"

There was a shimmer in the air, as if a portal was opening, before a male stepped out to stand directly in front of Levet. Levet blinked. The stranger was huge. Perhaps not as tall as a troll but just as wide, with a strapping chest that was left bare to reveal the light coating of fur. He was thankfully wearing leather pants and heavy boots. Levet was seeing all he wanted to see of the creature. He had long brown hair that flowed down his back like a mane, and dark eyes that appeared too big for his face. Most interesting were the horns that stuck out of the sides of his head and curved toward the sky.

With a frown, the creature leaned down, as if to study Levet more closely. "Are you Levet?"

Levet snorted. That was a silly question. "Who else would I be?"

"I've been searching for you."

"For *moi?*" Uh-oh. It was never a good thing when someone was searching for him. Especially a stranger.

"It was not my fault."

The male looked confused. "What wasn't?"

"Whatever I am being blamed for."

"I don't know what you're talking about."

Levet cleared his throat, shifting from foot to foot. "What do you want from *moi?*"

The demon tilted back his head, as if contemplating the spattering of stars flung across the midnight sky.

"The precise details have yet to reveal themselves, but—"

"Oh, there's going to be a revelation?" Levet interrupted, clapping his hands together as he swiveled his head from side to side. "Where? When?"

The male grunted. Did he have an upset tummy? Levet was feeling a little queasy. But that was because he was hungry. It had been far too long since his last meal.

"Are you sure you're Levet?" he demanded.

"Almost positive."

"Is there another Levet?"

Levet widened his eyes. "Certainly not. I am quite unique."

"That is one way to put it."

"Who are you?" Levet placed his hands on his hips, his tail twitching. There was something sunny about this unknown creature. No, wait. Shady. *Oui*. The male was shady.

"Odige," he said.

"Odige." Levet searched his memory. He'd been alive a very, very long time but he'd never met an Odige before. "That is an unusual name."

"Not where I'm from."

"Where is that?"

"Beyond the labyrinth."

"I do not know where that is…oh." Levet abruptly realized that the male was revealing the place of his homeland. "Are you a minotaur?"

The male dipped his head. "I am."

Levet pressed his hands together, excitement searing away his suspicion of the strange beast. He'd assumed that minotaurs were creatures of mist and legend. Now one was standing directly in front of him.

"I have always longed to meet one of you."

The male stretched his lips in a tight smile. "Then it's your lucky day."

"It is?" Levet bounced on his toes. Having a lucky day seemed like a very good thing. "Why?"

"You are going to meet a lot of minotaurs."

"Truly?" Levet bent to the side, trying to peer around Odige's massive girth. "Are they here?"

"No, I'm going to take you to them."

Levet's wings fluttered with a soul-deep pleasure. He'd never encountered anyone who could claim they'd been through the labyrinth to see the minotaur homeland. He was going to be famous. *More* famous, he silently corrected. He was, after all, the savior of the world.

Then his wings abruptly drooped. He couldn't go through the labyrinth. He already had plans for the night.

"Oh…wait. I cannot."

"Yes, you can."

"*Non*." Levet shook his head. "I mean, I am on a very important mission."

The male folded his arms over his chest. The gesture emphasized the fact that he was triple Levet's size.

"The queen will have to wait."

Levet folded his arms over his much smaller chest, refusing to be intimidated. "She cannot…oh." He froze, suddenly suspicious. "How did you know that I was referring to Inga?"

The male waved an impatient hand. "We know a great deal about you."

"How?"

"We have been trying to track you down for a long time. That meant following rumors and gossip and various reports of your whereabouts."

Levet blinked. "Like a stalker?"

Odige ground his teeth. "Like those who have a wish to find you."

"Hmm." Levet wasn't convinced. "Seems suspicious to *moi*."

"There is nothing suspicious," the male growled. "I was sent to retrieve you and that is what I have done."

Levet narrowed his eyes. "And if I do not wish to be retrieved?"

"I do not understand why you are being so stubborn."

"I am not stubborn, I am firm in my resolve," Levet protested. "And my resolve warns me that it is dangerous to travel to unknown destinations with strangers."

"There is no danger to you," the male insisted.

"Well, you would say that, would you not?" Levet flapped his wings. "Especially if you intended to do me harm."

The male lifted his hands toward the heavens. "Why me?"

Levet scrunched his snout. "Demons say that a lot around me. I am not entirely sure what it means."

They exchanged fierce glares, both refusing to be the one to back down. The stare-off might have lasted the rest of the night if Levet hadn't gotten a cramp in his foot.

"Enough." Levet flexed his toe claws, attempting to ease the knot.

Odige muttered a curse, holding up one large hand. "What if I swear on my goddess that no minotaur will offer you violence?"

Levet shook his head. "It does not matter. I will have to meet the minotaurs another time. Tonight, I must discover a means to open a portal to the merfolk castle."

There was a heavy silence, as if Odige was debating whether to squash Levet beneath his massive foot, or perhaps see how far he could toss him across the field.

Instead, he shrugged. "I can do that."

Levet blinked in confusion. "You can do what?"

"Open a portal."

"Not to the merfolk castle. It is protected by layers of magic. Only a creature with the ability to create portals and permission from the queen can penetrate the illusions without a formal invitation. That is why I was in need of Troy." Levet wrinkled his snout. "The horse-patootie."

The minotaur shrugged. "It's no problem for me. I can walk through any shield, no matter what the source of the magic."

"Truly?" Levet was genuinely shocked. "I did not know that minotaurs possessed that particular talent."

"We prefer to keep our magical abilities a secret."

Levet tapped a claw against the side of his snout. "Ah. It is wise to remain secretive. Mystery is also a part of my unique charm."

"Allow me."

Levet stepped back as the male waved his arm in a dramatic gesture. There was the crackle of power before a shimmer rippled around him. Leaning forward, Levet studied the unfamiliar magic. The opening looked more like a gateway than a portal, and there was a distinct scent of ripe wheat and ale. Where was the salty tang and soft ocean breeze?

"Wait." Levet took another step backward. "This does not smell right."

He was on the point of turning away when a large hand reached down to grab him by the horn. Before he could react he felt himself being hoisted off the ground, and with one mighty swing he was being tossed into the gateway like a Frisbee. Or perhaps it was more like a sack of potatoes, he conceded as he flapped his wings and windmilled his arms in a futile attempt to avoid landing on his derrière. "Help!"

Chapter 2

Spring in Chicago was a volatile time for Styx, the King of Vampires. The unpredictable weather, combined with the breeding season for many demons, ensured that there was rarely a night without some disaster that needed his immediate attention. Not to mention the fact he'd just endured yet another near-end-of-the-world event.

Tonight, however he was off duty. Off with a capital *O*. And he intended to enjoy every second of his rare respite.

Pretending he didn't feel like an idiot, he'd swapped his usual leather pants and knee-high shitkickers for a white satin shirt and black silk pants. He'd even allowed his black hair to flow down his back. He would never look civilized. He was a six-foot-five vampire with the bronzed skin and proud angular features of an Aztec warrior. And the very air shimmered with the force of his power. But he was doing his best to have a romantic evening with his mate, Darcy.

The slender, almost fragile female walking next to him didn't look like the mate of the most powerful vampire in the world. And she most certainly didn't look like a pureblooded Were. Her heart-shaped face was pale and unbearably vulnerable and her blond hair ridiculously spiked like a human teenager's. She was even wearing casual jeans and a sweatshirt that emphasized her youthful appearance.

At the moment, her eyes were squeezed shut as he led her through the maze of marble corridors lined with fluted columns. His lair on the outskirts of Chicago was a gilded monstrosity that should have belonged to an aging rocker with questionable taste. Not the Anasso, King of Vampires. In fact, as far as Styx was concerned the estate would have been improved with a match and several sticks of dynamite. Unfortunately, Darcy was convinced that the place suited his position. And Styx was willing to endure any amount of torture if it pleased his mate.

"What are you up to?" she complained as he turned into a short hallway that ended in a lavish set of double doors.

"Don't you trust me?" Styx demanded.

"With my life? Without hesitation. With my heart? Always. With the choice of my evening entertainment?" Her lips pinched. "Hmm."

"I'm not that bad."

"You took me to watch two trolls mud wrestle for our anniversary."

Styx clenched his fangs. Viper, the current clan chief of Chicago, was one of his closest advisors and a male he considered a friend, but there was no doubt the vampire could be a pain in the ass.

"Viper told me that the Trolls in Mud were a new musical group."

Darcy snorted. "And you believed him?"

"It made as much sense as Hoobastank or Smashing Pumpkins," Styx protested, not adding that he'd been relieved to discover that it was actually trolls in a mud battle. That was a lot more fun than humans screaming into a microphone.

"Fair enough," Darcy conceded.

"I did good this time. I promise."

Styx pushed open the library door and led her inside. It was a beautiful room. The long space was framed with heavy wooden shelves that were loaded with rare books and a large window that overlooked the moon-drenched rose garden. In the center of the Persian carpets that covered the floor was a table that was decorated with candles, a dozen roses, and an ice bucket that was chilling a bottle of Dom Pérignon. There was also a silver serving plate that was currently covered with a linen napkin.

"Open your eyes," he commanded.

Slowly Darcy lifted the heavy sweep of her lashes, her lips parting in appreciation.

"Wow," she breathed.

"Good?"

"Very good." She crossed the carpet to pull the linen off the dinner plate. "Eggplant parmesan. My favorite. Yum." She sucked in a deep breath, her gaze widening as she caught sight of the massive fireplace where logs were burning with a bright light. Styx rarely allowed a fire in his presence. Vampires were highly flammable creatures. Then she pointed toward the empty sheath attached to the wall above the mantel. "Where's your sword?"

"Gone," he said, keeping his answer vague.

She turned back with a worried expression. "Levet didn't sell it on eBay again, did he?"

Styx ground his fangs. The aggravating miniature gargoyle had tried to hock his massive weapon more than once. Idiotic pest.

"No. It's put away." Styx moved to wrap his arms around his beautiful mate. "Plus, the doors are locked and I put out word that if I'm interrupted I will rip off heads first and ask questions later."

Darcy smoothed her hands over his chest, the warmth of her palms searing through the thin fabric of his shirt.

"Very dramatic."

A low growl rumbled in Styx's throat. The touch from this female was as exciting tonight as it had been fifteen years ago. And would be a hundred years from now. Fate had created him to adore her for all eternity.

"For one night I refuse to be the Anasso," he murmured, his large hand following the curve of her spine to cup her slender neck. Already his fangs were fully extended in the anticipation of tasting her sweet, addictive blood.

Her lips twitched. "If you aren't the Anasso, then who are you?"

"Darcy's mate." He lowered his head to brush his lips over her mouth. "The male who worships the ground she walks upon. The male who is determined to devote his attention—"

"Um, Styx," she interrupted.

Styx lifted his head to frown down at her upturned face. "I'm not done telling you how devoted I intend to be. I spent all afternoon practicing the words."

"Do you smell that?"

He shook his head. "All I smell is your intoxicating scent."

"It's…" She sniffed the air. "Granite. Levet?"

Styx's brows snapped together. "No way. I have my Ravens keeping a very close eye on that…" He struggled to find words that wouldn't offend his mate. She possessed an unreasonable loyalty to Levet. "Aggravating creature. He's not allowed to come within a mile of this lair."

"Then perhaps it's another gargoyle."

"Impossible."

Darcy arched a brow. "Excuse me?"

Styx wisely scrambled to ease his mate's quick temper. "What I mean is that nothing is allowed in or out of the estate.…" His words trailed away as the ground shook as if it'd been hit by a meteor and the moonlight was blocked by a humongous object. "Shit."

Marching across the room, Darcy pointed out the window. "There. I told you. Gargoyle."

Styx stared at the massive gray form that was folding its ten-foot leather wings against its muscular body. A second later it hunched forward to peer into his library with a fierce expression on its lumpy features.

"That's not Levet," he muttered.

"Not unless he's grown considerably since I saw him a few days ago," Darcy agreed in dry tones.

Styx struggled to comprehend what he was seeing. Gargoyles were reclusive creatures who rarely left their homeland in France. Then, with a muttered curse, he realized exactly who was currently destroying his garden.

"Aunt Bertha." He shook his head. Just a few days ago Levet's relative had been wandering around Chicago, unsure how she'd been transformed into a human shape. During a massive battle against an evil ifrit, she'd reverted back to her original form. He'd assumed that she had returned to Paris. Or continued her travels around the world.

What was that saying? Assuming would make an ass out of a vampire?

Styx dropped a kiss on the top of Darcy's head. "Eat your dinner while it's warm. I'll get rid of Bertha and be right back."

"I've heard that before."

"This is our night." Styx moved to the large desk in the far corner. Bending down, he pulled out the sword that had been hidden beneath it. "Nothing is going to ruin it."

Darcy eyed the huge weapon. "I thought you said the sword was gone."

"Just because I want a night off doesn't mean my enemies do." Styx headed toward the door with long strides. "I'll be back before dessert arrives."

"Famous last words," Darcy called out.

Styx didn't respond. Mostly because he didn't have any defense. He couldn't count how many times he'd promised to be there for his mate only to have some emergency drag him away.

Using the back exit, he entered the garden, halting a judicious distance from the towering demon. Gargoyles were traditionally foul-tempered, stubborn, unreasonable creatures who were quick to use their large size and immunity to magic to their advantage.

Pausing to debate the best means of approaching the beast, Styx was distracted as a sharp chill in the air warned him that another vampire had joined him in the garden. He turned his head to watch a vampire with pale gold hair that reached his waist and ice-blue eyes stride toward him, his leather duster flaring around his six-foot-three frame. Jagr had been a Visigoth chief while he was a human and a feral fury continued to smolder around him.

"Jagr." Styx pointed his sword toward the looming gargoyle. "Is there anyone else about to drop in uninvited?"

The vampire grimaced. As the head of the Ravens, Styx's personal guards, he took his duties seriously.

"Not that I could detect. But I didn't sense the mountain-size gargoyle until it landed."

Styx shrugged. He didn't blame his companion. "They have the ability to shield their presence even from other demons."

Jagr wasn't pacified. "Do you recognize it?"

"Aunt Bertha. A relative of Levet."

"I assume this is a surprise visit?"

"That's one way to put it." Styx tightened his grip on the hilt of his sword. "Watch my back."

"Always."

Styx didn't have any doubt that the vampire would eagerly sacrifice his life to keep Styx safe. At one time that would have been a comfort, but now Styx realized he had to be twice as careful. He didn't want the male's death on his soul.

Darcy had made him soft, he silently accepted. And honestly, he wouldn't have it any other way.

"Hello? Bertha?" He called out, inching closer and closer to the creature. "Can you hear me?" There was no response. Wait. That wasn't true. Styx could feel an odd pressure inside his skull. As if something was trying to crawl into his brain. He hastily backed away. "Shit."

Jagr was instantly at his side. "What's wrong?"

Styx lifted a hand to touch his forehead. As if he could ward off the weird sensation.

"In this form I think they communicate telepathically."

Jagr shuddered. Vampires had a natural ability to use mental compulsion on lesser creatures, but they were careful to create shields to prevent their own minds from being entered. There was no way he could converse with the gargoyle.

Jagr glanced over his shoulder at the nearby house. "Maybe Darcy—"

"Absolutely not." Styx hesitated before he forced out the words he hoped never to say again. "Go get Levet."

Jagr's lean features tightened. "That is going to be a problem."

"I asked you to keep an eye on him."

"I did. That's why I returned in time to see the arrival of your oversize lawn ornament. I thought you should know what I witnessed."

Styx narrowed his eyes. He already sensed this was bad news. "Tell me."

"When I finally tracked down the gargoyle, he was at the Hunting Grounds attempting to convince Troy to open a portal to the merfolk castle."

Styx swallowed a growl. If Levet had disappeared through a portal, there was no way to locate him. At least not for a vampire.

"Did Troy open one?"

"No, he slammed the door in the gargoyle's face."

"The imp is smarter than I gave him credit for," Styx drawled. "What happened to Levet?"

"He headed away from the Hunting Grounds. I assumed he was on his way back to Chicago, but as he wandered through an empty field a stranger approached him."

Styx's unease deepened. He'd been annoyed by the thought that Levet had disappeared through a portal. Who knew how long it would take to track down the creature? But he should have suspected that was too simple a problem. Levet was a disaster magnet.

"How strange was the stranger?"

"Very strange." Jagr confirmed his worst fear. "A minotaur."

Styx stared at his most trusted guard, wondering if the male had taken a blow to the head.

"A minotaur." He shook his head. "Seriously?"

Jagr shrugged. "I've never seen one in person, but I'm sure that's what it was."

Styx had been around for countless centuries and traveled from this world to distant dimensions. And never once had he ever encountered a minotaur. Until this moment he would have sworn that they never left their homeland.

"What's it doing in my territory?"

"I think he was searching for the gargoyle."

"Of course he was." Styx's mood went from sour to downright rancid. He couldn't care less what happened to the stupid gargoyle. In fact, he hoped the minotaur ate him for dinner. But the idiot's aunt was currently perched on his roses and he had no way to get rid of her without the pest. "What happened?"

"He opened a gateway and they disappeared."

"A gateway?" Styx considered his limited options. "Can one of the fey follow them?"

"Not if the minotaur was going back to his people," Jagr said. "There's not a lot of information about the species, but what I've read indicates that they have layers of protection surrounding their homeland that have never been penetrated."

Styx didn't have the vast knowledge that Jagr did, but he'd done his share of research over the years.

"The labyrinth."

"Yes."

Styx shook his head. "Why the hell would the minotaur be interested in Levet?"

"I don't know, but he didn't go willingly."

"Crap." Styx reluctantly turned back to the hovering gargoyle. "Levet isn't here. Go look for him in the labyrinth." He stepped closer, studying the bumps and lumps of the gargoyle's face. Was she asleep? Styx waved his sword, trying to catch her attention. "Did you hear? He's with the minotaurs."

A searing heat blasted through the air and the night seemed to rip apart as a male form appeared directly in front of Bertha. He was large. Even bigger than Styx, with long hair that shimmered with a metallic, platinum sheen in the moonlight. His eyes were a piercing ebony. But it was the fire that danced over his skin and the heavy pulse of power beating through the garden that captured Styx's full attention.

"Get that sword near Bertha and I'll burn this city to the ground," the male growled. "Along with you and your clan."

Styx grimaced. He didn't have any trouble identifying the intruder. Levet had spent the past few days boasting that his aunt had captured the attention of a god. And there was only one god who walked around with flames.

Hades.

"What does she want?"

The god folded his arms across his chest. "Levet."

Styx didn't bother to repeat the obvious fact that Levet wasn't there. He was beginning to suspect that Bertha had sensed her nephew was in danger and now expected him to somehow rescue the stupid creature.

He turned back to Jagr. "We need that gargoyle."

Jagr spread his hands. "The only way into the minotaur homeland is through the labyrinth. No one can get in or out."

Styx pressed his fingers against his right temple. It was throbbing with the threat of a looming migraine. Hard to believe his night was about to get even worse. After all, his romantic evening with his mate had been interrupted. His rose garden was being squashed by a seven-foot gargoyle. And he was being threatened by an angry god who could destroy him with disturbing ease. Now, he had to somehow find a way to rescue his personal pain in the ass from beyond the labyrinth.

"There's one." He had to force the words past his stiff lips.

Jagr frowned before shaking his head in horror. "No. No, no, no."

"I need Ryshi," he growled.

Chapter 3

The lair in the Kunlun Mountains in Tibet was isolated even by vampire standards. The series of caves was impossible to reach without days of climbing on foot and protected by thick layers of illusion. Inside they were barren of all but the most essential needs. A few pieces of furniture, a collection of opera soundtracks, and a vast cavern where Sofie spent her nights chiseling works of art into the rock walls.

Most creatures would consider the stark surroundings more a prison than a home, but Sofie cherished the sense of peace. She'd made the choice to be alone a long time ago and she never regretted that decision.

She didn't like people. Unless they were dinner. And she liked demons even less.

Unfortunately, her personal preference for solitude was a source of utter indifference to the Anasso. As he proved when he stepped out of a portal created by some unknown fey creature at the base of the mountain and called for her to join him. Even if Sofie wanted to ignore the command—and blessed goddess she wanted to ignore it—the tremors shaking through the ground were creating fissures large enough to destroy her lair.

Only one creature possessed that sort of power. The Anasso.

Exchanging her loose satin gown for a pair of jeans, a heavy sweater, and thick boots, Sofie used the tunnel system she'd dug out of the stone to make her way down the towering mountain, stepping out of a hidden cave to stand directly in front of Styx.

He was wearing his usual leather pants and coat with a massive sword strapped across his back. He easily towered over her slender frame as she approached. Not a surprise, as the king probably towered over most demons, but she'd always been small for a vampire. With her blond hair cut in a pixie style and her crystal-blue eyes that were rimmed with bright silver, she was often mistaken for a fey creature. Or a human. The image was only intensified by the crescent-shaped scar with a small circle that was carved into the middle of her forehead.

The mark of a witch.

Sofie didn't mind. She preferred to be underestimated. It gave her a distinct advantage in any unwelcome battle.

"Styx." She offered a respectful bow of her head. "I assume you weren't in the neighborhood and decided to drop in?"

The male deliberately glanced around the rugged landscape that was eerily silent.

"Is anyone ever in this neighborhood?"

"Not if I can prevent them."

He pursed his lips, but thankfully didn't offer yet another tedious lecture on the dangers of isolating herself. For once, he came straight to the point of his visit.

"I need your help."

Sofie narrowed her gaze. "Help with what?"

"Not what. Who."

"I don't understand."

"Ryshi."

Sofie hissed, suddenly wishing she'd stayed in the privacy of her caves. So what if the damned mountain collapsed on her? She'd rather be buried under rock than be plagued by the memory of Ryshi. The half-jinn/half-imp male had given her nightmares for the past ten years.

Not that it would have changed her fate, she acknowledged ruefully. Styx would just have dug her out of the rubble and forced her to do what he wanted. The Anasso was nothing if not stubborn.

"No." She took a step backward. "No way."

Styx tightened his jaw, his expression grim. "I'm sorry, Sofie, but you're the only one capable of controlling him."

He was referring to her unique ability to lock her mind with another demon and hold them captive. It wasn't a compulsion that could bend the creature to her will. Or the talent of implanting false memories. Once she had a grip on another's mind, they couldn't travel more than a few feet away from her. Not until she released them.

"I thought he was locked in your dungeon?"

Styx nodded. "He is."

"Then why do you need me?"

"I want to retrieve a creature who's been taken into the labyrinth. Ryshi is the only one I know who has managed to navigate his way in and out of the maze."

Sofie wasn't surprised that the male had managed to do the impossible. He was a notorious thief who'd eluded capture for centuries. There was no place he couldn't enter.

"Then send him. Why include me?"

Styx arched a brow. "Do you honestly think that I would trust the thief on his own? As soon as I opened the door to his cell he would disappear in a cloud of smoke."

Sofie shivered. She didn't like the thought of the male roaming the world without restraint. Not when he blamed her for the decade he'd spent in Styx's dungeon.

"Leash him."

"Nothing can leash a jinn." He held her wary gaze. "Except you. I wouldn't ask if there were any other options."

His words held an edge of sincerity, but Sofie's talent also allowed her to detect when another creature was lying to her.

"That's not true," she murmured. "At least not entirely."

A wry smile twisted his lips as if he belatedly remembered her skill. "It's true that you're the only one who can help with the thief. But I'm not opposed to forcing you out of your lair." He waved a hand toward the mountain range that was still coated in snow even though spring had supposedly sprung. "It's fine to desire privacy, but this extreme isolation isn't healthy."

"It's what makes me happy."

"You can't avoid the world forever."

She stared at him in confusion. "Why not?"

His lips parted, but clearly deciding that he was wasting his time trying to convince her that the world wasn't an utter trash fire, he gave a resigned shake of his head.

"Complete this task for me and you can return to your self-inflicted prison."

"Do I have a choice?"

"No."

Sofie clenched her hands into tight fists. She wanted to beat them against the nearest boulder. Instead, she tilted her chin to a defiant angle.

"Then let's get this over with."

* * * *

Ryshi sprawled on the narrow cot, twirling the tip of his finger to create wisps of smoke in the air. It was one of his few means to break the monotony of the long nights spent in his cramped cell. Not as fun as infuriating the guards who brought him his meals, but it was better than nothing.

The days were better, of course. The vampires had been careful to place a dampening spell in the cells, which meant that he couldn't use his magic, but he was half jinn. That meant he could shift into his incorporeal form and float his way out of the lair. From there, it was a simple matter to use his imp magic to create portals that would take him anyplace in the world.

Eventually he was going to have to stop pretending to be a prisoner, he acknowledged with a faint sigh. It was slowing down his efforts. But for the moment, he was willing to choose caution over speed. The vampires were convinced he was safely locked away, so they had no reason to protect their lairs against a thief, and no reason to suspect him even if they did notice there had been a trespasser.

Besides, he'd enjoyed the knowledge that the leeches assumed they'd managed to capture him when he could disappear in a puff of smoke anytime he wanted.

Time, however, was ticking away. He didn't want to waste any more by having to return to this cell each night. And there was a niggling voice in the back of his mind that warned the vampires were touchy about their security. If they discovered he could easily move in and out of their dungeons, he might find himself trapped in a place that he couldn't escape.

An unacceptable risk.

As if the goddess had read his mind, there was the sound of heavy footsteps entering the dungeon. Ryshi recognized those size thirteen boots slapping against the stone floor. This wasn't just another guard. It was the Anasso.

Rising to his feet, Ryshi ran his fingers down the long tunic he wore over loose silk pants. Then, lifting his arms over his head, he stretched out his lean, supple muscles. He'd inherited his slender form from his imp father, as well as his long copper hair. The haunting darkness of his eyes, however, had come from his jinn mother along with his ability to shift to smoke.

He was leaning nonchalantly against the wall of his cell when the door was thrust open and Styx stepped inside.

"Ah. It's the big man himself," Ryshi drawled. "What an honor. Shall I bow or do you prefer for your sycophants to drop to their knees and kiss your ass?"

The Anasso bared his fangs in warning. "You try to kiss my ass and I'll chop off your head."

"Always so violent." Ryshi studied his nails, pretending to be unaware of the power thundering through the air. "I blame a lack of vitamin D."

Styx cursed, but thankfully the vampire resisted any urge to stab Ryshi with his big-ass sword.

"I have a task for you."

Ryshi buffed his nails on his tunic. "I'm listening."

"I need you to enter the labyrinth."

Well…that was a surprise. Ryshi had only revealed his ability to slip in and out of the minotaur homeland in an attempt to keep the vampires from locking him away. He'd assumed they would realize his worth as a thief and send him on a mission to pay for his sins. Instead, the idiots had tossed him in their dungeons.

Now he wondered if his boast was about to come back and bite him in the ass.

"A dangerous request," he pointed out.

Styx narrowed his eyes. "It's not a request."

"That doesn't make it any less dangerous."

"You would rather remain locked in this cell?"

Ryshi rolled his eyes. The male was no doubt a powerful creature, but he was as subtle as a raging troll. He had no concept of all the delicious grays between white and black.

"I'm setting the baseline for our negotiations," Ryshi informed the leech.

Styx scowled. "What negotiations?"

"You need something from me. I get something from you." Ryshi spoke slowly. "That's how it works."

A layer of ice suddenly coated the cell. The Anasso wasn't subtle, but he also wasn't stupid. And he was clearly in no mood for Ryshi's mockery.

"Not in my world." With blinding speed, Styx was standing directly in front of Ryshi, the tip of his sword biting into the center of Ryshi's chest. "I tell you to do something and you do it or I stick this big knife through your heart."

Ryshi smiled. The sword wouldn't kill him. Then again, it would hurt like a bitch. Something he preferred to avoid.

"Fine. But if you want someone to enter the labyrinth, you'll be shit out of luck if I'm forced to regrow my heart. No one except a minotaur can penetrate the magic." He deliberately paused. "And me."

Styx appeared magnificently unimpressed with Ryshi's logic. "So you claim."

"Are we going to negotiate or are you going to waste both our time with meaningless threats?"

Styx lifted the sword to press it against Ryshi's lips. "I swear I'll cut out that tongue."

"You wouldn't be the first." Ryshi shrugged. "Probably not the last."

Styx released a low roar, ice swirling through the air as he stepped back and lowered the weapon.

"What do you want?" he demanded.

"To start with, I want my freedom." Ryshi's voice hardened, the scent of amber filling the cell. "I spent the past decade locked away for a petty crime."

Styx made a sound of disbelief. "Petty crime? You broke into the lairs of vampires to steal their belongings."

"It was a game," Ryshi lied smoothly. If Styx discovered exactly why he'd been searching through the vampire lairs, the male might actually find a way to kill him. "I never took anything of value."

"And even after you were warned to stay away, you continued to sneak in."

Ryshi shrugged. He'd laughed when he'd discovered the warning scrawled outside this massive lair. It'd been like waving a red flag in front of a bull. Ryshi had been twice as determined to enter.

"I like the challenge," he admitted. "It keeps my skills sharp."

"And that's why you're locked in a dungeon."

True enough. Ryshi's arrogance had been his downfall. But it had been only a temporary inconvenience.

"What if I promise that I learned my lesson? Release me and I'll never bother you again."

It wasn't a lie. Ryshi had not only grown sloppy in his searches, but he'd conceitedly assumed that nothing and no one could ever capture him. He intended to be more careful in the future.

"Complete this task and we'll talk."

Not exactly a promise. But better than nothing.

"What do you want from the labyrinth?" Ryshi asked.

"A miniature gargoyle has been taken to the homeland of the minotaurs. I need him back."

Ryshi's mocking smile faded. This was a trick. It had to be. "A miniature gargoyle?"

Styx looked oddly uncomfortable. "It's a long, tedious story."

"I've got the time."

"I don't."

Hmm. Ryshi had heard vague rumors of a small gargoyle who'd supposedly saved the world from some mysterious evil, but he'd dismissed them as fairy tales. It seemed too weird to be real.

"Let me see if I have this straight. You want me to navigate the labyrinth, track down a miniature gargoyle that I presume has become lost in the maze, and return it to Chicago?"

"Correct."

Ryshi folded his arms over his chest. "Any other miracles while I'm out and about? Capturing a unicorn? Digging up a leprechaun?"

"Nope." Styx shook his head. "Just the gargoyle."

Ryshi swallowed the demand to know what the hell was going on. Did it matter? Not to him. He had no intention of entering the labyrinth. Not when he could create an elaborate ceremony that would convince the leeches he was headed into the maze. Once he was through a portal he would disappear. As long as he was careful not to be seen, the vampires would presume he was lost among the minotaurs along with the gargoyle.

A perfect solution to his current problem.

"Got it." He waved a slender hand. "Step aside and I'll begin preparing for my journey."

"Not without a chaperone."

Ryshi froze. "You didn't say anything about a chaperone."

The vampire made a sound of disgust. "You didn't think I would actually trust you to do what I asked without having someone keep an eye on you?"

"Why Styx, I'm wounded."

The massive sword was once again pressed against Ryshi's heart. "You will be if I so much as suspect you're attempting to flee before you've done as I asked."

Ryshi did his best to disguise his annoyance. A companion was an unexpected bother, but it didn't change his plans.

"So who's my...oh." Ryshi's heart lurched as he caught the icy scent that had haunted him for the past decade. "Sweet Sofie. Why didn't you say that in the beginning? I have no objections to spending oodles of time with that particular leech."

For once, he wasn't lying. The beautiful female had fascinated him from the moment he'd caught sight of her. It didn't matter that she'd been hunting him. Or that he'd spent the past ten years stuck in this cell because of her. His jinn nature was obsessed with the rare and unique. He had a lair filled with his collection of extraordinary objects. The fact that Sofie was also a lethal predator only added to his tingles of anticipation.

In contrast, Sofie appeared less than enthusiastic as she stepped into the cell and glared at him with her ice-blue eyes.

"Please stop talking," she muttered.

Ryshi offered a deep bow, allowing his gaze to sweep over her slender curves revealed by the jeans and her soft pink sweater.

"Your wish is my command. I have far more pleasurable ways to communicate—*argh*."

Ryshi jerked upright, his hands clenching as he felt Sofie's presence wrap around his mind. It wasn't painful, but it was unnerving as hell.

Sofie turned her head toward her king. "You're going to owe me for this, Styx."

The large male grimaced. "I hear that a lot."

Chapter 4

Levet should have been terrified. After all, if the myths about the minotaurs were true then there was no way to escape from their homeland. But terror wasn't what he was experiencing as he paced from one end of the long room to the other.

It was irritation.

How much time had passed since he'd been hauled through the gateway? It felt like an eternity, but it was possible that it'd been just a couple of hours. He didn't even know if time moved the same in this dimension. It might have been weeks or months or even years since he'd disappeared. What if Inga believed that he didn't want to come back? She might have turned her attention to that stupid Prince of Imps. The goddess knew that Troy was always sniffing around the merfolk castle.

Plus, it was boring. The room was perfectly comfortable, with a glossy wooden floor and heavy, hand-carved furniture. In fact, it was downright cozy. There was a large fire blazing in a stone fireplace at one end and windows that offered a view of rolling hills and a moonlit meadow. All very pretty, but Levet was ready to leave.

More than ready.

The sound of a door opening had Levet spinning around to watch as a tall female wearing a silk robe walked toward him. She had long dark hair that matched her eyes and a pair of magnificent horns that curled from the sides of her head. Levet resisted the urge to touch his own stunted horns. Instead, he glared at the female with simmering impatience.

"Hello, Levet." The female offered a bow. "I am Joya. Your guide."

"At last. I have been stuck here forever."

Her expression was difficult to read. "Forgive us. There were certain preparations that had to be completed."

"Preparations? I do not like the sound of that."

Joya straightened, looking confused by his words. "You are our guest of honor. Of course we must ensure that everything is perfect."

Levet wasn't entirely reassured. "The last occasion in which I was the guest of honor I was also the main course," he said, his wings drooping as he recalled his invitation to the goblin festival, which had included him tied over an open fire with an apple stuck in his mouth. "You do not intend to eat me, do you?"

If possible, she looked even more confused. "We do not consume meat."

"Oh." Levet heaved out a sigh. "That is a relief."

"If you'll follow me, I will lead you to the gathering."

Without waiting for Levet to agree, the female whirled around and marched out the door. Levet scurried to catch up. The last thing he wanted was to be trapped again.

They entered a long corridor with exquisite tapestries covering the walls and open beams overhead. The air was warm and scented with the tantalizing aroma of fresh bread and roasting vegetables. Not as good as a steak and potatoes, but Levet's stomach growled in appreciation. He was starving.

His stomach, however, was going to have to wait.

He cleared his throat, flapping his wings as he scurried to keep pace with his companion.

"While I am pleased to be the guest of the minotaurs, I am impatient to be on my way to the merfolk castle." Levet puffed out his chest. "You see, I am a close and personal friend of the queen and she is in urgent need of my services."

The female never slowed as they turned into another corridor. This one was wider with even more elaborate tapestries and fur rugs on the floor.

"I am not surprised that the queen would seek out your company," Joya murmured.

Levet flushed. "Perhaps I was not entirely clear," he conceded, his wings drooping. "While it is true that Inga is a dear friend, she is not precisely *seeking* my companionship. You see, I have been terribly busy and while it was not my fault that I was trapped in the netherworld, there is a teeny-tiny chance that Inga might believe that I abandoned her."

"Then she must be a fool," the female sniffed.

"*Non*, not a fool."

Levet hastily glanced over his shoulder. His luck had been exceptionally bad lately and he wouldn't be at all surprised if Inga appeared behind him and bashed him on the head with her oversize trident. When she didn't appear, he breathed a sigh of relief.

"You are special," Joya insisted. "Any female would be honored to have you as a companion."

"Honored?" Levet considered the word.

It was true that he'd been saving the world, he told himself. *Again.* And while it could be argued that if he'd stayed at the castle with Inga he would never have been sucked into the underworld, who knows what might have happened? The ifrit might have opened the gates of hell and the world would have been overrun with evil. Including the merfolk castle.

Inga should be thanking him, right?

Levet grimaced. Perhaps thanking him was wishful thinking. But she should answer his mental calls. How could he explain if she wouldn't even talk to him?

"Very honored," his companion insisted.

"That seems unlikely," Levet conceded. "But I do need to find a means to return to the merfolk castle. I am quite certain once I explain why I have been missing Inga will agree I had no choice."

"Once you have performed for us, I am certain you can continue your journey," she assured him.

Performed? Levet blinked in surprise. He assumed he had been snatched for some horrible reason. Now he felt a surge of excitement.

"Ah, *oui.* So you have heard of my skills?"

"Of course. They are etched in our histories." Without warning his companion came to an abrupt halt, pointing toward a heavy curtain hanging on the wall. "And woven into the fabric of our tapestries."

Levet leaned toward the image that was stitched into the rich cloth. He could make out what appeared to be a large wooden structure on the top of a hill. Was it a fortress? *Oui.* A very large fortress. It was surrounded by meadows filled with wildflowers and golden fields of wheat. Beyond that was a thick forest that was dark and menacing, as if the artist was offering a warning to the unwary. Levet shivered, returning his attention to the fortress, where the balconies were overflowing with various minotaurs. They were crowded together, all of them pointing toward the sky where a tiny gargoyle was floating above them, his wings sparkling in the glow of the fireballs that swirled around him.

Levet shook his head, barely capable of accepting what he was seeing. That had to be an image of him. As he'd said earlier, he was quite unique.

But how? He'd never been to this place. At least, not that he could remember. Like any demon, he'd had a few years during his youth that were lost in a haze of party excess. But even if he had drunkenly stumbled his way through the labyrinth, why would anyone create a tapestry to commemorate his visit?

"That is…" Levet didn't have the appropriate word. "Astonishing," he finally muttered. "Most creatures do not possess a proper appreciation of my talent."

"It is the most important thing in the world to us."

Levet scratched his snout with the tip of one claw, genuinely baffled. "Well, I am not certain it is that good," he protested. There was nothing worse for a performer than overpromising and underdelivering. It was one certain way to ensure the audience became a surly mob intent on violence. He'd discovered that fun fact when he'd been asked to entertain a horde of brownies during the great plague. "I mean, I can create stunning fireballs despite the complaints from the stupid Prince of Imps, but they cannot compare with the magic of the fairies."

Joya resumed her brisk pace down the corridor, headed toward the heavy double doors at the end.

"We have no need of fairy magic," she informed Levet. "The prophecies are very clear."

"Prophecies?" Levet stumbled over his tail, barely paying attention as she shoved open one of the doors and urged him to go ahead of her. They'd gone from him performing to being a part of their prophecies and he wasn't sure how they'd taken that rather colossal leap. "I am not certain that I understand what you desire of me…." His words trailed away as he realized that he was in a vast arena that was surrounded by crescent-shaped benches that soared toward the thatched ceiling far above his head. The floor of the oval-shaped arena was dirt, but in the center was a large dais with a massive throne encrusted with thousands of tiny gems that shimmered in the light from the torches that circled the opening.

Enchanted by the priceless throne, Levet didn't notice the large minotaur approaching him. It wasn't until a shadow fell over him that he glanced up in time to see a male attired in a fur cloak with a crown stuck between his horns offering a deep bow.

"Welcome, Levet," he said in a deep voice. Then straightening, he hefted a golden scepter high over his head. "Savior of the Minotaurs."

Without warning the gathered minotaurs jumped to their feet, releasing a roar that threatened to bring down the roof.

"Levet! Levet! Levet!"

Levet watched the shocking display with his mouth hanging open. Oh...*mon dieu.*

This couldn't be good.

* * * *

Sofie stepped out of the portal created by one of Styx's fey servants and turned in a cautious circle. She was carrying a long dagger that was wicked sharp and cursed by a Sylvermyst. The dark fey creatures were capable of creating a blade that would poison even a demon. A rare and dangerous weapon.

Just like her.

Her gaze swept over the empty fields, her senses searching for any trace of a hidden enemy. When she was confident that they were alone aside from a coyote hidden in the distant trees and a few dew fairies who danced in the moonlight, she turned to watch Ryshi step out of the portal.

He was wearing a dark green satin tunic stitched with gold thread and loose pants that ended at his ankles. His feet were bare, but there were wide copper cuffs around his ankles and wrists. The shimmery metal perfectly matched his hair, which was pulled into a braid. The style emphasized the stark beauty of his male features. It was his eyes, however, that sent odd tingles of awareness through her.

They were completely black, the liquid ebony giving the impression of bottomless pools of pagan power.

Spreading his arms, Ryshi tilted back his head and sucked in a deep breath. "Ah. The sky. And fresh air." He shuddered with pleasure. "Glorious."

Sofie shivered as an unexpected heat spread through her body. As if the sight of the decadent male was warming parts of her that hadn't been warmed in a very, very long time.

Disturbed by the sensations, she forced herself to turn away. It was disturbing enough to have her mind wrapped around his. The last thing she wanted was to be distracted by her unwelcome awareness.

"How do we get to the labyrinth?" she demanded.

"So impatient." Ryshi strolled to stand next to her, the warm scent of amber lacing the night air. "I've been locked away for a decade. Can't I have a moment to appreciate my freedom?"

"No."

His low chuckle brushed over her like a caress. "As charming as ever."

She clenched her fangs. "I'm waiting."

"I thought about you, you know," he drawled, clearly enjoying the knowledge that he was annoying her. "During the long days of pacing my cell I would imagine your beautiful face and your enticing scent."

"That's..." She deliberately allowed her words to trail away, slowly turning to face him. "Creepy."

His smile went from wicked to rueful. "Okay. That might have come out a little more stalkerish than I intended," he conceded. "But it's true that I never forgot you."

She shrugged, not about to reveal that he'd been in her dreams far more than she wanted to admit.

"I don't imagine you did forget me. I was the one who captured you."

"You caught me by surprise. I didn't know a vampire could snare a mind. And certainly not *my* mind."

Sofie didn't doubt his shock. Ryshi had been leaving the lair of a vampire in Chicago when she'd approached. He'd been strolling down the street with the confidence of a male who had no fear of predators. Even when she'd appeared he'd been more curious than alarmed. It wasn't until she'd actually grabbed his mind that he'd realized he was in danger. Even then, he'd maintained his arrogant attitude. She was fairly certain he'd have it even in death.

"Are you going to take us to the labyrinth before the gargoyle manages to escape on his own?"

Ryshi heaved a deep sigh. "Are you always so testy?"

"Yes."

"Why?"

"I don't like being away from my lair."

The words were out before she could halt them and something that might have been sympathy simmered in the ebony depths of his eyes. Thankfully, he was wise enough to keep his lips shut as he turned to wave his hand in a languid motion. The sudden scent of wildflowers filled the air, revealing he'd opened a portal, although Sofie couldn't see it.

"Our first stop is through there," Ryshi told her, pointing at a spot directly in front of her.

Sofie sent him a wary glance. "What do you mean, our first stop?"

"The labyrinth is made up of layers of illusion. It's those layers that create the maze."

"My lair is hidden by illusion. What makes this one different?"

"Once you enter a particular portion of the labyrinth, you can't leave. You must go forward and discover the opening to the next section."

Sofie considered the explanation. She'd never given the minotaurs or the stories that spoke of them much thought, but if the maze was as insurmountable as the myths claimed, then there had to be more to them than just illusions.

"I assume the doorway is hidden?"

"Not only hidden, but also protected."

"Protected by what?"

"Sometimes creatures who live inside the labyrinth. Sometimes it's magical snares."

Sofie grimaced. She would prefer to battle a horde of trolls than to deal with magic. Vampires had no defense against spells.

"What happens if you get caught in a snare?"

"You remain trapped for eternity. If you're lucky. If not..." He held her gaze. "You die."

She tilted her chin. He was deliberately attempting to frighten her. Why? Because he didn't want to enter the portal? Maybe his boast of being able to outwit the minotaurs was nothing more than a lie.

"If it's so difficult, how did you manage to navigate it?" she demanded.

"My imp blood allows me to see through illusions."

"Then any fey creature can get through?"

He sent her a startled glance. As if it was a ridiculous question. "Of course not. I'm the only one capable of that particular feat."

"Why?"

The wicked smile returned. The creature even had the audacity to step closer to her, his gaze locked on her lips.

"Because I'm multitalented. Would you like a demonstration?"

Sofie hissed. She didn't know what bothered her more. Ryshi's arrogance or his potent sensuality, which was threatening to destroy her shell of detachment.

Both, she finally decided, touching the hilt of her blade strapped around her waist.

"Are you trying to piss me off?"

"I don't have to try." He arched a mocking brow. "I'm guessing that pissed-off is your go-to mood setting."

Sofie snapped her fangs together. She was a vampire. A lethal predator and a demon who stood on top of the evolutionary ladder. She wasn't going to embarrass herself by squabbling like a child with this male.

No matter how annoying he might be.

"Tell me why you can get through and no one else can," she commanded.

His smile widened, but thankfully he answered her question. "Jinn are creatures of mist and magic. I become part of the illusion."

"It doesn't sense you are an intruder?"

"Exactly." His smile faded, his beautiful face suddenly hard with an unmistakable warning. "You, however, sweet Sofie, will set off all sorts of alarms."

There was an unmistakable sincerity in his voice. "What are you saying?"

"It would be better for both of us if you would wait for me here while I retrieve the gargoyle."

Her brows snapped together. A part of her was willing to accept that he was telling the truth. It seemed perfectly plausible that his jinn blood allowed him to pass unnoticed by the magic of the labyrinth. And that her own presence was going to be far more dangerous. Unfortunately, she didn't have a choice. Styx had ordered her to retrieve the gargoyle. And that's what she was going to do. No matter how difficult the job.

"I'm sure it would be better for you if I stayed here," she said dryly. "Then you could disappear in a puff of smoke."

"Why, Sofie," he drawled. "Are you implying you don't trust me?"

"I don't trust anyone."

He stilled, as if her words had caught him off guard. Then he lifted his hand, as if he intended to touch her cheek.

"I'm sorry."

"Don't be." She jerked away, desperate to avoid his touch. "Let's get this over with."

He lowered his hand, his expression impossible to read. "Fine." He folded his arms over his chest. "Obviously you're as stubborn as your king, but if you wish to survive, you'll listen to me once we're in the labyrinth. It's the only way both of us will return."

"Agreed," she said without hesitation. This male was the only one who supposedly entered the labyrinth and lived to tell the tale. She would have to depend on him to survive. That still didn't mean that she trusted him. She narrowed her eyes. "But I promise that if you try to escape or lead me into a snare, you'll regret it."

The sensual scent of amber drenched the air as the dark gaze moved slowly down the length of her body.

"One thing you should know about jinn, Sofie, is that we are captivated by a challenge."

Her fingers tightened on the hilt of the dagger. "Get this straight, Ryshi. I am not a challenge."

"Too late." His fingers brushed her cheek. A caress as light as the sweep of a butterfly wing and yet it seared her as if he'd used a branding iron. "Stay close."

He turned to disappear through the portal and Sofie grudgingly forced herself to follow.

"Like I have a choice?"

Chapter 5

Ryshi came to a halt as soon as he was through the portal, glancing cautiously from side to side. There was a blast of icy power as Sofie entered the labyrinth and stood at his side. Her eyes widened as she took in the sunny meadow surrounded by a frame of thick cedar trees.

It wasn't the daylight that brought the confusion to her face. It was easy to detect it was magic, not the real sun that would have turned her to a pile of ash. Or even the bucolic village across the field that was circled by cottages with thatched roofs and freshly scrubbed windows.

Her confusion was clearly directed at the sight of the numerous demons who were gathered in the center of the village, eating at the long wooden tables. Ryshi understood her bewilderment. The place appeared to be the perfect setting for a tribe of fey creatures, but there were more than fairies and imps among the large group. There were at least three orcs, a couple of trolls, and even a few goblins. There was also a vampire standing alone in the shadow of a large oak tree.

Sofie shook her head. "This isn't what I was expecting."

"Don't be fooled," Ryshi murmured, leading her through a thick patch of wildflowers. There were no pathways leading to the village. As if encouraging any trespasser to head in the opposite direction. "The moment they detect an intruder they'll attack."

She gave a sharp nod, staying close to his side as they walked forward. She wasn't afraid. Her scent would have revealed her fear. But she was wisely cautious as they approached the gathering.

"Where is the opening?"

Ryshi shrugged. "I have to look for it."

She sent him a sharp glance. "Don't you remember?"

"The illusions are never exactly the same. Sometimes they change while you're still in them." He wrinkled his nose. "Sometimes they disappear altogether. That's when you better hope you're close to an exit."

"Great. So we just wander around until you manage to find it?"

"Pretty much. Oh, and try not to die." Ryshi came to a halt, turning to face her. "Speaking of which." He waved his hand over her, close enough to feel her biting chill without actually touching her skin.

She stiffened. "What are you doing?"

Ryshi watched as his power floated and swirled through the air before coating the vampire in a layer of magic.

"Hiding you in my essence," he told his companion. "You should be able to pass through the magic without being detected."

She glanced down, as if unable to sense the masking spell. "I'm invisible?"

His lips twitched. "Not quite. But it will hopefully prevent the minotaur spell from recognizing you as an intruder. At least until we can find the exit."

He turned to continue toward the village, feeling Sofie hesitate before hurrying to catch up with his long strides.

"Why are we going toward the demons? Wouldn't it make more sense to start at the edge of the meadow and work your way in?"

"The entrance can be a tree, a flower, or one of the creatures in the maze. The only common denominator is that it's always in a place that most intruders would prefer to avoid." He nodded toward the village. "Like a hungry troll."

It'd taken him precious time and a near-death experience to discover the secret of the labyrinth.

"I suppose that makes sense," Sofie grudgingly admitted.

"Trust me."

"Never."

Anticipation swirled through Ryshi, igniting the passions that had been suppressed for far too long. This female was beautiful, of course. Vampires were always gorgeous. It was the bait they used to hunt their prey. It was Sofie's defiant independence and hint of mystery that fascinated him. She was complex and elusive and fiercely dangerous.

"A challenge," he breathed.

The chill in the air deepened, but Sofie didn't respond as she nodded toward the delicate wood sprite who was leaving the village to walk in their direction. The female was as tall as Sofie, with a slender frame that was covered by a sheer robe and long hair that held tints of green.

"Is she real?"

It was a question that Ryshi had considered long after he'd managed to escape from the maze.

"Yes. I'm not sure if they were captured by the minotaurs and forced into the labyrinth or if they entered on their own and were ensnared in the spell," he revealed. "But however they got here, they don't appear to realize they're stuck in this place. They simply repeat a moment in time over and over. In this case, it's obviously eating a meal together in the center of the village."

"They're like actors on a stage." Sofie shuddered. "Replicating the same performance."

Ryshi sensed her horror, but he couldn't allow her to sympathize with the creatures trapped in the labyrinth. Not if they were going to survive.

"Remember that those weapons aren't props," he said in a low voice, his gaze catching a glimpse of a silver blade hidden beneath the woman's robe. "One wrong move and she'll stick a dagger in your heart."

"I thought you said that your magic would protect us?"

"It allows me to move around like I'm one of them," he corrected.

"Just part of the cast?"

He clicked his tongue, sending her a chiding glance. "Hardly just another cast member. I'm the romantic lead."

As if on cue, the sprite sent him a smile of pure invitation. A smile that might have been a lot more inviting if her eyes hadn't been devoid of emotion. Like she was a puppet being controlled by an unseen master.

"More like the comic relief," Sofie informed him in sweet tones.

"Sweet Sofie. So beautiful and yet so cruel."

She flashed her fangs and he laughed. Unfortunately, their conversation was interrupted as the sprite performed a deep bow.

"Welcome to our village, strangers." Her voice was raspy, as if she didn't use it often.

Maybe never.

Ryshi offered a cautious nod of his head. "Thank you."

"I am Fassie." Her gaze darted toward Sofie, as if vaguely aware there was another creature in the area, before returning to Ryshi. She obviously realized Sofie was there, but her alarm hadn't gone off. Exactly what he'd hoped would happen. "Follow me. We are preparing lunch."

The female turned, heading back toward the village at a steady pace. Ryshi waited until there was some space between them before following. The female might act as if she was pleased by their arrival, but in the blink of an eye she could launch an attack. He'd had it happen before.

They'd reached the edge of the cottages when a soft breeze brought the scent of fresh fruit and figs dipped in honey. His mouth watered.

"Mmm." He licked his lips in anticipation. "Smells delicious."

Sofie nudged him with her elbow. "We don't have time to eat."

Ryshi laid his hand on his stomach. At heart he was a creature who gloried in self-indulgence. If fate hadn't interfered, he would no doubt have spent his existence in his demon club, the Oasis, surrounded by luxury.

"It's been a decade since I've had decent food," he complained.

"You aren't going to convince me that Styx tried to starve you."

He hadn't. Styx was no doubt a ruthless bastard, but he'd treated Ryshi remarkably well. And as a bonus, his mate, Darcy, was a vegetarian. Crazy for a werewolf, but crazy seemed to be an overriding theme at the Anasso's lair. She had a chef who specialized in meals that would please any fey creature. Still, there'd been a few things missing.

"No, but my meals didn't include ambrosia. Can you smell it?"

Sofie tilted back her head, her nostrils flaring. "I smell blood."

Ryshi's heart slammed against his ribs. He'd never been bitten by a vampire. Because he'd never *wanted* to be bitten by a vampire.

Not until this moment. Shuddering at the unexpected craving to feel Sofie's fangs sliding deep into his flesh, he slowed his pace.

"Do you need a sip?"

Her eyes dilated, as if she shared his aching desire for her to feed from his vein. "Are you offering?"

Ryshi traced his fingers down the side of his throat. It was a blatant invitation. "Anytime, anyplace."

Sofie's fangs pressed against her lower lip as the grass beneath their feet was coated in a thick layer of frost. Was her hunger for him threatening to escape her rigid control? Impossible to say. With a visible effort, she turned her head toward the approaching village and the demons who were eying them with various levels of interest.

Ryshi grimaced. It was understandable that he would have a hard time controlling his lust. He'd been so focused on his hunt that he'd neglected to seek out female companionship. But he sensed that it wasn't abstinence that had catapulted his desire into overdrive. It was all Sofie.

Leading them directly toward the long wooden tables, Fassie waved a hand at the bench. Instantly two imps jumped to their feet to make room for them.

"Join our feast," Fassie said. "We have plenty to share."

"Very generous," Ryshi said, settling on the bench and motioning for Sofie to join him.

She hesitated, her icy gaze sweeping over the large orcs who looked capable of crushing them with the massive cudgels they gripped in their hands. Then, as if realizing that refusal would give away the fact they weren't part of the illusion, she perched stiffly on the edge of the bench.

Fassie placed two large bowls of fruit in front of them before offering a bow. "A room will be prepared while you eat."

Ryshi grabbed a spoon off the table and dug into the fruit, licking the sticky honey from his lips.

"Mmm." He glanced toward Sofie. She looked as if she'd been carved out of ice as she sat in motionless silence, but Ryshi could sense that she was on full alert. It wasn't just the tension that hummed around her slender body. It actually vibrated through the bond that held his mind captive. He waved his spoon under her nose. "Are you sure you don't want a bite?"

Her gaze continued to scan their surroundings, constantly searching for danger. "I don't consume food."

"A shame." He scooped out a large fig and stuffed it in his mouth. Sweet pleasure exploded through him.

"Not really." She appeared to ignore his sigh of satisfaction as he polished off the last of his food. Then, without warning, she pointed toward a spot that was near a line of trees. "There."

He glanced in the direction she indicated, frowning at the sight of the nasty pile of garbage and filth that was attracting the attention of hundreds of buzzing flies.

"There what?"

"The opening."

Ryshi sent her a startled glance. Vampires were supposedly incapable of detecting magic.

"You can see it?"

"No, but you claimed it would be a spot that an intruder would avoid," she reminded him. "What better place than a pile of trash?"

"You're right. It's the only taint in the perfection of this place." He slowly smiled, fiercely pleased that she'd paid attention to his words. "So...not just another pretty face."

"Stop calling me pretty," she snapped, never allowing her gaze to leave the garbage pile.

He chuckled, unable to resist teasing her. It was the one certain means of slipping beneath her frigid composure. His amusement quickly faded, however, as he stepped away from the table.

"Let's check it out."

In a fluid motion, Sofie was standing next to him, clearly anxious to continue their journey. Side by side, they headed toward the edge of the village, the chill of her powers combining with his jinn magic to form a mist that danced around their feet. An unfamiliar sensation tingled through Ryshi at the sight.

Walking between two cottages, Fassie abruptly appeared beside them, her lips stretched in a smile.

"Your room is this way." She grabbed his arm, as if intending to pull him back to the village.

"I will join you in a minute," he promised, jerking out of her grasp.

Fassie grimly leaped ahead of them, spreading her arms. "This area is off-limits."

Without hesitation, they stepped around the sprite's slender form and continued forward.

"Wait!" Fassie called out. "You cannot go there. Stop!"

"We must be getting close," Ryshi murmured, his nose curling as he caught a putrid stench.

It wasn't just the garbage pile. The smell went deeper. As if there was a rot that crawled just beneath the pastoral beauty of the meadow. Was it the labyrinth? Impossible to know for sure. He hadn't noticed it the last time he was in the maze.

"Do you see the opening?" Sofie demanded.

Ryshi cautiously rounded the edge of the pile, his gaze searching for the shimmers of magic that would reveal the exit.

"Not yet," he said. "Watch my back."

Concentrating on his search, Ryshi didn't hesitate to trust Sofie to protect him. It wasn't just that she would be stuck in the illusion without him. He could actually sense her resolution. She'd made a pledge to her Anasso to return to Chicago with both Ryshi and the gargoyle. She would die to fulfill that promise.

A few seconds later, he heard the sound of heavy footsteps slamming against the ground and the grunts of an angry troll.

"The natives are getting restless," Sofie murmured.

Out of the corner of his eye, Ryshi caught sight of Sofie pulling out her dagger as two male sprites leaped over the garbage pile in a surprise attack. Grimly, Ryshi continued his search even as he monitored the battle. He wasn't worried about Sofie. As the sprites attacked, she was whirling in a blindingly fast motion, kicking one in the chest to send him tumbling into the garbage before crouching low to avoid the sword that was being swung at her head. She struck out with the dagger, slicing through the male's leg.

The sprite screamed in pain, collapsing as if some sort of poison raced through his body. Or a curse.

Sofie didn't watch the creature die. She was already leaping to the side as a troll tried to smash her with a heavy cudgel. Wisely, she didn't bother to try to stab the troll. Its skin was too thick for the blade. Instead, she grabbed the wooden club he was holding and used it to jerk the lumbering creature off balance. The troll roared in frustration, stumbling forward. Not waiting for the male to regain his balance, Sofie was darting between his legs, kicking his ankle as she rolled forward and flowed upright. The troll stumbled to his knees and Sofie leaped up to kick him in the center of his back. The blow sent him face-first into the garbage heap.

Ryshi wanted to stop his search and simply enjoy the show. Sofie moved with a quicksilver grace that was mesmerizing, flowing from one movement to the next as if she was performing a dance rather than destroying the throng of attackers that were piling up at an alarming rate.

Now, however, wasn't the time to admire Sofie's fighting skills. That would have to wait until they'd escaped the labyrinth.

At last discovering the faint shimmer between two large trees, Ryshi turned to grab Sofie's hand.

"Got it." He ignored her fierce glare, maintaining his tight grip as he pulled her toward the trees. "Let's go."

* * * *

Styx was in his office, searching through his old scrolls to discover any weaknesses that Hades, god of the underworld, might possess when a servant arrived to inform him that Viper was waiting for him in the library.

Styx scowled as he stomped his way through the house. Not that he was mad at the interruption. His eyes were starting to cross from endless hours of trying to decipher ancient texts. But hearing the empty echo of his boots against the marble floor reminded him once again that he was alone in his lair.

Darcy hadn't even argued when he'd suggested she travel to Kansas City to stay with her twin sister. She'd obviously decided that an oversized gargoyle and a deity from the depths of hell were more than she could bear.

They were more than *he* could bear. But there wasn't much he could do about them until they managed to locate Levet.

Stepping into the library, Styx spotted the clan chief of Chicago staring out the window. At a glance the two vampires appeared to be complete opposites. Viper was several inches shorter than Styx with a slender body that he kept attired in velvet jackets and satin slacks. His hair was as pale as moonlight and tumbled to his waist; his eyes, in contrast, were as dark as the midnight sky. But while their appearances might be different, they both possessed the sort of thunderous power that made the demon world quake in fear.

"Viper." Styx crossed toward the desk to pour himself a large shot of his favorite whiskey. He didn't doubt he was going to need it. "What are you doing here?"

Viper continued to stare out the window. "Have you noticed that there's a rather large gargoyle in your yard?"

"I noticed."

"And if I'm not mistaken—and I'm never mistaken—that's Hades, the god of the underworld."

"Yes."

Viper slowly turned, his lips twitching as he struggled to control his amusement. "Is there a particular reason that a gargoyle and a god from hell are smooshing your rose garden?"

Styx tossed the whiskey down his throat. "My best guess is that they're worried about Levet."

Viper's nostrils flared with distaste. It was Viper's mate, Shay, who'd encouraged Levet to stay in Chicago after he'd been rescued from the slave traders. And no one had suffered more than Viper at having the aggravating pest constantly underfoot.

"I heard that he managed to be captured by the minotaurs," Viper said, proving once again that the vampires were best at everything. Including sharing gossip. "Although I'm confused why you would care. Surely it's a good thing the creature has become someone else's problem?"

"I care because I have a seven-foot gargoyle and a god perched in my garden."

Viper shrugged. "If they're worried about the stupid creature then why are they here? Surely they should be doing something to get him back?"

Styx grimaced. "I'm assuming they expect me to take care of it."

Viper looked confused. "Why would you be able to..." Viper's eyes abruptly widened as he realized why Aunt Bertha and Hades were depending on Styx to retrieve Levet from the labyrinth. "No. Don't tell me you released the thief?"

"What choice did I have?"

"He stole my favorite dagger."

Styx rolled his eyes. Viper had been collecting rare weapons for several centuries. He had entire warehouses stuffed with them.

"You have thousands of daggers."

"That's not the point." Viper ran his hand down the black velvet jacket and layers of ice coated the priceless carpet on the floor. "I don't like a demon creeping in and out of my lair whenever he wants. Next time he might take more than a dagger."

Styx couldn't argue. When they'd first realized there was a mysterious burglar targeting vampire lairs, Styx had been annoyed. It wasn't like the creature took anything more than small objects that were more sentimental than valuable. And worse, it didn't matter how many times he left warnings for the bastard, he just wouldn't stop. At last he'd had no choice but to send Sofie to capture him.

"Once he returns, I'll make the decision of what to do with him," Styx assured the male, adding that to his very long to-do list.

The truth was, he didn't know what to do with Ryshi. Keeping him locked in his dungeons seemed excessive for such petty crimes, but he couldn't allow him to continue trespassing into vampire lairs. It would make him look weak as a king.

"If he returns," Viper muttered.

"He will." That was one thing Styx had no doubt about. "I sent Sofie with him."

"Poor Sofie."

Styx shrugged. He didn't regret forcing the reclusive vampire from her lonely mountain.

"She needs the distraction."

Viper arched a brow. "Easy for you to say."

Easy? Styx deliberately glanced toward the window. The moonlight drenched the seven-foot gargoyle in a pool of silver while Hades was cloaked in a darkness so thick it was impossible to penetrate.

"Trust me, there's nothing easy about this situation," he growled. "So why are you here?"

"Jagr contacted me."

Styx blinked. That was a surprise. "Why?"

"He's searching for information on the minotaurs."

"From you?"

Viper pressed his hand against the frilly lace shirt beneath his jacket. "Why do you look so surprised? I'm not a complete hedonist."

"Yes you are."

Viper chuckled. "Okay, I am. But while I don't stuff my lair with dusty old books I'll never read, I do collect rare weapons." He pointed toward an object on the leather couch near the bookcases.

Curious, Styx crossed the room to gaze down at the bundle that had been left on the cushions. Reaching down, he cautiously pulled off the soft leather blanket, not sure what to expect. What he revealed was a long spear with a heavy wooden shaft and a chiseled copper tip at the end. He arched his brows. There didn't appear to be anything special about the weapon.

"What is it?"

Viper joined him, reaching down to pick it up. "A minotaur spear."

Styx was still confused. "Fascinating, but I'm not sure how it's supposed to help."

Viper held the spear so the chandelier overhead could reveal the marks that had been scratched into the wood. They didn't possess the elegant beauty of fey hieroglyphs or the complicated patterns of a sorcerer's staff, but the simple symbols were easy to decipher.

"From what I could discover in my research, these carvings represent various prophecies for the minotaurs. I studied them centuries ago, but I'd forgotten about them until Jagr called. There's one I think you should see." Viper tilted the shaft toward Styx, pointing toward the symbols carved just beneath the copper tip. "Here."

Styx leaned forward, his gaze tracing the wavy line with smaller vertical lines that looked like fields of wheat. As Viper slowly turned the shaft, he could make out a round wooden building with a long balcony. "It looks like a castle. Or a fortress."

"The homeland," Viper explained. Then he pointed to the last symbol. "And there."

This one was more difficult for Styx to make out. It looked like a plump ball with dangly legs flying over the fortress. It wasn't until he noticed the horns that he realized what it was supposed to be.

"A gargoyle?"

"Look closer," Viper commanded.

Styx ground his fangs together, squashing his flare of impatience. Viper wouldn't be showing him the spear if he didn't believe it might help. Or at least he'd better not. Styx wasn't in the mood for jokes. He was in the mood for sticking things with his big sword.

Leaning forward, he continued to study the rough etching of the gargoyle. It took a full minute before he realized what had captured Viper's attention.

"It's an image of Levet," he muttered in disbelief.

"Unless there's another gargoyle with fairy wings and a habit of showing up in the most inconvenient places."

Styx shuddered. "Don't even joke about there being more than one." Stepping back, Styx considered the implications. "Does this mean that the pest has visited the minotaur homeland before?"

"These are prophecies." Viper ran his fingers down the shaft of the spear. "So even if he hasn't been there in the past, they certainly believe he has a reason to be there in the future."

"What reason?"

Viper glanced toward the window. "I have no idea, but it's bound to be awful."

Styx felt his stomach clench with dread. The tiny gargoyle had started wars, destroyed cities, and ripped holes in the fabric of time. The thought that he was about to create yet another disaster that would no doubt cause endless trouble for the vampires was enough to make Styx consider a long vacation. Preferably in an undisclosed location far from Chicago.

"Shit."

Chapter 6

Leaping through the portal, Sofie discovered she was shrouded in shades of gray. Not the shadows of twilight. Or even the gloom of a cave. Just a cold, monotonous gray that draped the empty landscape that was dotted with barren rocks and dead tree stumps. It was a complete contrast to the vivid colors they'd left behind. As if they'd entered a dimension that was utterly devoid of life.

Coming to a sharp halt, Sofie resisted the urge to turn her head and make sure that Ryshi was nearby. Not only did she refuse to reveal her fear of being abandoned in the strange labyrinth, but she didn't need to see the mongrel jinn to know he was standing a few inches away.

It wasn't just the warmth from his body, or the scent of amber. It was his presence that flowed through the leash she'd placed around his mind. The connection was more intimate than usual, as if he was more a partner than a prisoner, but Sofie dismissed the sensation.

She had more important things to worry about at the moment.

"What is this place?" she demanded.

"I'm not sure." Ryshi hissed as a large bolt of lightning zigzagged from the sky, striking the ground with sizzling force. "We need to find shelter," he rasped, his gaze scanning the desolate landscape as another bolt slammed into a large rock that instantly exploded. He pointed toward a low hill where there appeared to be a small opening into a cave. "Over there."

He took several steps before Sofie leaped forward to grab him by the arm. "Wait," she commanded, smelling the ozone before the lightning streaked across the lead-gray sky. The second it faded she called out, "Now!"

Together they raced forward, forced to leap over several wide crevasses before they were diving into the low cave. Directly behind them, lightning hit close enough to shower them with pebbles as it struck the hard-packed ground.

They crouched at the back of the small space, watching the lethal bolts that were systematically wreaking havoc.

"This is…" Ryshi paused when the dirt above their heads sprinkled down as lightning hit the hill. "Unexpected," he continued when the cave didn't collapse. "I wonder if the minotaurs created this area of the labyrinth because of me?"

"Because of you? That's a conceited assumption, even by your standards," Sofie mocked. "Why would you assume that you're so important?"

He shrugged. "I'm the only demon to enter the labyrinth and not only survive, but escape."

All right. Sofie couldn't deny he had a point. If he was truly the one and only creature to outwit the labyrinth, then it was possible they'd taken steps to make sure he couldn't do it again.

Not that she was about to agree with the aggravating creature. Instead, she waved her hand toward their bleak surroundings.

"Why would they create this?"

He turned his head, but not before she caught a glimpse of his annoyed expression. As if he realized he was giving away more than he intended.

"Lightning is one of the few ways to disrupt my powers," he grudgingly admitted.

It had to be his jinn powers, Sofie silently acknowledged. A fey creature was impervious to anything that was created from nature. Except iron.

"What happens?"

"I turn to smoke."

Sofie frowned. She thought jinn preferred to travel through the world in that form. Who wouldn't want to drift around, completely undetected?

"Would that be a bad thing?" she asked.

"I can't move through the exit when I'm incorporeal."

Oh. Okay. That made sense. Still, she wasn't prepared to pander to his ego by accepting that the minotaurs had created an entire section of the labyrinth because of him.

"You know, it's just as likely this area was created to protect against vampires." It was no secret that vampires were highly flammable and that a lightning strike could potentially turn her into a small pile of ash.

"True." He turned his head to study her with a curious expression. "I wonder if the magic sensed your presence."

"I don't intend to stay here long enough to find out."

"Good choice." She sensed him preparing to leave the cave. "Wait for me here. I'll search for the opening."

She grabbed his arm. "No."

He made a sound of impatience. "You have my mind trapped. I couldn't run away even if I wanted to." With a swift motion, he twisted his arm so he could grab her hand and press it to the searing heat of his lips. "And trust me, I don't want to."

Sofie jerked, shocked by the sensation of being branded by his touch. "I'm not worried about you fleeing. I'm worried about you doing something stupid and getting yourself killed."

He turned her hand over, nuzzling the sensitive flesh of her inner wrist. Hunger blasted through her as hot and explosive as lava.

"Why, Sofie." He stroked his lips up her inner arm, leaving behind a trail of fire. "I didn't know you cared."

Sofie shivered, dazed by the melting desire that threatened to drown her. Jinn were masters of seduction. It was rumored that a full-blooded jinn could manipulate any demon with desire.

But Sofie didn't believe he was using his power on her. This wasn't magic. It was the raw lust of a female who'd forgotten the pleasures the touch of a male could offer. Or maybe there'd never been another male who had managed to penetrate her defenses. At least not in a way to stir her deepest desires.

Her eyes closed as she allowed herself to briefly savor that intoxicating sensation, then the crack of lightning striking a nearby tree had her yanking her arm from his light grasp.

"I don't care," she informed him, turning her head to gaze out the opening of the cave. Ryshi had a unique ability to distract her. It was... aggravating. "But I'll be stuck here if you die."

"And you would miss me."

"Hush." She held up a hand, tilting her head to the side. "I'm trying to listen."

"Listen to what?"

"The pattern."

Ryshi pressed against her as he leaned toward the opening. "The pattern of what?"

Sofie refused to give him the satisfaction of shoving him away. Or at least that's what she told herself as his warmth wrapped around her and his scent seeped into her skin.

"The lightning," she said, keeping her gaze trained on the flashing bolts.

"There's a pattern?"

"You said yourself that the spell repeats itself over and over. If you're right, then there has to be a pattern."

"Of course." She didn't need to see his expression to sense his startled approval. "Very clever."

She frowned, annoyed by her surge of pleasure at his admiration. "It will take a few minutes to memorize it."

"I'm in no hurry." He turned to lean his back against the side of the cave, stretching out his legs. "Plus, this gives us an opportunity to become better acquainted. Tell me about yourself."

Sofie clenched her hands. His touch might be intoxicating, but there was no way in hell she was discussing her past. Not with anyone.

"Do you always talk this much?"

"I'm interested in you." There was a brief pause. "And honestly, I haven't had a decent conversation in a decade."

"Neither have I." She silently counted between the flashes of lightning. "It's been fabulous."

Ryshi sucked in a sharp breath at her blunt honesty. "You don't like vampires?"

"I prefer my own company."

"Why?"

"Because I have the opportunity to think without constant interruptions," she snapped. It wasn't entirely a lie. She did prefer the quiet. But that wasn't the true reason she avoided other vampires. "Something I could use right now."

He ignored her less than subtle reprimand. "The world has become a crowded place. How do you avoid interruptions? Do you have a lair in the Fortress of Solitude?"

Her lips twitched. Despite her isolation, she did have a computer and access to modern technology and pop culture. It was imperative to be able to blend with the humans. They were her food source, after all. Plus, she liked watching movies on occasion. And Superman was one of her favorites. He was a creature who hid behind a mask, accepting that the truth of his identity was his greatest weakness.

"That's a good description."

"And you never get bored?"

"Never."

"Hmm." He tapped his fingers against the hard ground. "Sounds to me like you're hiding from something."

Her jaw clenched. "I am. Infuriating creatures like you."

Tap, tap, tap. "That's not all."

Sofie continued to monitor the lightning, memorizing each strike. Unfortunately, that didn't keep the painful memories from forming in the back of her mind.

Memories that she devoted a great deal of time and energy to keeping buried.

"You know nothing about me," she rasped.

"I can sense there's more. Through our bond."

Sofie jerked in shock, turning her head to glare at his searingly beautiful face.

"Impossible."

He held up his hands, as if trying to soothe her burst of temper. "I didn't notice it the first time you captured my mind, but now…" His brows drew together as he considered what he was experiencing. "Now, I can feel the bitterness that simmers deep inside you. It has something to do with this."

Without warning, he leaned forward, his fingers brushing over the center of her forehead. Sofie hissed, flinching back as his touch ignited a cascade of pain that had nothing to do with the actual wound.

Her hands curled into tight fists. He was just guessing, right? He had to be.

"You don't have to be able to read my mind to guess having a mark carved into my forehead doesn't make me happy."

"It's not the mark." His fingers brushed through the soft strands of her hair, which she kept deliberately short, before he was settling back against the wall. "You obviously wear your scar with pride. It's the male who carved it who is responsible for your bitterness. Your sire?"

She snapped her fangs in his direction. "Stop."

"I can't help it," he protested. "You created the link between us, not me."

"I have your mind imprisoned; there is no link between us." She stared grimly at the lightning that continued to strike. "Now let me concentrate."

There was a blessed silence before Ryshi spoke in soft tones. "You're standing on a mountain. There's an icy breeze tugging at the fur cloak you have wrapped around you. You tilt back your head to view the vast sky that's studded with stars. Ah. You smile."

Sofie knew the exact memory he was describing. She'd been forced to travel to the nearby city to acquire the blood she needed to survive, along with a few supplies. When she'd returned to her lair, she'd climbed to the top peak and simply savored the beauty that surrounded her.

"How did…" Her words died away along with her anger as she tried to block his ability to peer into her thoughts. She couldn't shut the connection, not without releasing him from her hold. But amazingly, she realized that she could catch glimpses into Ryshi's mind. "Oh."

He leaned forward. "What is it?"

"You're right."

"Always."

She shook her head, unnerved by how entwined their thoughts had become. The connection was supposed to be a leash. Like a human would put on a dog. It was a means of keeping Ryshi under her control, but without any actual link that might leave her vulnerable.

"I can sense you. Why?" She spoke her thoughts out loud. "It's never happened before."

"Have you ever held the same mind more than once?"

Sofie considered her answer. When her powers first manifested as a young vampire, she'd been capable only of coercion. More of a suggestion than a compulsion. As she matured, she discovered she could actually trap a demon with her mind. She couldn't force him to do anything, or distort his thoughts, but she could keep him from fleeing. It'd proved to be a handy skill and quickly made her a favorite of her sire. He enjoyed having her hold his enemies captive while he tortured them. But then her powers took another leap. One that led to her downfall. Was it possible her powers were evolving yet again? The explanation didn't bring her any comfort.

"I've held the same mind several times, but usually not for this length of time," she admitted.

"It could be that." He flashed his sexy smile. "Or more likely, it's the fact that I'm very, very special."

Sofie flinched. Was it possible that Ryshi's magic was altering her powers? Or that he was able to manipulate her through the bond? That seemed even worse than all the other options.

"It goes both ways," she warned with a frown.

He looked more curious than alarmed. "You can read my mind?"

Sofie paused before giving into temptation. Instantly she was flooded with a vivid image. An explosion of colors and scents burst through her, but at the same time, it had the transparent sensation of a mirage.

"I see a large open space that's framed by golden trellises," she murmured. "There's a high, domed ceiling that's painted blue with silver stars and a large fountain in the middle of a mosaic tiled floor."

"My Oasis." Ryshi heaved a deep sigh. "It's been too long."

"Around the edge of the opening are piles of satin pillows, and low tables with…" It took a moment for her to recognize the tall copper pipes with long hoses and mouthpieces. "Hookahs."

"My shisha parlor."

Sofie snorted. It was the perfect setting for Ryshi. Lush. Decadent. Drenched in luxury. Then her brows abruptly snapped together as the image transformed. The room was the same, but it was no longer empty. There was a beautiful female with long brown hair and midnight eyes lying on a pile of satin pillows.

Surprise and something that was ominously close to outrage jolted through Sofie as she studied the unknown creature.

"And a companion," she rasped.

"Oh yes," Ryshi purred, reaching out to run his fingers down her arm. "If you insist."

She shook off his hand. "I see a female." Ice crawled over the floor of the cave. "Your mate?"

Ryshi's sensual features abruptly hardened at her sharp question. It wasn't shock that she'd managed to peer into his mind. It was fear. As if she was seeing something he didn't want seen.

"I don't have a mate."

"A lover then," she countered, only to shake her head as she caught a vision of Ryshi sitting at the low table with the female sharing a meal. His feelings toward her weren't sexual. They were a mixture of fond exasperation and aching regret. "No. It's your sister. What happened to her?"

"Nothing." He turned away, staring out the opening of the cave as if trying to shut off their connection.

An impossible task.

Unfortunately.

"I'm not the only one who is bitter," she murmured, shivering as she touched the raw, painful emotions bundled in the center of his heart.

"Maybe you should concentrate on the lightning."

Sofie could have forced her way past his barriers, but she didn't. It wasn't that she was concerned about invading the male's privacy or stirring up painful memories, she hastily assured herself. She was a ruthless vampire who didn't give a shit about anyone or anything. She simply didn't have the time to probe.

Yes. That was it.

She shook her head at her idiotic thoughts and watched the lightning spear toward the hillside. It had happened in that precise location twice before.

"I have the pattern," she announced.

"You're sure?"

"It's not very complicated." She crouched at the entrance of the cave, sending Ryshi a warning glance. "Stop when I say stop. Run when I say run. And stay close."

Ryshi didn't protest. Instead, he pointed toward a spot that was north of where they were hidden. Or at least, what felt like north to Sofie. It was impossible to know for certain surrounded by the strange illusion.

"Head toward the rock formation over there," he said.

"Do you see something?"

"Not yet, but the lightning is driving everything toward this area."

Sofie considered the pattern of the lightning. He was right. After entering this section of the labyrinth, they'd been herded like cattle away from that particular location.

"The opening will be in the most dangerous area," she said dryly.

"Yep."

"Run toward that dead tree stump to the right," she commanded, not waiting for Ryshi to agree before she was sprinting out of the cave and across the hard ground. Ryshi quickly caught up despite her blinding speed, racing beside her. "Stop!" They skidded to a halt as a bolt hit a rock directly in front of them. The explosion of dirt smacked into Sofie's face, but she remained focused. Becoming distracted now could mean the death of her. And Ryshi. "To the left," she called out. They dashed toward a wide fissure, easily vaulting over it as the lightning struck just inches behind them. "Stop." Another bolt. This one a few feet to the side. "Forward."

Together, they zigzagged their way toward the rock formation. "Can you see the opening?"

Ryshi swiveled his head from side to side, a tension vibrating around him. At last, he gave a sharp nod.

"Yes." He stretched out his arm. "Give me your hand."

Sofie wrapped her fingers around his, squeezing them in warning. "Hold on." She counted to three, waiting for the lightning to strike just in front of them. The flash was blinding, but it didn't matter. She couldn't see the opening anyway. "Now!"

Ryshi took the lead, tugging her toward a large stone formation perched in front of a jagged cliff. Sofie followed without hesitation, placing the trust she claimed she didn't possess in her companion as he jumped directly into the pile of rocks.

Chapter 7

Bertha grumbled as she searched for a comfortable position. It was impossible. The rose garden had a dozen marble benches, statues, fountains, and other knickknacks that poked and prodded her backside. It was like sitting on a pincushion.

Landing in Styx's backyard probably hadn't been her best decision, she ruefully conceded. It wasn't precisely designed for comfort. At least not for a gargoyle of her impressive size. But she hadn't known what else to do after she felt Levet being taken from this world.

As soon as she'd sensed his distress, she'd flown to the spot where he'd disappeared. She'd intended to follow his trail and smoosh whoever had dared to attack her tiny relative. But once she'd arrived in the middle of the field outside of Chicago, she'd been shocked by the unmistakable scent of minotaur.

What were the reclusive creatures doing there? And more importantly, why had they taken Levet?

The questions had no answers. Even worse, she had no means of navigating the labyrinth, not even in her current form. Thankfully, she'd heard rumors of a jinn mongrel who claimed to have survived the journey. And she had known exactly where to find him. Flying the short distance to Chicago, she'd landed behind the Anasso's lair, not considering the fact that she wouldn't be able to communicate with Styx. Vampires were too thick skulled to receive telepathic messages.

Unfortunately, she'd also failed to consider the awkwardness of being squashed in such a cramped space.

Not her fault.

In the first place, the King of Vampires should have a more expansive estate. If she were a queen she'd insist on a garden the size of Versailles. And in the second place, she'd spent the last months stuck in the shape of a human. Now that she was once again in her demon form, she occasionally forgot that she needed adequate room for her fabulous girth.

She supposed that she should take comfort in the knowledge that eventually the stupid vampire had realized that Levet was in danger and had sent the thief to rescue him. Plus, he was no longer waving around his big sword. She didn't want to have to smoosh him unless absolutely necessary.

Stretching out her wings, Bertha tried to knock away the stupid ornaments that were stabbing into her tender bits. A wasted effort, she acknowledged with a flare of annoyance. And to add to her irritation, the outrageously gorgeous god who was hovering around her like a mother hen instantly moved to stand directly in front of her.

His dark eyes smoldered with flames as he glanced around in the hope of finding some enemy to battle.

"Is something wrong? Are you in pain?"

"I think a sundial is poking my…" Bertha cleared her throat, snapping her wings back to fold them against her body. "Tail."

The flames remained dancing in the dark eyes as a wicked smile curved his lips. "I can remove it."

Bertha shivered at the thought of having his long, slender fingers in such an intimate spot. She knew from experience they created searing pleasure as they…

No, no, no.

She wasn't here to be fondled by the god of the underworld. As much as she might want to be. She was here for Levet.

"Don't even think about it," she warned.

His smile widened. "Too late."

Bertha rolled her eyes. "Why are you here?"

His smile faded, as if it was being wiped away by his dark thoughts. "You were being threatened."

"I've spent endless centuries being threatened by one creature or another. Usually by my older sister who happens to be a bitch with a capital B. One time she—" Bertha bit off her words. She could spend several years describing the torments she endured at the hands of Levet's mother. The female was a cruel, vindictive gargoyle who took pleasure in causing pain. At the moment, she was more interested in discovering exactly why

Hades was there. "Never mind. You've never made an appearance before tonight. So why now?"

"Does it matter?"

"It does if you intend to fiddle with my life again."

"Fiddle?"

Hades arched a brow, obviously caught off guard by her chiding words. He was no doubt used to creatures tumbling to their knees and begging for his mercy, not warning him to stay out of their business.

"You know exactly what I'm talking about." There was no apology in her tone. This male was responsible for her months of wandering around stuck in a fragile human form, prodding her to travel from place to place with no memory of where she'd been or where she was going. She'd feared that she would be roaming in confusion for the rest of eternity. "It's a wonder I didn't end up dead. Or worse."

His brow inched higher. "Worse?"

"I might have been enslaved."

The flames flared in his eyes. "There was never any danger of you being harmed."

Bertha pursed her lips. "How was I supposed to know that?"

Hades tossed his head, his metallic silver hair shimmering in the moonlight. He looked more like a male who was being unreasonably harassed than a powerful god.

"I do not understand why you continue to dwell on the past," he chided. "You were an essential tool to prevent utter catastrophe. You saved the world."

Bertha wasn't appeased. Unlike Levet, she didn't want to be a hero. She wanted…

Hmm. Actually, she wasn't sure what she wanted. At one time she was easily satisfied. She would explore the world, enjoying the sights before finding a comfortable spot to nap for a century or two.

Now she felt an odd niggle of dissatisfaction. At first, she assumed it was hunger. Usually, a platter of Peking duck and Mandarin pancakes would banish any weird pangs. When that didn't work, she'd tried traveling to Vienna to distract herself with a few nights of culture. Honestly, it was lovely, but it didn't ease her disgruntlement. It was like having an itch she couldn't quite scratch.

Bertha clicked her tongue in annoyance. She blamed Hades for her irritable mood. Before he'd crashed into her life everything had been fine. Not exceptional, but fine.

"I'm no fan of catastrophe, but I don't like being treated as if I'm a puppet on your strings," she groused.

He held up a hand as if making a pledge. "I don't have any plans to make you my puppet."

"Then what are your plans?"

His flawless features twisted into a grimace. "Would you believe me if I say that I'm not sure?"

"No."

He abruptly laughed. "You're odd."

"I'm odd?" She clicked her tongue. "Really, Hades. You are the worst at giving compliments."

"You didn't allow me to finish."

"Fine. Finish."

He stepped closer, his ruthless heat cloaking her like an embrace. Bertha trembled in pleasure. This was better than any platter of Peking duck.

"I'm a god."

"That's it? I'm odd because you're a god?"

Flames danced over his body. Was he struggling to contain his temper? Probably. She often had that effect on males.

"I'm a god, which means I have visions of the future," he continued, his tone warning that he didn't want any interruptions. "Especially if there's going to be an event that might change the world." The flames disappeared as he studied her with a steady gaze. "That's how I knew that you were going to be necessary to keep the gates of hell closed. And of course, just touching a creature allows me to see their death, no matter how distant it might be. But now—"

"No!" Bertha slapped her hands over her ears. She didn't want to know if she had a fiery, painful fatality in her future. She didn't want to know even if it wasn't fiery. Or painful. Immortals possessed an arrogant belief that nothing bad would ever happen. "Don't tell me, don't tell me, don't tell me."

He lifted his arms, then spread them to the sides. Bertha felt her hands being tugged away from her ears despite the fact that Hades wasn't actually touching her.

"I can't tell you because I can't see it," he informed her.

"Oh." Bertha glanced toward her hand, which was still warm from his invisible grasp. "How did you do that?"

"I'm a god."

"You say that a lot."

He sent her a scolding frown. "Bertha. I'm trying to explain why I am here."

"Okay, okay. No need to get pissy. I'm listening."

There was a pause, as if Hades was counting to ten. Or maybe one hundred. Then he spoke in a tone that was carefully devoid of emotion.

"I was able to see your future up to the point of battling the ifrit. It was very clear what you needed to accomplish. As well as what would happen if you failed." He shrugged. "But after that everything else is a mystery."

Bertha considered his words. Should she take offense? No. Not this time.

"I like being a mystery," she informed him. "It's better than being odd."

Hades's tension visibly faded as a smile played around his lips. "I assume that it means our futures are connected."

"Really?" Bertha blinked in confusion. "Why would you assume that?"

"The only future I can't see is my own."

"Hmm." Bertha wasn't a god. Or an oracle. But the lack of visions didn't feel like the best indicator of whether or not there was going to be a love match. She'd rather take her chances on Tinder. "That seems to be a leap."

"One I'm willing to take."

Once again he spread his arms wide. This time a layer of flames spread over her, dancing and swirling as it caressed her skin. It didn't burn, but it was hot enough to penetrate her thick hide, seeping to her very soul. Bertha groaned, melting beneath the searing pleasure that engulfed her. She'd lived a long time. Centuries and centuries and centuries. But she'd never felt anything like this.

Obviously being a god came with a vast plethora of skills. Including the ability to bring a gargoyle to her knees. In the very best way.

"That's..." She sighed, unable to come up with the words to express what she was experiencing. "Warm," she finally muttered.

Hades tilted his head to the side. "Just warm?"

Bertha was on the point of admitting that it was gloriously sinful and that he could scorch her anytime he wanted when she was distracted by a movement at the edge of the garden.

She swallowed a sigh. Playtime was over. At least for now.

"Incoming," she muttered.

Hades frowned. "Incoming what?"

"Vampires. Two of them are headed this way."

The flames that had been caressing her abruptly disappeared. A shame. They really were lovely. Then Hades turned his head to glare at the tall, dark-haired male who was accompanied by another vampire. This one was smaller with pale hair and the appearance of a Regency dandy.

"Leeches," Hades snarled. "What do they want?"

"Maybe they are out for a midnight stroll. This is their lair, after all."

"I'm a god."

Bertha heaved a sigh. "Again with the god thing?"

Hades tilted his chin, looking every inch a deity. "It means that I can claim any territory I want. For now, this garden is mine."

"Um. I wouldn't mention that to Styx. He's already cranky."

"I'm not here to make Styx happy." Hades glanced back at Bertha, his expression impossible to read. "I'm here to make *you* happy."

"Oh."

For once in Bertha's life she was speechless. A god was there to make her happy? That seemed...unlikely. So was this a trap?

Before she could demand an explanation, Styx stopped directly in front of Hades.

"We have something you need to see," the Anasso said, his tone respectful, but determined.

Hades folded his arms over his chest, fire swirling around his feet. "Doubtful."

The silver-haired vampire took a cautious step backward, but Styx ignored the less than subtle warning. In fact, he held out a long stick, as if expecting Hades to take it.

"This is a spear that belonged to the minotaurs. It's etched with what we believe are prophecies."

Hades narrowed his eyes at the male's arrogance, but he didn't char him into a briquette. Progress.

"Why show it to me? The minotaurs aren't my disciples. I have no authority over their divinations."

"We need your interpretation," Styx said.

Hades glanced toward the staff. "Asking a favor from a god is a risky business."

"Not a favor," Styx hastily corrected. Had he made a deal with a god before? If he had, it obviously hadn't turned out well. "Just a...sharing of information."

Hades made a sound of disgust. "You believe I can be manipulated with clever words?"

"Styx, maybe we should reconsider this," the silver-haired vampire hissed.

Styx pretended not to hear his companion, his gaze never wavering from Hades. "I suspect that the etchings might explain why the minotaurs kidnapped Levet."

Bertha's mild amusement was instantly replaced with a fierce flare of hope. "Hades."

The god glanced in her direction, his expression exasperated. He didn't want to give the vampire what he desired. Bertha was guessing that Hades didn't offer his service to anyone without demanding compensation. Probably in the form of a soul. But he knew how desperately she wanted to track down her relative.

Grinding his teeth together, Hades held out his hand. "Give it to me."

Styx cautiously placed the spear on Hades's palm. The god spun toward Bertha, holding the weapon so she could see the pictures that had been carved into the wood. She leaned forward, her gaze skimming over the various symbols. From what she could see they devoted most of their prophecies to battling an unseen darkness that was consuming their homeland. It wasn't until she reached the top of the staff that she noticed the carving of a tiny gargoyle.

"Levet." She turned her attention to Hades, who was running his fingers over the shaft, as if absorbing the essence of the weapon. Or perhaps the essence of the minotaur who had carved the symbols. "What does it mean?" she demanded.

"The minotaurs believe this gargoyle is going to save them," he murmured, speaking out loud so the vampires could hear his words.

"Save them from what?" Styx demanded.

Hades touched a deep hole that had been drilled into the wood. "Extinction."

"Levet?" Bertha was more resigned than shocked. She loved her relative, but he was a disaster magnet. If there was going to be an end-of-the-world event, her nephew was somehow going to be involved. "How?"

"It doesn't reveal how he manages to accomplish the feat, but this proves they have elevated him to god status."

The silver-haired vampire widened his eyes in disbelief. "You can't be serious?"

Hades sent him a grim glare. "I'm always serious."

"Levet a god?" Styx shook his head. "If that stunted pest is a god, then I'm the tooth fairy."

Bertha dismissed the grumbling from the vampires. Clearly they were jealous of Levet.

"That's not so bad," she said to Hades. When she'd realized that Levet had been taken by a minotaur, she'd immediately assumed the worst. Now she breathed a sigh of relief. "Maybe I overreacted."

Hades hesitated, as if debating whether to allow her to cling to her newfound hope, or to destroy it. In the end, he destroyed it.

"I wouldn't be so certain," he warned.

"Why do you say that?" Bertha demanded.

He pointed toward the image of a fortress where a gathering of minotaurs were gazing up at the gargoyle flying over their heads.

"These minotaurs are worshipping the gargoyle," Hades said.

Bertha eyed Hades, not sure why being worshipped was a bad thing. "Okay."

His fingers swept down to point at a separate group who were gathered around a long table.

"These minotaurs are preparing for a sacrifice."

"Oh." Bertha's heart sank to her toes.

* * * *

Levet sat on the humongous throne as a table was carried into the arena and placed directly in front of him. It wasn't the most comfortable chair. In fact, the hard gems poked into the tender flesh of his backside and his legs dangled off the ground, reminding him that he wasn't nearly large enough to fill such an impressive chair.

Even worse, he was increasingly uncomfortable at the knowledge that hundreds of minotaurs were watching him from the surrounding bleachers. The male in the fur cloak and crown had called him the savior of the minotaurs. A title that Levet was certain came with all sorts of duties and complications. Probably even danger.

Exactly what he didn't want.

He was supposed to be comfortably settled in the merfolk castle, watching Inga paint her extraordinary murals or sneaking into the kitchens to steal a cup of nectar before the chef could chase him away. The simple life of a retired knight in shining armor.

Trying to decide the best way to convince the strange creatures that he was no longer in the business of saving the world, Levet was distracted as Joya stepped toward the table and pulled aside the silk cloth to reveal the silver platters beneath.

"Your dinner," she told him.

Levet's stomach growled in appreciation as he leaned forward. Okay, maybe being a savior came with a few benefits.

"Roasted pig?" The smell of fresh meat made his mouth water. Just the thing he needed to keep up his energy. "I thought minotaurs didn't eat meat."

"We do not, but we wished to please you."

"Oh." Levet found that the gems didn't bite into his flesh quite as badly as before. It was a pleasant change to have someone be concerned about his happiness. Not that Inga didn't care, but she was currently treating him with a cold elbow…wait, that wasn't right. Knee? *Non.* Shoulder? *Oui*, that sounded better. "Roasted pig pleases me very much."

Joya waved her hand toward the rest of the bounty. "There is also freshly baked bread and garlic potatoes and—"

"Apple pie?" Levet interrupted, clapping his hands together as he caught sight of the round pan with a cinnamon crumble on top. "I adore apple pie."

The female grabbed a tall pitcher that was beaded with condensation and poured an amber liquid into the mug set directly in front of Levet. The rich scent of hops and fermented yeast teased his nose.

"And our finest ale."

Levet stretched out his hand, intending to grab the mug. He was parched from his trip. And there was nothing like a good ale to wash down roasted pig. But even as he leaned forward, he forced himself to stop and consider what he was doing.

It wasn't an easy task. Levet wasn't much of a thinker. He liked to jump headfirst into situations without bothering to consider whether it was a good or bad idea. How was a demon supposed to enjoy his life if he was forever avoiding disaster? Besides, some of his best adventures had come from situations any sane gargoyle would have avoided.

Now, however, there was a voice in the back of his mind that warned him that Inga wouldn't be happy if he did something stupid and got himself killed. And the last thing he wanted was to disappoint the Queen of the Merfolk.

Sitting back, he cleared his throat. "I fear there's been some confusion," he forced himself to say.

Joya appeared alarmed by his words. As if she feared that she had somehow offended him.

"You don't like the meal?"

"*Non.* It is perfection," Levet hastily assured her.

She breathed a sigh of relief. "Then why do you believe I am confused?"

Levet nodded toward the table. "This cannot be for me."

"Of course it is. We have been preparing a very long time for your arrival."

"You keep implying that you were expecting me."

"We were."

Levet shook his head. The conversation was going in circles. It was starting to make him dizzy. Or maybe it was his hunger making him dizzy. Hard to say.

"How is it possible for you to expect me? I have no connection to the minotaurs." He wrinkled his snout. "At least, none I can recall."

His companion waved a hand toward a figure who was seated in the front row, the hunched body covered by layers of fur. The horns were stunted like his own and there was a heavy veil across the face, preventing him from getting a good look at the mysterious creature.

"Our seer had a vision of you."

"Really?" Levet parted his lips in pleasure. Most of the time he got tossed into danger because the other demons considered him expendable. Who cared if something terrible happened to Levet? It was amazing to think that he was important enough to feature in his very own vision. Always assuming this wasn't some terrible mistake. "And you are certain it's *moi?*"

Joya nodded emphatically. "Quite certain."

Levet scratched the tip of his snout with a claw. "And what am I doing in this vision?"

"Saving the minotaurs from utter destruction."

"That is..." Monumental. Astonishing. Improbable. Levet coughed, trying to find a word that wouldn't reveal his disbelief. "Nice. Um. Do you know how I achieve this miracle?"

"Me?" The female appeared shocked as she pressed her hand against the center of her chest. The question obviously troubled her. "How can we know the ways of gods?"

Gods? Levet shook his head. He had to have misheard. "Did you say clods, *peut-être?*"

"Why would I say clods?" The female abruptly bowed deeply enough to brush her horns against the dirt floor. "You are Levet. The God of Salvation."

"Levet!" The ridiculous crowd once again surged to its feet. "Our savior!"

"Sacrebleu."

Chapter 8

Ryshi clutched Sofie's hand in a fierce grip as he lunged headfirst through the portal. There was no need for the dramatic exit. The gateway didn't close. Or at least, he'd never had one close after he'd found it. But even as they were flying through the opening, he had an unreasonable fear that it might snap closed and trap Sofie on the other side. Without him to reveal the gateway it would be a certain death sentence for a vampire.

Why the possibility bothered him was a mystery. Being in different sections of the labyrinth might sever her hold on his brain. From there he could navigate his way out of the maze and continue his hunt that had been so rudely interrupted by the leeches a decade ago.

But there was no way in hell—or any other dimension—he was leaving Sofie behind. He would risk his own life to make sure she survived.

Why?

Ryshi allowed a wry smile to twist his lips. He could be wild and reckless and occasionally self-destructive, but he wasn't stupid. He wasn't going to dwell on the reason this female was becoming a vital part of his world. Better to tell himself he was too busy preparing for whatever they were about to face next than to ponder his strange fascination with his companion.

Tumbling through the gateway, they landed on a hard patch of ground. Ryshi grunted at the sharp impact, but with one graceful motion he was on his feet, prepared for an attack.

Nothing happened.

There were no demons, no lightning, no hint that there was anything or anyone in the area. That should have eased Ryshi's tension. Instead, he muttered a curse as he caught sight of the high hedge that surrounded them as far as the eye could see. Overhead a thick blanket of clouds hung in sullen stillness, as if longing for a breeze to stir them to life.

Sofie tugged her fingers out of his tight grasp, glancing around with obvious approval. "Now this is what I expected when we entered the labyrinth."

"Don't be fooled," Ryshi warned.

"Fooled by the hedges?"

Ryshi frowned at her dry tone. He'd been equally confident when he'd first arrived in this spot. What could be hard about a mundane human maze created out of a bunch of bushes? It'd taken hours, or perhaps it'd been days and weeks—time moved oddly in the labyrinth—before he realized he was in genuine danger.

"This area took me the longest to escape."

Sofie touched the dagger at her side, no doubt expecting some hidden monster to leap out of the hedge.

"Why?"

"The exit keeps moving."

"Then how do you find it?"

"Luck."

She sent him a glance of disbelief. Clearly she didn't like the thought of depending on a fluke to get out. He didn't like it either.

"Seriously?"

"Yeah. And that's not the worst."

"I'm afraid to ask."

He nodded toward the three separate openings that were visible in the hedge. They were arched, and neatly trimmed, and wide enough for a troll to easily enter. They were also identical. It made it impossible to know which one might lead to the exit.

"If you take the wrong path it dumps you back to this entrance," he said.

"Are there hidden dangers?"

"Not physical dangers, but there's something in the air."

There was a long pause, as if Sofie was waiting for him to continue. "Poison?"

Ryshi didn't blame her for appearing confused. Demons were impervious to toxins that might pollute the air. Not to mention the fact that vampires didn't breathe. He forced himself to recall his journey through the hedges, a shiver racing through him at the memory. It was something he'd done his best to forget.

Turning his head, he studied the nearest entrance. Once he stepped inside the maze, there was a thick shadow that had pressed against him like a death shroud, threatening to destroy his will to continue.

"It's hard to describe."

"Try," she commanded.

Another shiver inched down his spine. Ryshi adored hot nights in his desert Oasis, surrounded by satisfied guests who came to his parlor to enjoy the hookahs and the sand sprites who swayed and danced in the moonlight. The soft music, the hum of low-spoken conversations, and the constant buzz of demon magic that filled the air. Even during the day there had been the chatter of his staff as they'd bustled through the large club, cleaning away the debris from the night before and preparing for another evening of entertainment.

He hated being alone. And the thick silence of this place only added to his misery.

"It feels as if you're being smothered in defeat," he finally muttered.

"That's dramatic."

It was. But it still didn't capture the invisible burden that had pressed down on him with a grinding weight.

"Before I managed to find the exit I just wanted to give up. It was... crushing."

He expected her to dismiss his words of caution, but Sofie instead frowned, her expression worried.

"Then let's find the exit quickly."

He sent her a wry glance, but he couldn't deny his relief that she accepted his warning without argument. She might claim she would never trust him, but a part of her already did.

"Easier said than done." Ryshi turned toward the hedge, pointing at the closest entrance. "Let's start there."

With a nod, Sofie followed him through the arched opening and into the shadowed tunnel. They traveled straight, unable to see anything but the leafy hedge and dirt pathway. Then abruptly the tunnel came to a T, forcing Ryshi to make the decision to turn right or left. He chose right, knowing it didn't make any difference. Either he would be lucky enough to discover the exit, or they'd be dumped back to where they started.

They continued in silence, turning left and right when they came to an intersection. Ryshi didn't bother trying to keep track of their path, or even how much time was passing. There wasn't a pattern that could be memorized. Not when the exit was continually moving from one location to another.

Instead, he concentrated on the cool brush of Sofie's power as she walked next to him. He wasn't alone, he silently assured himself, forcing one foot in front of the other. And eventually they would find their way out of this bleak maze.

As if sensing the cloud that threatened to overwhelm him, Sofie abruptly broke the silence.

"Tell me about your sister."

Ryshi flinched. He desperately needed a distraction, but the last thing he wanted was to discuss his sister. Especially with a leech. Yet, even as his hands clenched in frustration, he discovered his anger fading away as a voice whispered in the back of his mind.

If Sofie was merely hoping to lighten his dark mood, there were a thousand conversations they could have that had nothing to do with their personal lives. The current state of human politics, the threat of global warming, the decade he'd spent trapped in the Anasso's dungeons. The mysterious reason the minotaurs would kidnap a gargoyle...

So why bring up his sister?

"Are you interested?" he demanded.

Sofie shrugged. "If we're going to be stuck here for any length of time we might as well be civilized."

He sent her a chiding glance. "That didn't answer my question. Are you interested?"

Her lips pinched. He didn't need to be able to read her mind to know she wanted to tell him that she couldn't care less. She took pride in her ability to remain aloof from those around her and revealing her curiosity would destroy that image.

"Fine," she snapped as they came to yet another intersection. "I'm interested."

Ryshi paused, as if debating which direction to go. In truth, he was bracing himself to open wounds that he'd kept buried for a very long time.

Why was he opening them? Well, that was another one of those questions he didn't want to consider. Probably because it would mean accepting that he wanted this female to be interested in him. Not as a prisoner. But as a desirable male who she found fascinating. And sexy. And irresistible.

Turning to the left, he entered the shadowed tunnel to continue their seemingly endless wandering.

"Zena is the only daughter of my mother," he told his companion. "She's a full jinn."

Sofie easily kept pace next to him, her gaze locked on him rather than looking for hidden dangers. Ryshi hid a smile of satisfaction. She either trusted his word that there were no monsters in the hedges, or she was more interested in what he had to say than in worrying about potential dangers.

"How many siblings do you have?"

"One sister and probably twenty brothers. At last count." Ryshi shrugged. Talking about the flighty, impetuous fey side of his family was easy. He rarely had contact with them, but when he did it usually ended in a drunken brawl. The typical fun and games of any demon family. "My father is committed to producing the next generation of imps and there are plenty of females to provide him assistance in his goal."

Sofie rolled her eyes, obviously familiar with imps, but she didn't allow him to divert the conversation.

"If you have such a large family, why can I only sense Zena?"

He trained his gaze back on the dirt pathway, knowing that the tumultuous feelings his sister stirred inside him would be visible in his eyes. Unlike Sofie, he didn't have an icy grip on his emotions.

"I was raised by my mother." His words were low and grimly controlled. "Zena and I shared a lair with her."

"You were close?"

"I loved her, of course. We were family. But I was much older and I left while she was still a youngling."

He could feel her gaze searching his profile, no doubt wondering why he was so reluctant to discuss Zena if they barely knew one another.

"Where did you go?"

"I traveled for several centuries."

Despite his tension, Ryshi smiled at the memory of his carefree existence. He'd bounced from one dimension to another, indulging his every desire without worrying about the future. It had been glorious. Eventually, however, he'd developed the urge to settle down. It wasn't a nesting instinct, more a desire to build a lair where he could entertain his wide variety of friends. That's when he'd created the Oasis. He hadn't expected it to become a raging success. Or that he would have to create a waiting list for demons who were eager to become members of his exclusive club.

At last Sofie broke into his memories. "What about your sister?"

Ryshi's mood swiftly soured as he forced himself to dredge up the day he'd discovered his world was about to be turned upside down. Although, at the time, he hadn't realized anything was about to change.

Otherwise he would have fled in horror.

"I didn't see her again until my mother arrived on my doorstep and asked me to take Zena."

"She abandoned her?"

He shrugged. "Jinn rarely remain in one location for more than a few centuries. It's our nature to wander and my mother had decided it was time for her to move along."

Sofie was silent for several minutes. Finally, she gave a shake of her head. "I'm trying to imagine you being responsible for an impressionable young female."

He snorted. He'd been shocked out of his mind when his mother had blithely announced she was leaving and that he was now responsible for an adolescent jinn. He wasn't a nurturer. Most of the time he could barely take care of himself. Then Zena had actually moved in and all hell had broken loose.

The pampered female was exactly like him. Spoiled, impulsive, and headstrong. And like any teenager she also had extreme mood swings that terrified his staff. Honestly, they'd terrified him as well. Worse, she refused to obey his rules.

"It was challenging," Ryshi admitted, an edge in his voice revealing that he was trying to downplay the infuriating years they spent together. "For both of us."

"Does your sister still live in your lair?"

Ryshi managed not to stumble as her question pierced his heart. "No."

He wanted his sharp answer to be the end of the conversation. He'd already forced himself to say more than he wanted. But of course, it wasn't. For whatever reason, Sofie wanted to know the truth about Zena. And she wasn't going to be satisfied until she had it.

"Why not?"

"I forced her to leave."

Something that might have been comprehension flared in her blue eyes, emphasizing the silver rim. Had she sensed that this was the source of his pain? Probably.

"Was there a particular reason you forced her to leave?"

"A thousand reasons. She was at the age where she was insisting on testing her boundaries."

"How does a jinn test her boundaries?"

"By creating chaos. My Oasis was a place of serenity for the demons who gathered there, but Zena couldn't bear the tranquility. She demanded loud music so she could dance on the tables. She destroyed priceless treasures I'd collected during my travels. She stole money from the club and harassed my staff until they refused to return. I tried to be patient."

Her brows arched. "You? Patient?"

"I didn't throttle her in her sleep," he said dryly. "Trust me, that took an extraordinary amount of patience. But when I returned one night to discover she'd snuck in a dozen slog demons to party in the Oasis, I was done."

Sofie made a soft sound of shock. No one with a shred of sense would have anything to do with a slog demon. Not only did they smell like the pits of the underworld, but their thick skin was covered in a toxic slime that destroyed anything it touched. Being around them was like standing in the middle of a pool of acid.

"What happened?" she asked.

Ryshi's jaw clenched. By the time he'd returned from a short trip to Paris, he'd discovered his parlor empty of customers as well as his staff. They'd all fled the moment the slogs had arrived.

"The slogs assumed I was dinner and I had to kill them before they could bite me." Slog teeth were coated in a poison that could kill demons. "The battle left gaping holes in my floor where their bodies leaked their toxic blood and contaminated the fountain that supplied the Oasis with water. I knew that it would take years and a large chunk of my fortune to repair all the damage."

"Where was Zena during the battle?" Sofie asked.

"She was standing on the bar, laughing at the destruction."

A sudden layer of ice coated the hedges that formed the tunnel, as if his explanation had angered Sofie. Why? Had she endured a similar situation in her past? Or did it trouble her that he'd been hurt by his sister's callous behavior?

Either way, it revealed she did have feelings beneath that frigid exterior.

"I'm sure that didn't make you happy," she finally said.

"I've never been so furious in my entire life," he admitted. "I ordered her to pack her bags and leave the Oasis."

"What did she do?"

Ryshi's steady pace never faltered, but tiny tendrils of mist formed around his feet. It was his jinn nature to turn into smoke form when he was under extreme stress. He had to concentrate to maintain his corporeal form.

"At first Zena was certain that I was teasing. After all, she'd destroyed my lair a dozen times before without consequences. But eventually I convinced her that I was serious." Ryshi shook his head. The arguments between the two of them had always been epic, but after the slogs had destroyed the Oasis, Ryshi had refused to speak or even glance in Zena's direction. He'd acted as if she didn't exist. No matter what outrageous stunt she pulled, or how loud she screamed. It was the worst punishment possible for a young female who had to be the center of attention at all times and the one certain way to drive her away. "She packed her bags and left."

"Where is she now?"

Ryshi came to a halt as they reached an intersection. "I don't know," he muttered.

"She disappeared?"

"That's exactly what happened." More mist swirled around Ryshi as the painful memories threatened to overwhelm him. "After Zena stormed out of the lair—and she quite literally stormed out—I spent the next few years savoring the quiet. There was no more drama, no sense of impending doom when I left my private quarters. Just the soothing sound of workers as they restored the Oasis."

"You didn't hear from her?"

Ryshi shook his head. "I assumed she would eventually return and beg for forgiveness. I even fantasized that she would have learned her lesson and accept my rules."

Sofie snorted. "Seriously?"

"She'd never been on her own," he responded, his tone defensive. "It was possible that she might mature when she was forced to take care of herself."

"Did she return?"

She hadn't, of course. Every night that'd passed he'd become more and more concerned. And along with the concern had come a shitload of guilt.

At last he'd decided to go in search of her. He was still angry, but she was his sister. It was his duty to provide her with a home, right? And he had to admit, he actually missed Zena. Not her ridiculous pranks and demands for attention, but his lair had been too quiet since she'd left.

He traveled to the locations they'd visited during her time with him, but he couldn't find any trace of her. He'd widened his search to other dimensions, and even sought out his mother in the hopes that Zena had gotten in contact with her.

It was as if she'd vanished in a puff of smoke. No trail to follow. No rumors of her passing. No hint that she still existed.

A terrifying fear that something terrible had happened settled in his heart. Zena should be easy to locate. She left behind a trail of chaos wherever she went. So the fact that there was nothing meant that she'd been captured. Or was dead.

Finally, he'd decided to take extreme measures to discover exactly what'd happened to her.

That, however, was a story he wasn't going to share with anyone.

Especially not Sofie.

"This way," he said, turning to the right and heading down the tunnel with firm steps.

Sofie hurried to catch up, her lips parting to demand he continue the story. Before the words could leave her lips, however, a burst of magic shuddered through the maze. Ryshi cursed, already bracing himself as the earth beneath their feet abruptly disappeared and they were falling through an endless blackness.

Chapter 9

Levet licked the sticky cinnamon goodness from his lips as he polished off the last of the apple pie. He couldn't deny that he was enjoying himself. Halfway through the lavish feast, he forgot about the gathered onlookers and even the fact that he'd been more or less kidnapped. The meal had been delicious and there was a welcome warmth flowing through his veins.

As if he was floating in a warm bath.

He was slumping in his seat, drifting into a lovely snooze, when Joya abruptly appeared beside him, holding a large pitcher in her hand.

"More ale?"

Levet roused himself, leaning forward to grab his mug. He hadn't even realized it was empty. In fact, he had no memory of how many times he'd emptied it only to have it quickly filled to the brim by the hovering Joya.

More than was precisely wise.

At least a part of his delicious haze was directly connected to the ale he'd consumed.

"It is delicious," he said, watching as she poured the deep amber liquid into the mug.

"We brew it ourselves."

Levet lifted the mug toward his lips. He caught the unmistakable scents of hops and yeast and malt.

"Does it have magic in it?" he asked.

Joya looked confused. "Why do you ask?"

Taking a deep gulp, Levet leaned forward to replace the mug on the tray in front of him. He grunted as he nearly slid off the chair. Desperately flapping his wings, he managed to avoid the embarrassment of tumbling off the throne.

"I seem to have lost my balance." He leaned back, lifting his hand to touch the center of his face. "And I cannot feel my snout. Is it still there?"

"Yes, it's there."

Levet continued to poke at his face. "In this area?"

Joya blinked. "It is attached in the proper place."

"Thank the goddess." Levet blew out a huge sigh of relief. "I would be sad if I had misplaced it."

There was an awkward silence, as if Joya was trying to decide if Levet was playing some sort of joke on her. When Levet simply stared at her in a daze, she lifted her hand and motioned toward the corner of the arena.

"We have prepared entertainment for you," she announced.

"Oh." With a blink, Levet watched the massive minotaurs leap and twirl toward the center of the arena. They were wearing heavy crimson cloaks that looked like something a human matador would wear and thick boots that created small clouds of dust as the dancers moved in perfect unison. "I am not to perform?"

Joya sent him a startled glance. "Do you wish to?"

"My balls are quite spectacular."

"I...um...I'm sure they are."

Levet smiled. Or least he tried to smile. His lips were now as numb as his snout. It made it difficult to know exactly what they were doing.

"I can twirl them and make them float and—"

"Perhaps another occasion," Joya suggested, grabbing him by the shoulders as he swayed and smacked his head against the side of the throne. "For tonight you should rest and prepare yourself."

"You might be right," Levet ruefully conceded. "My balance has gone missing along with my snout."

Joya waved her hand toward the minotaurs who were now directly in front of Levet, leaping high in the air and performing spectacular flips.

"These are our finest dancers," Joya murmured.

"They are *très* colorful." Levet's eyes widened as he realized their horns were glittering in the torchlight. He thought at first they were painted, but as they came closer he could see the unmistakable flash of priceless emeralds and rubies. "Perhaps I should have my horns encrusted with gems."

"The process begins when they are still calves," Joya explained. "I am told it's quite painful, but the results are spectacular."

"Painful, eh?" Levet lifted his hand to touch one stunted horn. He was not a fan of pain. Especially when he was the one in pain. "Maybe the natural approach to beauty is best."

"Indeed," Joya quickly agreed. "You are flawless."

"Right?" Levet heaved a sigh. How many times had he attempted to convince others of his sheer perfection? It seemed absurd that he was the only one who recognized his excellence. "I wish you could convince Inga of that."

Joya tilted her head to the side, a strange expression on her face. "Is this Inga your mate?"

Levet's wings fluttered, a lump forming in his throat. That felt like a dangerous question.

"She is..." He shifted uncomfortably on his throne, a large amethyst poking into his unmentionables. It was difficult to define his relationship with Inga. Not until he had an opportunity to discover why she would no longer answer his calls. "A friend," he finally conceded.

"There are many females here who would be willing to be your friend. They are prepared to worship you in whatever way you desire."

Levet considered her soft promise, temptation whispering through the back of his mind.

"I have never been worshipped before."

Joya stroked a hand over his wing. "It is your destiny."

Levet shivered in ecstasy. There was nothing better than having his wing stroked. Well, obviously it would be better if Inga was doing the stroking, but still...

"Worshipping does seem appropriate considering I am a hero," Levet agreed.

"As you wish."

Levet wasn't sure what he expected. Perhaps a few minotaurs kneeling at his feet, or a song in honor of all his great deeds. He'd once tried to hire a minstrel to wander around the world and spread the word, but the stupid fairy had taken his money and disappeared. There was a teeny-tiny chance that the creature had been eaten by a dragon, but that didn't excuse his lack of success.

Instead, Joya gave another clap of her hands and a dozen female minotaurs appeared from an entrance across the arena. They were wearing long robes that sparkled in the torchlight. Levet watched in fascination as they started to dance, grabbing their robes and tearing off pieces of cloth. No, wait. He frowned. They weren't wearing robes, they were covered in flimsy scarfs. And each time they passed in front of him they were pulling one off and tossing it toward the throne.

"Wait." The fuzzy pleasure that lingered from the potent ale was abruptly shattered as Levet held up his hands, waving at them in a stop-it-now gesture. "What is happening?"

"These females are here to please you."

"Why are they taking off their clothing?"

Joya looked confused. "You prefer males? That can be arranged."

"I prefer everyone to leave their clothing on." Levet grimaced. There had been a time when he would have fully enjoyed the show. The minotaurs were lovely creatures, even if they had kidnapped him. But he wasn't interested in other females. Not now. "If Inga were here, she would bash me with her very large fork."

"Fork?"

"Her Tryshu," he explained, referring to the fabled trident that only the true leader of the merfolk could touch.

Joya's jaw clenched, as if she was becoming aggravated with Levet's refusal to enjoy the dancers.

"If you will tell me what sort of entertainment you desire, I can arrange for it."

Levet hopped off the throne. The feast had been fun and he wished he had the recipe to make a few barrels of that ale. It was worth its weight in gold. But now he was done. He wanted to take a little nap, then travel to the merfolk castle to see Inga.

"I believe I should return to my rooms."

"But..."

Levet didn't allow her to finish her protest. He had been polite, had he not? Even after he'd been kidnapped. He hadn't used his impressive magic to harm his captors or burned down the fortress with his mighty fireballs. Nothing was stopping him now.

"I will take over, Joya," a rumbling male voice said from behind him.

"Yes, master," Joya murmured.

The tall male wearing a crown and fur robe appeared beside Levet as he waddled toward the exit.

"Allow me to escort you," he said.

Levet snorted. As if he could halt the oversize bull-man. Besides, he was still worried that he couldn't feel his face.

"Can you see my snout?"

The large male coughed, as if he had something stuck in his throat. "Excuse me?"

"Joya assures me that it is there, but I am not entirely convinced."

They crossed the arena, which had fallen unnervingly silent, as if the minotaurs were stunned by an unexpected turn of events. Or maybe they'd all had too much ale and blacked out in their seats. At last, they stepped through the open doors and entered the hallway.

"You're worried about your snout?" the male next to him abruptly demanded, as if he'd been pondering Levet's last words.

"*Oui.* It is a very fine snout."

The minotaur shook his head. "The ways of gods are odd."

"You can say that again." Levet readily agreed, puzzled when the male turned down a narrow hallway. He was almost certain his rooms were in the opposite direction. With a shrug, he followed his companion. Surely the creature knew his way around the fortress. "There was this Dark Lord that convinced creatures he was a god and nearly destroyed the world," he continued his story. It was a fabulous tale, after all. One that he would share with anyone who would listen. Which wasn't nearly as many as there should be. "You probably heard about him. But what you might not know is that if it had not been for me, the veil would have parted and evil would have taken over."

"Ah." There was a proper expression of satisfaction on the male's face. "So you have performed miracles before."

"*Oui.*" Levet tried to wrinkle his snout, only to sigh in exasperation when he still couldn't feel it. "The miracles were not precisely planned, and most did not occur in the way I would have desired, but there is no question that I am a hero."

"Good. Then it is time."

Levet frowned as the male took another turn and entered a short corridor that ended in a narrow staircase.

"Time for what?"

"For you to deliver us from doom."

"What sort of doom?"

"You will see."

The male swiftly climbed the steep stairs, his boots making the wood shudder beneath the impact. Levet scrambled to keep up, his heart sinking to the tips of his toes. There was a small part of him curious to know more about his role as the savior of the minotaurs. It was, after all, pretty special to star in a seer's vision. And it would make a great story to tell once he returned to his world. Inga was certain to be impressed if she knew he was a god.

But a larger part of him sensed that the sooner he could escape from this place the better. It wasn't modesty that had made him confess that most of his miracles had been accidents. It was the honest-to-goddess truth. Usually, he was simply trying to survive when he'd been swept up in a tidal wave of events.

"Actually, I would rather not see," Levet said in apologetic tones, reluctantly following as the male reached the top of the stairs and headed toward the ornately carved double doors straight ahead of them. "I mean, I really am busy at the moment. Perhaps we could reschedule this particular doom until a more convenient date." Levet shivered. "As in never?"

The minotaur halted in front of the doors, sending Levet a confused glance. "I don't fully comprehend your humor."

"It isn't for everyone." Levet clicked his tongue. "Or so I've been told. I assume they are just jealous of my quick wits and overabundance of charm."

The male was momentarily speechless. Then he gave a sharp shake of his head. "No matter. Once you have performed your duty I promise you can return to your busy schedule."

Levet's wings drooped. "Doom duty," he muttered. "Why *moi*?"

"You were foreseen."

"It could be a mistake, you know. There are many other gargoyles." Levet's wings perked up as he was struck by a sudden inspiration. "My mother, for instance. She is much stronger and far better suited to facing doom. And I am certain she would be delighted if you were to kidnap her and—"

"Does she look like you?" the male rudely interrupted.

"Um, well. She might be a tad larger."

"And her wings?"

Levet heaved a resigned sigh. "Leather."

"You are the chosen one."

"That sounds like such a good thing in books," Levet muttered. "But I suspect it will not be as fun as I imagined it would be."

Ignoring Levet's grousing, the minotaur turned and placed his hands against the doors. The muscles of his wide shoulders bunched and he released a low grunt as he pushed against the carved wood. It'd obviously been a while since anyone had bothered to grease the hinges, Levet silently decided, as they squealed in protest before slowly allowing the doors to swing open.

"Follow me."

The male stepped through the opening and Levet hesitated. What to do, what to do...

He could turn and try to make a run for it. He didn't doubt that he could disappear among the numerous rooms in the fortress. His compact size allowed him to be very good at hiding. But then what? He wasn't arrogant enough to believe he could make his way through the labyrinth. It was very likely he would become trapped in the maze and spend the rest of eternity roaming around. Not the most pleasant future for a demon with his adventurous spirit.

For the moment, he had no choice but to go along with the minotaurs and hope they would eventually send him home.

Forcing his reluctant feet to carry him forward, Levet stepped through the open doorway and onto a long, narrow balcony built from wood. He scowled as he realized that the timber balustrade was too high to see over, and with a flap of his wings, he lifted himself off the ground to land on top of the wide railing.

Prepared to see hordes of demons charging in their direction, or perhaps magical fires circling the fortress, Levet was relieved when there was nothing to cause him alarm.

In fact, the pastoral landscape seemed perfectly normal. Beneath the silvery moonlight, Levet could easily make out the rolling fields golden with ripening wheat and the babbling brook that danced through the meadow. In the distance, he could see orchards where the trees swayed in the breeze, the fruit-ladened branches dipped toward the ground.

"I am no horti-torti, but—"

"A what?"

"You know. One of those creatures who know about planting stuff in the ground." Levet waved his hand in a vague motion. "But everything looks fine to me. Indeed, it looks like a bumper-car crop. If that is all, I will be on my way."

The male grabbed Levet's wing before he could hop off the railing. "Not the fields. That."

The minotaur pointed his finger toward the sky and Levet reluctantly tilted back his head. His gaze swept over the stars that were spattered like diamonds against the velvet backdrop, admiring the beauty before he at last located the spot that the male was indicating.

It was directly over the fortress and utterly barren. As if it was sucking away every star or speck of light that came near.

"Ah." Levet's stomach twisted with dread. "You mean the big black hole in the sky?"

"That is exactly what I mean."

Chapter 10

Sofie sat on the hard pathway, her legs crossed as she used her dagger to carve a branch she'd chopped off and stripped of leaves. She wasn't sure how long it'd been since they'd been whisked back to the entrance of the maze. There was a weird, sluggish sensation in the air that suggested that time moved slower in this particular area. Beside her, Ryshi was slumped against the hedge, his eyes closed.

Through their mental connection she could sense his struggle against the dark atmosphere that hung over them like a shroud. It wasn't just the fact that his imp blood craved sunshine and fresh air. It was a soul-deep hatred for the thick silence and smothering sense of claustrophobia.

The emotions vibrated through Sofie with shocking intensity. She still had no idea why her connection with Ryshi was so…intimate. It could be because it was the second time she'd trapped his mind. Or the length of time they'd spent together. But neither answer felt right.

It was more like the familiarity she might have shared with a clansman. Or a mate…

Sofie muttered a curse, returning her attention to the figure she'd carved out of the wood. Clearly the atmosphere was affecting her as well. What other excuse could there be for the tingle of excitement sizzling down her spine?

Perhaps sensing her sudden unease, Ryshi sat up and stretched his arms over his head. Sofie stifled a groan as he arched his back, looking like a sleek, sensuous cat.

Was he deliberately drawing attention to the lean muscles that moved beneath his satin tunic? If so, he had succeeded in spectacular fashion.

Slowly, he leaned forward to study the figurine in her hand. His warm scent of amber swirled around Sofie along with a wisp of smoke that brushed against her skin like a caress.

"Who is that?" he asked.

"A rock sprite who lives in the mountains near my lair," she said, eagerly returning her gaze to the smooth piece of wood in her hand.

She stroked her fingers over the delicate features that were an exact replica of the fey creature who for years she'd watched scamper over the rocky pathway just outside her lair. Until this moment she hadn't realized just how closely she'd observed the creature. As if she'd been lonelier than she wanted to admit.

"It's exquisite." His gaze lifted to sweep over her face, his eyes filled with pleasure. "You are very talented."

She shrugged, pretending that his words hadn't warmed her icy heart. Her art was the one thing she took pride in.

"It helps to pass the time."

The smoke continued to swirl around her, the light caress sending shivers of pleasure through her.

"If you are searching for a way to pass the time, you should come to the Oasis with me," Ryshi murmured. "There are a wide variety of options to titillate you."

The image of the lush room with the sparkling fountain and mosaic tiled floor seared her mind. And lying on the satin pillows was Ryshi, his tunic gone to reveal the width of his chest, his hand held out in invitation.

Sofie hissed as desire slammed into her with the force of a rabid troll. She couldn't determine if she'd come up with the fantasy or if she was reading Ryshi's mind. And right now, she didn't care. She just wanted to be at the Oasis. Alone with this male so she could join him on the pillows and forget this awful place.

She was actually swaying toward him when she abruptly recalled that this male was her prisoner. What was wrong with her? Was she tired? Or was the connection between them lowering her usual barriers?

"I don't want to be titillated," she said, speaking more to herself than the male who was stirring needs that she didn't want stirred.

He arched a brow. "Never?"

"Never."

He reached out to brush a finger down the side of her neck. "A shame."

Yes, it is a shame, a renegade voice whispered in the back of her mind. A voice she sternly ignored.

"Will you return to the Oasis when Styx releases you?"

As she hoped, Ryshi was distracted by the question. He leaned back, although the smoke continued to circle her. Like a temptation that was just out of reach.

"Eventually." He tilted his head to the side, studying her with genuine curiosity. "Will you return to your lair?"

"Of course."

He clicked his tongue. "Such a waste."

She narrowed her eyes at the typical male response, the temperature dropping several degrees.

"Careful."

"We make formidable partners," he hastily explained. "If we survive it would be interesting to see where it might lead."

Partners? Sofie stiffened at the odd ache that opened in the center of her unbeating heart. She'd once had a clan. A family. But that had all been destroyed by her powers. The memory was a reminder that she was destined to be alone. Ever since the moment she'd woken as a vampire.

"I can tell you exactly where it would lead." Her voice was grim. "Nowhere."

He frowned, easily sensing the tension vibrating in the air. "Are you afraid of me?"

"You do like to live dangerously."

"You have no idea," he said dryly.

"That wasn't a compliment."

He shrugged. "At least I live."

Sofie flinched at the direct hit. "As do I."

"No." He shook his head. "You hide."

She turned her head, refusing to meet the unnerving black gaze. He was right, of course. She'd been hiding for years. But that's the path she'd chosen, and she wasn't going to change now. Not even for this male who was reminding her that she had needs that went beyond food and shelter.

"You know nothing about me," she informed him in sharp tones.

Predictably, Ryshi ignored the warning chill in the air. In fact, he boldly reached out to grasp her hands in a light grip.

"I know these fingers create beauty." Without warning, he lifted her hand to press it against his lips. Heat raced through Sofie. His touch felt as if it was searing her skin. And it wasn't just his natural warmth. It was the magical smoke that swirled and sizzled as it brushed over her. The sensual pleasure it created was intoxicating. Releasing her fingers, his hands skimmed up her arms and over her shoulders. "And I know that there is power in this body as well as a fluid grace. Watching you fight those demons was mesmerizing. I've never seen anyone move with such elegance."

A treacherous shiver raced through Sofie, undermining her determination to keep this male at a distance.

"Ryshi."

"I know that you were hurt, but that you battle to overcome your wounds." He overrode her protest, his hands gently cupping her face as his gaze settled on the mark carved into her forehead. His eyes smoldered with a sudden emotion. As if the sight of the scar infuriated him. "And that your battle is easier when you are alone in your mountain."

Sofie knew she should pull away. She never discussed her past. And more importantly, she never, ever discussed the wound on her forehead. But she was lost in the dark gaze. As if he'd somehow managed to hypnotize her.

"Everything is better when I'm alone in my mountain," she forced herself to say.

Smoke wrapped around her, like an embrace. "You don't miss the touch of a friend? Or a lover?"

She didn't try to lie. Even if he couldn't sense the ache he'd created inside her, the scent of her frustrated desire spiced the air. Instead she lowered her lashes, futilely trying to leash her emotions.

"Sometimes."

The word came out like a curse. No surprise. Sofie hated admitting a weakness. And desire was most certainly a weakness. Especially when it was focused on this particular male.

"And do you have one?"

She deliberately misunderstood him. "A friend?"

"A lover."

"Not currently."

His thumb traced the curve of her lower lip, pressing hard enough to trap her tender skin against the tip of her fang. The tiny pain was oddly erotic.

"That could be corrected," he assured her in husky tones.

She stiffened, her gaze lifting to glare at his obscenely handsome face. "It's a choice, not a mistake that needs to be corrected."

"Very well. A choice," he smoothly agreed. "One that could be changed."

"Changed by you, I suppose?"

His fingers suddenly tightened as if he was battling back a fierce emotion. "By me and no one but me."

There was a possessive edge in his voice that should have pissed her off. So why didn't it?

"Arrogant," she muttered.

"Obsessed," he corrected without apology. "You have haunted my dreams, sweet Sofie." He traced his fingertips over her brow. "Those amazing eyes, as blue as an arctic sky and circled with frost." He brushed a light caress down her cheeks. "Your satin skin. Your sweet scent."

"Sweet?" Sofie arched a brow. She was many things. Sweet wasn't one of them.

He leaned forward, pressing his face into the curve of her neck and breathing in, as if savoring her scent.

"Chamomile," he murmured. "My favorite."

Her hands lifted, but instead of pushing him away, Sofie grasped his shoulders. It was that or melt into a puddle of desire.

"How many females have you used that line on?" she demanded.

"One." He nibbled a path down the length of her neck, the feel of his teeth against her skin sending jolts of delight through Sofie.

She ached for him to break through her skin and drink her blood. Not because she wished he was a vampire. The feel of his scorching heat was oddly addictive. But because...

No. She squashed the dangerous thought. This place was obviously messing with her head. Or maybe it was Ryshi who was toying with her. Either way, she needed to concentrate on why they were in the labyrinth in the first place.

"Ryshi." She pressed her hands against his chest. "This isn't the time or place."

He lifted his head to study her with those stunning eyes. "Will there ever be a time and place?"

She tried to say no, but the word wouldn't form. As if it was stuck in her throat. Or maybe she was just unwilling to close the door to the possibility of taking Ryshi as her lover.

"Maybe," she finally conceded.

"Better than no." Ryshi brushed a light kiss over her lips before slowly pulling back. His expression hardened as he glanced toward the nearby hedges. "All right. I suppose we should try this again."

* * * *

Bertha was attempting to process what was etched onto the spear. It was a difficult task. Not only because she hated processing anything, but because it was next to impossible to imagine anyone believing Levet was some sort of god.

Not that her nephew wasn't a wonderful creature. He was loyal and funny and he had a heart bigger than his brain. But he was also a magnet for disaster and more likely to create a catastrophe than to offer salvation. How desperate did the minotaurs have to be to choose such a creature?

With a shake of her head, Bertha dismissed her amazement. Right now, the only thing that mattered was the fact that someone was going to be sacrificed. And knowing her nephew, it was probably going to be him.

"I have to do something," she muttered as the vampires returned to their lair, leaving her alone with Hades.

Hades shrugged, his expression revealing his indifference to Levet's ultimate fate.

"The leeches have sent a creature to retrieve your relative."

Bertha snorted. "A thief who was so untrustworthy he was locked in the Anasso's dungeon? Hardly the sort of hero I would depend on to rescue my favorite nephew."

A faint smile curved his lips. "We can't always choose the tools we're given to accomplish our goals."

Bertha sniffed. Obviously, he was referring to her and the part she'd played in stopping the ifrit. He should be on his knees in gratitude. Who else could have performed such a miracle? Still, she refused to allow herself to be distracted.

She needed a way to get to Levet and pull him out of the labyrinth. Which meant that she was going to have to have some help.

"You're a god," she said.

He nodded. "I am."

"Why can't you get him?"

"I can't penetrate the magic of the labyrinth."

"Why not?"

"It was created by Gaia."

Bertha furrowed her brow as she searched through her very long memory. Demons had a variety of gods they worshipped. Some were so obscure she'd never even heard of them. Gaia, however, was fairly popular among the fey and elemental creatures.

"Mother Earth."

"That is one name she uses."

Bertha studied her companion. Despite her growing sense of familiarity with Hades and her dangerous habit of treating him as if he was just another male, there was no doubt that he was a god. The very earth seemed to sag beneath the weight of his power. It seemed unbelievable that there were other deities out there who were more formidable.

"Her magic is greater than yours?" she demanded.

Hades was immediately offended. Fire swirled over his body, sparking and snapping in reaction to his burst of temper.

"Don't be ridiculous."

"Then why can't you break through the labyrinth?"

His handsome features tightened. He was clearly annoyed that she would ever doubt his superior strength.

"The same reason another god can't enter the underworld unless I allow them," he informed her sternly. "There are rules."

Bertha clicked her tongue. "Stupid rules."

"Not really," he protested. "It prevents any nasty misunderstandings. Trust me, you don't want to witness a war between gods."

She didn't, of course. The Dark Lord had been bad enough before he'd been trapped beyond the veil. His explanation, however, didn't ease her need to rescue Levet.

"Then I need to speak with Gaia."

Hades shrugged. "You can try, but I don't think she'll answer."

"Why do you say that?"

"You're not one of her worshippers."

Oh. That made sense. If a god was forever answering the requests and pleas of a bunch of strange demons, they wouldn't have time to take care of their own people. That didn't mean, however, that they were completely unavailable to others. She knew from her own experience they dabbled in lives that had nothing to do with them.

"I wasn't one of yours either," she reminded him in dry tones. "That didn't stop you from trespassing in my mind."

A provocative smile curved his lips as he allowed his flames to dance over her. "You were always destined to be mine."

Bertha arched her back as the heat seared over her. Like a cat being stroked. And that's what she felt like. A cat that was being offered a big heaping bowl of cream.

She cleared the sudden lump from her throat. "We're not discussing you, we're discussing Gaia. There must be some way I can ask for her assistance."

His expression was distracted, as if he was concentrating on something beyond their conversation. Whatever it was had a hungry anticipation burning in his eyes.

"To be honest, I haven't felt her presence in several centuries."

Bertha waited for him to continue. When he didn't, she sent him a puzzled frown. "What does that mean?"

He shrugged. "She's no longer in this dimension."

"Why not?"

"Gods occasionally retreat and seek peace from the demands of the world."

"You take a vacation?"

"It's more like a temporary hibernation."

"Oh." Bertha released a small, longing sigh. She'd spent several lovely centuries napping in the Alps. And once she'd been buried beneath an erupting volcano and managed to sleep in peace for nearly a millennium. "There is nothing better than a nice long hibernation."

"I can think of a few things that are better."

Hades stepped closer, stroking his hand down the curve of her wing. A shockingly intense sensation blasted through her at his touch. His flames were seductive. The heat brushed over her, teasing her with its light stroke. His actual touch was like a thunderclap, ricocheting through her with enough force to send her to her knees.

Bertha jerked away before she could make a fool of herself. "Stop that."

He frowned, appearing genuinely concerned by her reprimand. "You don't like it?"

"Too much," Bertha admitted without hesitation. "I can't concentrate."

Hades's smile returned. "I like the sound of that."

So did Bertha. She could use a few mindless hours of pleasure. Maybe a few mindless years. Decades. Centuries.

It'd been a while for her. Unfortunately, she had other matters to deal with first.

"I intend to focus on Levet until he is safely retrieved from the minotaurs," she warned in stern tones.

"Stubborn," Hades muttered.

"Excuse me?" Bertha widened her eyes. This male had ruthlessly used her to achieve his goals. He'd even sucked her into the underworld without asking if she wanted to go. So rude. Now he had the audacity to claim that she was the obstinate one. "Did you just call *me* stubborn?"

He folded his arms over his chest, staring at her in disbelief. Clearly, he wasn't accustomed to creatures daring to talk back to him. Probably because most creatures had enough brains to avoid offending a god.

But thankfully, there wasn't any anger in his amazing eyes as he stared at her. Instead, there was a sparkle of something that might have been fascination as he accepted she wasn't going to leave Levet's fate in the hands of an unknown thief.

"I might be able to help," he offered reluctantly.

"How?"

"I can contact Gaia."

"Even if she's hibernating?"

His lips twisted, an unreadable expression on his flawless features. "She'll answer if I call."

Chapter 11

Ryshi placed one heavy foot in front of the other, trying to ignore the fear that they were trapped in the bleak maze. He'd found the exit before. Granted, he'd stumbled on it by accident. But it was proof that it was there.

Somewhere…

Reaching an intersection, he turned to the left and led them down the endless pathway. It was exactly the same as the hundreds of pathways they'd already traveled down, and while they hadn't been whisked back to the entrance, they were no closer to getting out.

Ryshi grimaced, trying to concentrate on the icy power that swirled around him and the sweet smell of chamomile that scented the air. It was the only thing keeping him from dropping to his knees and conceding defeat. Unfortunately, it couldn't entirely ease the heavy sense of doom that pressed against him like a shroud.

"I hate this place," he muttered. It was that or scream at the top of his lungs.

Sofie closed the distance between them. "Is it the silence?"

He tilted back his head, glancing toward the sky where the clouds hung so low he could almost reach up and touch them. They added to the oppressive atmosphere that threatened to choke him.

"It's the sense of being trapped," he said, glancing toward his companion. "Don't you feel it?"

She sent him a wry glance. "Being trapped isn't my nightmare."

Ryshi nodded. Many vampires chose dank lairs that were buried deep underground or hidden in the darkest crevices of a mountain. Places that made his imp soul cringe in horror.

"Then what is your nightmare?" he asked, in desperate need of a distraction.

"The Anasso showing up on my doorstep."

He released a sharp laugh. "That is a nightmare for anyone."

She continued to study him, her expression one of genuine curiosity. "If being trapped bothers you, then how did you survive being locked in Styx's dungeon?"

Ryshi turned his head, pretending to search for the exit. He didn't want to lie to Sofie. Not when he was suddenly hoping that there might be a future for them that didn't include chasing miniature gargoyles and braving the labyrinth. But he couldn't be sure that the Anasso didn't intend to throw him back into the dungeon as soon as he returned to Chicago. He couldn't risk being truly locked away. And not only for his own sanity.

For now, he had no choice but to keep the truth to himself.

"I entertained myself by tormenting the guards," he said. It wasn't a lie. He'd spent many enjoyable hours teasing the leeches until they threatened to carve out his tongue. "And if I became overly bored I would create enough trouble for Styx to pay me a visit."

Her eyes narrowed, the silver band around the blue shimmering in the muted light. "There's something you're not telling me."

Ryshi jerked his thoughts away from his time in the dungeon, concentrating on their surroundings. The growing bond between them allowed her to see more than he wanted.

"There's lots of stuff I'm not telling you." He released a tendril of smoke, sending it to brush against her cheek. "I have to maintain some air of mystery."

Her jaw tightened, as if she wanted to demand an answer. Then she shrugged. Was she accepting that she couldn't force him to tell her the truth? Or had she lost interest?

"Okay, then tell me why you were sneaking into the lairs of vampires," she commanded.

Ryshi swallowed a chuckle. This female had a talent for asking questions he didn't want to answer. She also had a talent for stirring his desire, a voice whispered in the back of his mind. And fascinating him in a way he couldn't entirely explain. As if he'd been waiting for her for a very, very long time.

"To pass the time," he said in a deliberately offhand tone.

She shook her head, disbelief etched on her beautiful face. "You have your demon club."

Ryshi clicked his tongue. "It's not a demon club, it's a shisha parlor."

"What's the difference?"

"A style. A vibe. A certain je ne sais quoi that isn't available in any other demon club," he explained. "Any idiot can serve grog and offer naked dancers or fighting pits to sate the masses. I offer a place of tranquility. It's…"

"Special," she offered.

"Exactly." He flashed an approving smile. "Just like the owner."

She rolled her eyes, but didn't allow herself to be sidetracked. "It had to be more than a means to pass the time."

Ryshi slowed his pace as they neared yet another intersection, searching his brain for a lie that she would accept.

"I told you," he said at last. "Jinn are addicted to the rare and unusual. On occasion I feel the urge to search for items that capture my interest. Where better to look than the lairs of leeches who are notorious for plundering treasure from lesser demons?"

Her disbelief never wavered. "If you really wanted treasure you would seek out a dragon."

Ryshi glanced at her in genuine horror. He had heard stories of the outrageous wealth that could be found in a dragon's hoard. Not just gems, but priceless magical artifacts. And when he was young and foolish, he'd occasionally dreamed of trying his luck sneaking into a dragon lair. Always assuming he could find one. But as he grew older he wisely realized that no artifact was worth being consumed in a fiery blast of flames.

"I desire excitement, not certain death," he said in dry tones.

"You don't fear vampires?"

His gaze skimmed over her pale, perfect face. Fierce sensations jolted through him. A tangled combination of lust, enchantment, and a sizzling sense of anticipation that was intoxicating.

"Only one."

Their gazes locked and held as an emotion that seemed too large to name flowed through the bond that connected them. Ryshi trembled, allowing the sense of destiny to wash through him. What was the point in fighting? Besides, he didn't *want* to fight. From the moment he'd first seen Sofie there'd been a part of him that had known their futures were bound together.

Sofie, however, was obviously still struggling to deny the inevitable. Turning her head, she tilted her chin to a stubborn angle.

"You were searching for something in the vampires' lairs. I just can't tell what it was."

Ryshi didn't bother to argue. Instead, he studied the intersection, attempting to decide what direction to take. Not that it really mattered. He was wandering through the maze like a drunken troll. Left, right, left, right, and boom...whisked back to the beginning.

Rinse and repeat.

Thankfully his attention came in handy. They were stepping into the intersection when he noticed a black hole in the middle of the pathway.

"Careful," he said, grabbing Sofie's arm to bring her to a sharp halt.

Ryshi leaned forward, studying the opening in confusion. It wasn't large. Perhaps three feet wide, but from his angle, Ryshi couldn't see the bottom. Was it because there was no end to the darkness?

Sofie inched closer to him, as if instinctively sensing that something was wrong.

"I don't suppose that's the opening, is it?"

"No." Ryshi shook his head. "It wasn't here before."

Sofie wrinkled her nose, leaning forward. "Maybe it's a shortcut."

A sharp shiver raced through Ryshi as he took a step backward. He wasn't sure why he was afraid of the hole, but there was no denying the urgent need to be far away from it.

"This isn't a gateway," he said, taking another step back. "Or a portal. It's empty."

"That might be a good thing," she suggested. "I don't want anything crawling out of it."

"Not empty of creatures, although it is," he corrected. "It's empty as if it's a void."

Sofie tilted back her head, obviously using her powers to search for an answer to the strange opening. At last she made a sound of frustration, shaking her head in defeat.

"I can't smell anything. Could it be a trap?"

"Possibly." Ryshi shrugged. From what little he'd seen of the minotaurs, they didn't seem capable of this sort of magic, but he'd be a fool to underestimate what might be lurking in this god-awful place. "I'm not eager to find out. Are you?"

"No. But we might not have a choice."

Ryshi sent her a startled glance. "Why do you say that?"

"It's growing."

Growing? Ryshi muttered a sudden curse. He'd been so intent on discovering what was inside the hole that he hadn't paid attention to the fact that it was spreading wider and wider. As if it sensed they were nearby and was attempting to suck them into the darkness.

"You're right," he rasped. "It feels hungry."

She visibly shuddered. "Hungry?"

Ryshi struggled to find the words that would capture the low pulse that seemed to reach out toward them. It was like the maw of a gigantic beast that had been awakened after a millennium of slumber and was in dire need of sustenance. Or a black hole that threatened to consume the entire maze.

The only thing he knew for certain was that it had to be some sort of magic or Sofie would be able to detect the weird sensation.

"I don't know how else to explain it," he muttered. "But we need to get out of here."

"I agree." She sent him an expectant glance. "You have to find the entrance and you need to do it quickly."

He shook his head in frustration. Did she think he'd been randomly roaming around because he enjoyed being in this miserable place? If he could've gotten out they would be long gone.

"I told you, finding the exit is a matter of luck."

She turned to face him. "We've already established that the labyrinth is built on a pattern. We just have to figure it out."

Ryshi concentrated fiercely on the female in front of him, trying to ignore the heavy pulse of the void.

"I've tried. The maze keeps shifting, creating new pathways." He waved an impatient hand toward the clouds above their heads. "There's no sun or stars to follow and there are no scents beyond the stench of these stupid hedges."

She stepped closer, reaching out to place her hands on his shoulders. Any other time, he would have taken advantage of her proximity to wrap his arms around her and haul her tight against his body. Right now, he was far more interested in what she had to say.

"What do you hear?" she demanded.

He frowned. The place was eerily quiet. "Nothing."

"Exactly."

"Exactly?" He ground his teeth. "What does that mean?"

"Ryshi." She held his gaze, her expression somber. "If you can't find the pattern it's because it's hidden in the silence."

"That doesn't make any sense," he snapped.

She stubbornly refused to back down. "Instead of wandering aimlessly through the maze you should listen for the magic."

"You think it makes a sound?"

"Not one that I can hear." She peered deep into his eyes. "But you can. If you're willing to try."

Ryshi parted his lips to tell her that was ridiculous. He knew what magic sounded like. He heard it on a regular basis as he moved through the world. And there was nothing in this maze that indicated there was a spell nearby.

Then again, her words made a weird sort of sense. There had to be some sort of pattern. And it wasn't among the hedges. Plus, he'd been there twice and struggled to get out. It was possible that it had something to do with his reluctance to open himself to the heavy atmosphere that filled this place.

"Fine." He reached out to place his hands on her hips. He had a feeling he was going to need her support. In more ways than one. "I'll listen if that makes you happy."

Her features tightened. "Getting out of here and back to my lair will make me happy."

His fingers tightened on her hips. Her continued insistence that she couldn't wait to flee his presence and return to her home was wearing on his nerves. Granted, she'd been more or less forced into entering the labyrinth. And their time together had been a series of near-death experiences. Not the most romantic way to start a relationship. Still, he could sense that she wasn't entirely horrified to be with him. In fact, there'd been several moments when she seemed eager to spend time in his company. In his arms...

"Liar." He leaned forward to place a soft, lingering kiss on her mouth. She dug her nails into his shoulders. "Hey."

"You're going to miss me." The friction of their lips brushing together created electric tingles that danced over his skin.

"Like the plague," she stubbornly insisted.

Ryshi smiled. They both knew her desire wasn't a figment of his imagination. She was hungry for his touch. He could smell it on her skin and feel the need humming through her body. All he had to do was pull her into his arms and she would melt.

"Eventually you'll admit the truth."

He could feel the tremor of excitement that raced through her body, but with a soft hiss she pulled away, sending him a chiding glance.

"I don't think we should waste any time."

She was right, of course. As much as he wanted to concentrate on Sofie and her sweet scent, he had to find a way to get them out of there. Even now he could feel the darkness spreading closer and closer.

Closing his eyes, he opened himself to his surroundings. He instantly felt the dense press of the air. As if it was a tangible weight that was trying to force him to his knees. Behind him he could smell the nearby hedges, and even the clouds gave off a scent of rain that never fell.

Beyond that...nothing.

"I don't hear anything," he said.

"Listen."

He ground his teeth at her dogged insistence. "I am."

Without warning he felt her arms wrap around him, as if she was using her presence to battle back his demons.

"Listen," she whispered in his ear.

Ryshi stilled, allowing her icy power to seep deep inside him. Her touch not only banished the sensation of being slowly smothered, it also allowed him to focus his mind. Suddenly he wasn't battling the silence. Instead, he allowed himself to sink deeper, simply drifting as he strained to hear any hint of magic.

He kept his eyes closed, using Sofie as an anchor as the memories he kept hidden crashed over him in a furious wave. This was why he'd created his elegant parlor. And why he surrounded himself with guests and servants. And why he'd been willing to risk everything by daring to enter the labyrinth all those years ago. Not to mention stealing into the lairs of vampires.

It wasn't simply guilt, although he had plenty of that. He would never forgive himself for driving away his sister. And he fully intended to spend the rest of eternity searching for her.

But there was more to his restless need for constant entertainment than remorse, he grudgingly conceded. It'd started when he was very young, long before his sister had been born. Back then he'd been alone with his mother in their lair. His father had taken off with a wood sprite and Ryshi had suddenly realized how quiet it was with no one around.

It wasn't that his mother had completely abandoned him. She spent enough time in the lair to make sure he wasn't stolen or killed by one of her enemies, but jinn were by nature solitary creatures. It didn't occur to her that he might need companionship. And if Ryshi had been a pureblood the endless years he'd spent alone in his palatial rooms wouldn't have bothered him. But he had the blood of an imp in his veins. That side of him had craved the love and physical affection that the fey shared with their children. He needed laughter and sunshine and the camaraderie of a large, boisterous tribe.

Over the years, he'd come to dread watching his mother walk out of the lair, knowing he would be alone in the silence for endless decades. Sometimes centuries.

After he'd created the Oasis, he'd thought he'd healed those wounds of his past. He had a thriving business and constant company to fill the void. And the arrival of Zena had given him the family he'd always desired.

But now, held tightly in Sofie's arms, he realized that he'd only masked the emptiness. The Oasis would always be his pride and joy. And he loved Zena despite her aggravating determination to drive him crazy. But deep inside, he'd still been alone.

What he truly needed was a mate. A partner who would fill his heart, his soul, and his bed.

The thought should have sent him into a panic. What could be more smothering than being eternally bound to one female? What happened was just the opposite. Accepting his bond with Sofie, Ryshi could physically feel the silence fracture and shatter, as if struck by a hammer.

With a sigh of relief, he wrapped his arms around her waist, finally able to hear the faint hum of magic. It was distant, and he took a second to be sure that it wasn't an echo coming from the expanding hole. Once he was confident that he'd locked in on the spell, he buried his face in the curve of her throat, taking a brief moment to immerse himself in her scent of chamomile before reluctantly pulling away.

"I found the doorway."

Sofie blinked, as if attempting to clear her mind. Obviously, she'd been equally lost in the potent awareness created by their embrace.

Not that she would ever admit it, he ruefully acknowledged, watching her expression harden as she squared her shoulders.

"Where?"

He didn't bother to try to force his way past her brittle defenses. That was going to take more time than they currently had. Always assuming it was even possible.

A worry for another time and place.

"This way."

He grabbed her hand and tugged her away from the gaping hole, retracing their steps toward the beginning of the maze. For once he didn't hesitate as he turned the corners, picking up speed as the hum grew ever louder. How the hell had he missed it before? It was as noisy as a freight train.

There had to be some sort of magic hiding the sound. Now that he'd broken through that spell, it was no longer muted.

They were nearly back to the entrance of the maze when he caught sight of the shimmering gateway hovering in the middle of the hedge. He came to a sharp halt.

"There," he said, pointing toward the magic that Sofie was incapable of seeing.

"The opening?"

He nodded. "Ready?"

"More than," Sofie muttered, glancing over her shoulder.

Belatedly, Ryshi realized that the darkness had followed, threatening to swallow them before they could escape.

Not giving himself time to consider what was destroying the maze, or even what might be waiting for them on the other side, he squeezed Sofie's fingers. If she'd been a human he would have crushed her bones, but she was a vampire and she didn't even flinch as she returned his grip, pressing against his side as they leaped directly into the hedge.

* * * *

Levet scratched his snout, studying the sky above his head. He'd seen many strange things in his very long life. Unicorns. An ogress who turned out to be the Queen of the Merfolk. The return of the Backstreet Boys. But he'd never seen a big hole that appeared to be sucking in the nearby stars. It wasn't a portal. Or a gateway. Or any other magical means of being transported that he'd used. It wasn't even a rip that could happen when mortals used magic to move between dimensions.

"I am not exactly certain what that is," he at last conceded.

"Neither are we," the minotaur next to him said in harsh tones. "It appeared almost a century ago."

"A century?" Levet grimaced. That was a long time to have that hanging over your head. Literally.

"At first it was nothing more than a pinprick of darkness."

"What did you do to stop it?"

"Nothing." The male shrugged. "We assumed it was a passing aberration."

Levet flapped his wings in disbelief. "You ignored a hole in your sky?"

The minotaur's features settled into a defensive expression. "We didn't ignore it. Obviously, we kept an eye on the thing. But it didn't appear to pose any danger to my people."

Levet clicked his tongue in disapproval. "I thought it was ostriches, not cows, who stuck their heads in the sand."

"Excuse me?"

The male stiffened, his hand lifting to touch the crown on his head. Was it a silent warning that he was in a position of authority? Or maybe he feared he'd lost it on the way to the balcony?

Levet didn't care either way. His thoughts were currently lost in the image of a minotaur sticking their head in the sand.

"It would be more difficult for you, right?"

"You aren't making any sense," the male snapped.

"Your horns. They would get caught in the sand." Levet sighed at the male's blank expression. Obviously, the minotaurs weren't blessed with a sense of humor. "Maybe we should return to your explanation of your holey sky."

"The darkness began to spread, consuming the stars. We feared it might destroy our homeland."

Levet glanced toward the rolling fields. He couldn't see any rot or disease. "It does not appear to have done any damage."

The heavy scent of bull swirled through the air, making Levet's snout wrinkle in distaste.

"Only because we discovered one means of keeping the darkness sated," the male said.

"How do you sate the darkness?"

Without warning the male lifted his hands and loudly clapped them together. Levet flinched. He wished they would stop doing that. It hurt his ears. Maybe he should buy them a bell. Or a gong. Anything had to be better than the clap, clap, clapping.

Levet's thoughts were scattered when the sound of footsteps echoed from beneath them. Leaning forward, he watched as a group of minotaurs appeared from beneath the balcony. They were attired in the same outfits that the performers had been wearing and their horns sparkled in the moonlight.

"More dancing?" Levet was surprised, and more than a little relieved at the unexpectedly simple solution to the problem. He assumed that it would be something awful.

"No," the minotaur swiftly burst his pimple. *Non.* Not pimple. Bubble. "Not dancing."

Levet continued to watch the creatures below him. They'd reached the center of a sunken garden and were spreading out to form a circle around a large, flat stone. From his angle it looked like a dinner table.

"A feast?" he demanded.

"No."

The male did another loud clap. Levet's lips parted to protest, but before he could speak, the sound of harsh screams echoed through the air. Levet snapped his wings back, peering over the edge. He wasn't sure what he'd expected. It sounded like someone was being ripped apart by a feral hellhound. What came into view was a female minotaur wearing a long white gown. There were two large minotaurs on either side of her who had their hands wrapped around her arms to drag her down the narrow pathway. They weren't having an easy time of it. The female was trying to kick and bite and scratch her companions. Not to mention continuing her ear-piercing screams as they headed toward the center of the garden.

"She is not happy." Levet pointed out the obvious. "Perhaps she would be quiet if they released her."

The male next to him folded his arms over the considerable width of his chest.

"We can't."

"Why not?"

"The darkness must be fed."

Fed? Levet was confused. He'd said there wasn't going to be a feast. So how could they feed the hole?

"Does she intend to scream at it until it closes?"

"You will see."

The male's expression was grim as he watched the female being tossed on top of the rock and the surrounding minotaurs moving forward to swiftly tie her down with thick ropes.

His first instinct had been right, Levet acknowledged silently. This was going to be bad. Really, really bad.

"Um...to be honest, I do not care to see," he said, his tail twitching as his claws dug into the railing of the balcony. The female continued to fight as her wrists and ankles were bound to the table, the sour scent of her terror thick in the air. "Please stop this."

"Only you can stop it." The male turned to face Levet, pointing toward the sky. "Close the hole."

"How?"

"You are the god, not me," the male snapped. "Use your magic."

Levet's mouth went dry. He had always been the underdog. The plucky hero that no one believed in. That was the position he felt most comfortable in. Not being a god.

Having someone put so much pressure on him was giving him performance anxiety.

Still, the poor female continued to scream, and he had a horrifying fear that she was about to sacrificed if he didn't do something.

"I do not believe my fireballs will do much good, but I suppose I could try."

He glanced toward his companion, secretly hoping the male would tell him not to bother. When the minotaur continued to stare at him with an expectant expression, Levet swallowed a sigh and lifted his hands.

Who knew? Perhaps in this particular dimension he was a god. And perhaps his magic would be as majestic as he'd always imagined it was supposed to be. Stranger things had happened.

Puffing out his chest in a pretense of courage, Levet gathered his magic and released it in one powerful surge. Thankfully, two impressively large fireballs formed, dancing just above his head. Not bad, he silently congratulated himself. Not bad at all.

They hadn't exploded. Or set the fortress on fire. And best of all, the minotaurs below had stopped what they were doing to watch him with varying degrees of wonderment.

Just maybe he was a god....

Feeling far more confident than he had a few seconds before, Levet gave a dramatic gesture of his arms to send the fireballs soaring toward the sky. They sizzled loudly as they traveled upward, leaving behind tiny trails of sparks. Like a comet streaking toward the heavens.

Levet could hear the soft oohs and aahs from the gathered crowd as his magic aimed straight for the hole. He wanted to ooh and aah himself. They were quite impressive. Levet tried to stay humble, even when he was yet again saving the world. He would allow the minstrels to sing of his great deeds. If only he could find one who was worthy of his story.

He was busy forming the precise words of glory that he wanted in the first verse of his epic ballad when the balls began to wobble. Understandable, he assured himself. They'd traveled a long distance. There was bound to be a wobble. Or two.

Maybe three...

Levet's wings drooped as he watched the fireballs reach the massive hole. He'd hoped they would choose that moment to explode and collapse the opening. Or catch any gasses inside the hole on fire. Anything that might help. Instead, they flickered before slowly fading into tiny embers that fell harmlessly to the ground.

Acutely aware of the disappointed glances that were now trained in his direction, Levet grabbed his tail and nervously began to polish the tip.

"Well, that is embarrassing," he muttered.

The minotaur abruptly stomped his heavy foot, making the entire balcony shudder beneath the impact.

"You must have another magic."

"I do," Levet assured the male, refusing to be blamed for the fizzling fireballs. "I have tremendous skills, but they are not the sort of power to repair a gaping hole in the sky."

"That can't be true," the male growled. "You were seen in a vision. You are our savior."

Levet glanced up, glaring at the male next to him. It wasn't as if he'd presented himself to the minotaurs claiming to be some sort of god. He'd been kidnapped, held captive, and was now expected to perform a miracle. It was all massively unfair.

"It must have been a faulty vision," he groused. "Like a dude."

"Dude?" The minotaur blinked in confusion. "You mean a dud?"

"*Oui.*" Levet stomped his foot with impatience. Wasn't that what he'd just said? "A dud."

The minotaur stared at him for a long time, as if waiting for Levet to concede that he was joking and that he really did have the magic needed to close the hole. Finally, he turned away.

"Then we have no choice." He lifted his hands and smacked them together, the loud clap ringing in Levet's sensitive ears.

Levet sucked in a sharp breath, watching the minotaurs below step away from the table, leaving behind the female who continued to scream at the top of her lungs. What was happening? Were they going to leave the poor female tied to the table?

Preparing for the worst, Levet tried to judge the distance between the railing where he was perched and the table far below. Could he reach the female before the minotaurs could grab him and—

His frantic thoughts were abruptly interrupted as a loud roaring noise filled the air and a black mist funneled out of the hole. Levet flinched. He didn't know what was in the mist, but he sensed it would be a very bad thing if it touched him.

It swirled downward, seeming to head toward the balcony before it was curving back to surround the table in a cloud of darkness. At first nothing seemed to be happening. The mist covered the female and simply swirled around. Heaving a premature sigh of relief, Levet was about to return his attention to the minotaur next to him when there was another loud roar and the mist simply disappeared.

Along with the female strapped to the table.

"*Non, non, non,*" Levet breathed in horror. "Where did she go?"

"We're not sure," the male next to him admitted. "They never return."

Levet's wings flapped in distress. The female had been a minotaur. One of their own people. It was the height of callousness to feed her to the hole as if she was a porky chop, not a valuable member of their tribe.

"Why would you do that?"

The male sent him a fierce glare. "A sacrifice is the only means to keep the darkness from growing." He pointed a finger directly into Levet's face. "Unless you can perform the miracle that we have been promised."

Chapter 12

Ryshi managed to land on his feet this time. A miracle. And just as miraculous was that they were dumped onto a soft patch of grass. Still, he was on full alert as he glanced around. They were standing near a thick forest of towering pine trees that perfumed the air with a refreshing scent. Lovely.

Unfortunately, the smell couldn't overcome the stench that floated from the nearby town. The reek from rotting food, brackish water, and filthy minotaur fur was too potent to be covered.

Ryshi clenched his teeth as he realized exactly where they were. It wasn't quite as bad as the previous maze, but it was close. And worse, this area was going to be the most dangerous for Sofie.

Turning his head, he watched as she wandered toward a nearby tree, reaching out a hand to brush her fingers over the green needles.

"Are you okay?" he asked.

She turned to face him, her expression icily composed. "This is no illusion."

A pang of regret that she was once again the aloof, unapproachable vampire sliced through Ryshi. He'd heard the expression one step forward and two steps back, but with Sofie it was like a teeny step forward and a mile backward. Not that he was going to concede defeat, he assured himself. It didn't matter how many steps backward, forward, or in between it took, he was going to have this female in his life.

Forever.

"No. It's very real," he assured her.

Sofie turned to study the nearby town. Her nose wrinkled as she took in the sprawling buildings constructed from wood with thatched roofs that sagged from the constant drizzle that fell from the gray sky. There were a few muddy lanes, but most of them meandered in strange curves and often ended without warning. Probably because the large population of minotaurs spent most of their time in the nearby colosseum, drinking their potent ale and enjoying violent battles between their chosen warriors. They weren't big fans of wasting time repairing their homes or cleaning the foul waste that clogged the sewers.

"We reached the homeland?" she asked in disbelief.

Ryshi shook his head. He hadn't actually entered the minotaur homeland when he'd been there before, but he very much hoped it was better than this place.

At least cleaner.

"My guess is that this is more like a suburb."

Her gaze remained locked on the town, where they could see several large minotaurs staggering down a muddy lane. One of them stumbled forward, smashing into a lopsided building that promptly collapsed beneath the impact.

"Is that a joke?"

"Not really."

"This doesn't look like any suburb I've been in." She sent him a suspicious glance. "At least not since medieval London."

Ryshi shrugged. "I was forced to stay here long enough to determine that this place is not the same as the labyrinth. There are no illusions and the only creatures here are minotaurs."

She wrinkled her nose. "That's what I smell?"

"Unfortunately." There was nothing pleasant about wet, moldy fur. "It's also unfortunate that they aren't held captive by the same spell that's inside the rest of the maze."

She snorted. "Thank the goddess. I hate magic."

"I'm not a fan of the labyrinth, but in this place there's no hiding the fact that we're intruders. As soon as one of the minotaur spots us we're going to be hunted."

Sofie shrugged, obviously not as terrified of the minotaurs as she was of magic. Understandable; any vampire would rather face a danger they could see and touch.

"How can you be sure this isn't the homeland?"

Ryshi waved a hand toward the squalid settlement. "It's a crappy homeland if it is."

"True." Her gaze skimmed toward the distant buildings that spread out as far as the eye could see. "But there might be nicer neighborhoods on the other side of town. Most cities have their slums."

"This city is all slum," he assured her. "Last time I had to hide for several days in my jinn form while I searched for—" He bit off his words as he realized he'd almost revealed more than he wanted. "The exit," he managed to mutter before clearing his throat. "I have seen more than enough of this place to be confident that there are no nice neighborhoods. Plus, I overheard two minotaurs discussing the homeland."

Sofie narrowed her eyes, but she surprisingly didn't press him for an answer on what he was looking for. She seemed more interested in how he'd managed to travel without being detected.

"I assume your jinn form means that you moved around the area in a cloud of smoke?"

He smiled at her blunt question. "That's one way to put it."

"Are you invisible?"

"Not completely. A demon searching for a jinn might be able to see me, but the minotaurs had no reason to suspect that I was here. It allowed me to overhear several interesting conversations."

She nodded. "What did you discover?"

"There were two minotaurs fighting over a barrel of ale," he told her. "They were complaining about being banned from the homeland and the fear they'd never get to return."

"Banned? They were kicked out?"

"I would guess that all the minotaurs in this area have committed some sin that placed them here."

The temperature dropped as she sent him a chiding glance. "So this is more a prison than a suburb?"

"Same thing." He shrugged. "From what I could gather, this outskirt area is the last layer of protection for the minotaurs."

With a roll of her eyes, she stepped back; then, tilting back her head, she turned in a slow circle. Ryshi didn't need the sharp chill in the air to tell him that she was using her powers. He could sense it through their mental connection.

"I don't smell the gargoyle," she at last said, her voice edged with frustration.

Ryshi felt his own share of irritation. As much as he was enjoying his time with Sofie, he wanted to be back in Chicago. Not only because he needed to return to his hunt, but he hated this place. There was something rancid about it. As if there was a rotting core that he could sense beneath the layers of illusion.

With an effort, he kept his emotions tightly leashed. The sooner they could find the stupid gargoyle, the sooner they could escape the labyrinth.

"There are dungeons protected by magic beneath the colosseum," he told Sofie. "If he's being held in one of the cells, we might not be able to detect his presence."

She sent him a suspicious glance. "How do you know about the dungeons?"

Ryshi grimly refused to allow his memory of being in this town to rise to his mind. He couldn't allow her to realize why he'd been searching every nook and cranny of this hellhole.

"I thought they might have hidden the exit there," he smoothly lied.

She didn't believe him, but once again she didn't press for the truth. A tiny fear bloomed in the center of his heart. Had she lost interest? Hell, maybe she'd never really had any interest. Maybe he'd imagined her reluctant fascination.

Sofie thankfully broke into his dark thoughts. "Which way is the colosseum?"

"It's on the other side of town."

"Of course it is." She shivered in disgust. "Is there a way to avoid the mess?"

Ryshi turned to lead her toward the nearby woods. "We can skirt along these trees, but we need to be careful. There are guards patrolling the area."

They entered the shadows of the towering pines, staying close enough to the edge to keep an eye on the town. Not only was Ryshi worried about guards, but there was always the chance some idiot would catch the place on fire and it would spread to the woods. He'd seen evidence the place had been burned to the ground more than once.

They'd walked nearly halfway around the town when Sofie at last broke the silence.

"I don't know anything about minotaurs," she admitted. "I know there are a few legends, but I never paid any attention to them."

Ryshi wouldn't have known anything about them either. They'd left this world so long ago that few creatures had memories of the mysterious tribes. Or were they herds? In any case, he'd only studied them because he'd heard of a magical item they possessed. An item that he'd desperately needed. The information had been sketchy at best and most of what he'd learned about the minotaurs had only come after he'd entered the labyrinth.

Too late to do any good.

"Obviously, they are reclusive to the point of absurdity," he said. "Not only did they create the labyrinth to protect themselves from invaders, but until Styx arrived in my cell to tell me that the gargoyle had been kidnapped, I assumed they never left their homeland."

"What else?"

"They have the strength of an orc and the endurance of a werewolf," Ryshi promptly answered.

He didn't want her to underestimate them. They looked slow and stupid, but he'd seen them in battle in the colosseum. They were intimidating fighters who had no sense of fear.

"Do they have magic?"

"They can create illusions. And a few have the ability to move through gateways."

"Like the fey?"

Ryshi shook his head. Fey creatures, including himself, could open portals that would lead from one place to another. Usually to a place far away. Or even another dimension.

"It isn't a portal. Or not like any I've seen before. They disappear and a second later they reappear a few feet away. It makes it almost impossible to defeat them. As soon as you think you have them cornered, they vanish and reappear standing directly behind you."

She arched her brows. Not so much in concern as in surprise. It was a unique talent.

"Is that it?"

"They aren't as stupid as they look." He emphasized the words.

Vampires were lethal predators who stayed firmly on top of the demon food chain. But their one weakness was arrogance. Even Sofie tended to believe she was invincible.

"Great," she said dryly. "They're as strong as an orc, they can appear and disappear, and they're smart."

"Not smart," he corrected. He'd once witnessed two minotaurs spend an hour trying to get through a doorway at the same time. "Just not as dumb as they look. Oh, and I almost forgot, they carry spears that can punch through steel."

They continued around the edge of the woods, the distant roar of minotaurs filling the air. With the thick cloud cover and heavy drizzle, it was impossible to know what time it was. Ryshi had assumed that time was irrelevant in this dimension since there didn't seem to be any day or night. But the sound of cheering meant the daily battles had started in the colosseum.

"Let's concentrate on how they can be defeated," Sofie suggested, her gaze focused on the village.

"They are fearless in battle, but they're also undisciplined," Ryshi said. "Plus, they have no control over their tempers. I suspect they could be easily goaded into a reckless mistake."

Sofie started to nod only to come to a sharp halt, reaching out to grab Ryshi's arm.

"Stop!"

Ryshi did as she commanded, his head swiveling from side to side as he searched for the approaching danger.

"A minotaur?" he demanded.

"There's one nearby," she said, her expression distracted as she tilted back her head as if searching the branches of the nearest pine tree. "But that's not what I'm worried about."

"Then what is?"

"I smell silver."

Ryshi didn't possess the same sensitivity to silver as a vampire, but he instinctively lunged toward her. If there was silver in the area it had to be a trap. He'd managed to wrap his arms around her, but before he could shove her to the ground he felt a heavy blanket fall from the branch above them. No, not a blanket, he realized as Sofie released a cry of pain. It was a net made from strands of silver.

Ryshi tried to use his body to prevent the metal filaments from touching Sofie, but the net was tightening as if controlled by a spell. There was no way to keep it from searing her with a sickening stench of burned flesh. He had to get the damned thing off her. Not only to stop the damage to her body, but to keep it from draining her strength.

Attempting to determine the source of the magic, Ryshi was interrupted by the heavy sound of footsteps heading through the trees. The guards had obviously realized their trap had been sprung and were now coming to investigate. He had only seconds to do something.

Muttering a curse, Ryshi accepted he couldn't help Sofie. Not while he was trapped in the net. The only way they were going to survive this was if he managed to escape. Once he was out of the net he would find a way to release her.

The question was whether or not she would release her hold on his mind.

"Sofie." Glancing down, Ryshi grimaced as he caught sight of her agonized expression as the silver burned her skin. Her eyes were squeezed shut, as if she was trying to shut out the pain. "Sofie, can you hear me?"

She hissed in response, assuring him that she was still conscious. "The minotaurs are coming. I need you to let go."

With an obvious effort she forced open her eyes. They were dazed with agony, but she managed to focus on him.

"What?"

"You have to trust me," he whispered, cupping her face in his hands. "Let go."

She stared at him a long time, as if reluctant to release her grip on his mind. Was she afraid he would abandon her? Or did she simply desire him to remain close? Both possibilities made his heart clench with regret. And the sense of guilt only intensified when the touch of her nestled in his mind slowly pulled away. It was like having a part of himself removed.

Dammit. The last thing he wanted to do was leave her with the minotaurs. Especially when he had no idea what they might do to her. But if he remained, then they would both be trapped.

He had to take the chance that he could save her.

Brushing his mouth over her parted lips, Ryshi savored his last taste of her before he released his magic and disappeared in a puff of smoke.

* * * *

Bertha muttered a curse as she wrestled her way through the thick vines. Since following Hades into this secluded dimension, she'd been drowning in vegetation. Not only from the looming trees that blocked out the sky, but the tall grass that reached up and wrapped around her ankles. As if it was deliberately trying to trip her.

Normally, she loved nature. She wasn't a fey creature, but what was better than a lush meadow? Or a craggy mountaintop. Or even a view of the ocean. Majestic.

But this...this was nature on steroids.

And while it was uncomfortable and sometimes painful to wriggle her extra-large body through the thick brush, she was thoroughly annoyed by the mold that covered her from head to toe. She didn't mind a bit of fungus, but this was ridiculous. It would take weeks to scrub away the green stains.

And if that wasn't aggravating enough—and it was—she had to watch Hades nonchalantly stroll ahead of her, the damned plants swaying to the side to give him a clear pathway. Not one blade of grass dared to brush against the crimson robe he had wrapped around himself, and the vines curled away in fear.

The sight not only a reminder that he was a god, but that he was way out of her league.

She swallowed a sigh. "Where are we?"

He slowed his pace, allowing her to catch up with his long strides. "Some would call it the beginning of time. Just as the underworld is the end of time," he told her, his exquisite face hard with a tension that made her stomach clench. "Neither is accurate. We each have our original source of power. This is Gaia's."

She glanced down at her moldy skin. "It does have a primordial vibe."

Without warning, Hades came to a halt, turning to face her. "Can I offer you a suggestion?"

Bertha stilled. She was old. And set in her ways. Some might even say that she was pigheaded. She didn't like anyone telling her what to do. Including this gorgeous, sexy-as-hell god from...well, from hell.

"You can. I don't promise that I'll like it."

His ebony eyes smoldered with power in the shadows, holding an unspoken warning.

"You won't. I think it would be better if you changed into your human form."

"I don't have a human form," Bertha instinctively protested. She was a gargoyle, not a shapeshifter.

A faint smile curved his lips. "You do now."

Bertha frowned before realizing he was referring to the human shape he'd forced her into to defeat the ifrit. It took nerve to remind her of being in such a weak and vulnerable form. But while she wanted to chide him for his past behavior, she was suddenly intrigued by his blithe assumption she could shift into that form anytime she wanted.

"I don't need your magic?"

Flames danced over her. "It's already inside you."

His magic was inside her? Should she be mad? Probably. But it wasn't anger that tingled down her spine. She liked the thought that she carried a portion of this male with her. It was... Comforting? No. It did comfort her, but that wasn't the exact word. Exciting, yes. Arousing, definitely.

More than anything, it was inevitable.

She shook her head. Now wasn't the time to think about her complicated relationship with the god of the underworld. Not when she could feel a terrifying power humming just below her feet. As if they were standing on top of a nuclear reactor.

"Why do you want me to change form?" she demanded.

He hesitated, clearly choosing his words with care. "Gaia can be temperamental."

"A temperamental god?" Bertha rolled her eyes. "Shocker."

"Even more temperamental than most."

"What does that have to do with me?"

"She insists on any petitioners always being lower than her," he reluctantly admitted. "Which means you will have to crawl on your belly if you stay in your current form."

Bertha narrowed her eyes. "Excuse me. Did you just say crawl on my belly?"

Hades shrugged. "That's what I said."

"Never."

"It's not my decision, Bertha." Hades spoke in an exaggeratedly soothing tone. Was he trying to tell her that she was totally overreacting? "This is Gaia's private lair. She can make any rules she wants."

Bertha stomped her foot. Who cared if she was overacting? Crawl on her belly? Unacceptable.

"Stupid rules," she muttered.

"Agreed."

They glared at each other for a long moment, until the distant call of some exotic bird trilling in the shadows broke the silence. Deep inside, Bertha knew she was being unreasonable. As Hades had pointed out, he wasn't the one who made the rules in this realm. And they were only there because he'd agreed to help her save Levet from the minotaurs. But that didn't keep her from feeling outraged at being treated as if she were a worm.

"Fine," she finally forced herself to mutter.

Closing her eyes, Bertha put aside her annoyance to concentrate. Changing form wasn't a natural talent for a gargoyle, and she wasn't entirely sure what she was supposed to do. It wasn't like it came with a manual or anything.

At first, she strained her muscles in an effort to transform herself into a different shape. Maybe she could physically force herself to shift. Unfortunately, the only thing that happened was a cramp in her ass. She grunted in pain, shaking her hind leg in an effort to ease the spasm. That didn't work. She clearly needed a new tactic.

Keeping her eyes closed, she told herself to relax. Last time she'd simply awakened in the shape of a human. Easy peasy. That had to mean that there was nothing she needed to do beyond letting Hades's magic to do its thing, right?

It was as good a plan as any.

She cleared her mind of everything but the aggravating male who was standing just a few inches away. Even with the drumbeat of power from Gaia beneath her feet, she could feel the massive pulses of magic that surrounded Hades. They washed over her like the waves of an ocean, surrounding her in the warm, enticing scent of cypress. She allowed the magic to flow through her, slowly feeling his heat burn her from the inside out. Was she melting? That's what it felt like. As if she'd become a gooey ball that he could transform into any shape he wanted.

Gooey gargoyle? Hmm. That didn't seem like a good thing, but it was the only way to explain what was happening. It wasn't until the sensation had passed and she was once again a solid shape that she opened her eyes and glanced down.

As expected, she'd shrunk by several feet and her sturdy arms and legs were now delicately curved. She was wearing a thin satin gown that did nothing to keep the thorns on a nearby bush from stabbing into her flesh. Curly gold hair tumbled over her shoulders and when she glanced over her shoulders, she could catch the faintest outline of ephemeral wings.

The form was perfect for traveling in the human cities, but it sucked in the middle of a jungle.

Slapping a mosquito that landed on her cheek, she glared at Hades. "Are you happy now?"

He took a step toward her, his fingers brushing the spot where the mosquito had stolen her blood. Instantly the tiny wound was healed.

"I'm always happy when you're near," he murmured, flames visible in the depths of his eyes. "And to me, you're beautiful in any form you choose."

"You're getting better," Bertha praised the god. It was the only way to properly train him.

His fingers brushed her lower lip. "Give me time. I'll be perfect."

"Hmm."

A shiver of pleasure raced through Bertha, but before she could wrap her arms around Hades's neck and properly reward him for his efforts, there was a rustle in the bushes behind her.

Jerking around, she watched a tall, reed-thin male with a bald head and eyes too large for his narrow face step through the vines. He was wearing a green robe. Or maybe it was a white robe covered in mold. Hard to say. As he reached them, he bowed deep enough for the top of his head to brush the weeds. Impressive.

"Lord Hades," the servant murmured as he straightened. "My mistress eagerly awaits your visit. Follow me."

Without glancing in Bertha's direction, the creature waved a bony hand and the trees parted to reveal the opening of a large cave.

Bertha arched her brows as she glanced in Hades's direction. His features were as beautiful as ever, but there was a remote hardness in his expression she hadn't seen before.

"Eagerly?" she asked, annoyed with the goddess before she even met her.

"Let's get this over with," he muttered, marching toward the cave.

Chapter 13

Sofie floated in a sea of darkness, desperate to avoid the beckoning light. She wasn't afraid it would lead her to death. She'd already died and been resurrected as a vampire. The next time she was destroyed it would be in a puff of ash. But the light meant a return to consciousness and the pain she could sense hovering just on the horizon.

Distantly she could hear waterdrops falling from over her head to plop against the floor. As if the roof was leaking. Odd. Her lair was deep enough in the mountain to avoid the rain. And even when the snow melted, the stone was thick and hard enough to prevent any leaks.

Where was she?

Careful not to twitch a muscle, Sofie reviewed her last memories. She'd been in her lair, carving her latest fresco into the wall when the Anasso had rudely interrupted her. Yes, that was right. And he'd demanded that she leave her home and travel to...

Chicago. And Ryshi.

The darkness began to recede as the memory of entering the labyrinth formed in her mind. They'd been searching for a gargoyle, but they'd been trapped as a silver net had fallen on them. Or at least she'd been trapped, she silently conceded. Ryshi had disappeared.

Cautiously she reached out with her powers, searching for any hint of the jinn. Nothing. The nearest creature was a minotaur who reeked of damp fur and sour ale.

Trying not to gag, Sofie finally forced open her eyes. She couldn't pretend to be unconscious forever. And the longer she waited, the more likely the word of her arrival in the private lands of the minotaurs would spread and the greater the danger. Besides, the hard stone floor wasn't the most comfortable place to rest.

The first thing she noticed as her gaze cleared was the damp rock above her. As if she was in a cave. Then she turned her head, discovering the heavy bars that blocked her exit. Not a cave. A prison.

Were these the dungeons beneath the colosseum that Ryshi had mentioned? If they were, then the gargoyle she was searching for wasn't here. There was no scent of granite. Or any other demon beyond minotaur.

A worry for later, she told herself, reaching for the dagger that had been strapped on her hip. No surprise to discover it'd been taken. Muttering a curse, she lifted her hand to her neck. The net was gone, but there was a burning pain that blistered her throat.

Sofie winced as her fingers touched the thin band of silver that circled her neck. It wasn't large enough to kill her, but it was draining her strength at an alarming rate.

And it hurt like a bitch.

"It's about time," a voice growled.

Still lying on the ground, Sofie watched a male minotaur approach the bars of her cell. He was large, but not much bigger than a vampire, with horns that stuck out of the sides of his head and curved upward. The hair between his horns was buzzed to his skull, but he had a shaggy beard that hung down to his impressive potbelly. He hadn't bothered to put on a shirt, but thankfully he had on leather pants and boots. In one large hand he carried a spear with a wooden shaft and a metal tip.

Sofie wasn't impressed.

"Where am I?" she asked.

"I'll ask the questions, leech," the male chided, reaching the spear through the bars to jab the tip into her leg.

The metal wasn't silver and the damage it caused was minimal, but it was enough to spark her anger.

"Don't poke me," she warned.

"Ha." The male stabbed her again, grinning in pleasure at tormenting her. Jerk. "How are you going to stop me?"

Ice coated the floor of the cell. "Last warning," she hissed.

"I'll do what I want—"

The male's boast was cut short as Sofie grabbed the spear just below the tip and yanked it out of his hand. Smoothly rising to her feet, she snapped the shaft in half and dropped it on the ground.

"Where am I?" she asked again.

The male managed to look like a petulant child as he stared at his broken weapon, but he at least answered her question.

"The homeland of the minotaurs." His gaze lifted to glare at Sofie. "The *private* homeland where intruders are not welcome."

Sofie didn't have to fake her disgust as she glanced around. The dungeons looked just as filthy and ill tended as the city above. There was a slimy coating of mold on the damp rock and the stench of rotting food wafted from the cell next door.

"This place is your homeland?"

The guard scowled, obviously offended by her revulsion. "These are the dungeons, not a palace."

Sofie paused. The silver collar around her neck meant that she couldn't use her powers to trap the male's mind. A damned shame. She sensed this beast would be easy to control. But she recalled Ryshi mentioning the best way to battle a minotaur was by prompting him to lose his temper.

If she could get the male close enough to the bars, she could grab him and physically force him to open the cell door.

"I caught a glimpse of the town. It's even nastier than this place." She took a step forward, a mocking smile curving her lips. "I can't imagine why you go to such an effort to keep creatures out. Who would willingly visit such a pigsty?"

The minotaur's nostrils flared in outrage. "The traditional lands are beautiful. Lush and green and..." The words trailed away as the male realized he was probably giving away more than he should. "How did you get here?"

Sofie tucked away the knowledge that Ryshi had been right. This wasn't the actual homeland. At the same time, she considered how she could get information as she continued to piss off the guard.

"I'm not sure." She took another step forward, standing just an inch from the bars. She hoped it would lure the male closer. "I was tracking a gargoyle through a field when I was sucked into this place."

The guard frowned. "Impossible."

"You think I used magic to get here?" she taunted. "I'm a vampire."

"I know what you are."

"Then you should realize that I couldn't open a gateway. It had to be one of your people who kidnapped me."

The male stuck out his lower jaw. "My people never leave. Especially not from this area."

Sofie shrugged. "Okay. Maybe the gargoyle did it."

"If there was a gargoyle hanging around here I would know."

Sofie studied the guard. Despite the silver collar around her neck, she could sense that his ignorance was real. He didn't have any knowledge of Levet. Or even the plot to kidnap the gargoyle.

Did that mean the gargoyle was in the homeland? Or maybe he was already dead. Either way, she had to get out of the dungeon to discover the truth.

"Well, if I didn't open a gateway, and you claim there is no gargoyle, then by process of elimination it had to be a minotaur who is responsible, right?"

The male blinked, clearly having difficulty processing her words. At last he gave up and stomped his foot in frustration.

"You're pissing me off, leech."

Sofie laughed. "Like I give a shit."

The guard stepped toward the cell. "You think I won't kill you?"

Sofie blew him a kiss, silently urging him closer. "You can try."

There was a brief hesitation, as if the male was battling his urge to charge into the cell and beat her into submission. Annoyingly, he managed to contain his brutish instincts. At least for the moment.

"First, I want to know what happened to your companion," he growled.

Sofie stilled, concentrating on keeping her expression from revealing her shock at his words. She'd hoped that the minotaurs hadn't caught sight of Ryshi before he disappeared. That would give him the best opportunity to hide in the shadows until he found a means to help her escape.

And if that was impossible, then to simply flee and save himself. The mere thought that the minotaurs might hurt him made her stomach clench with a sense of dread.

"Companion?" She blinked in faux confusion. "You mean the gargoyle?"

The guard stomped his foot. "Stop yammering about that damned gargoyle."

"You're the one who asked."

"I'm talking about the male who was with you just before you were captured."

"You're delusional." Sofie folded her arms over her chest, staring at the guard as if he'd lost his mind. "There was no male. At least, not with me."

"He was there." The beast's features tightened into a bitter expression. "And he's the same bastard who snuck in here before."

Sofie clenched her teeth. They not only knew that Ryshi was in their realm, they knew he'd been here before. It added yet another layer of danger. The last thing they needed.

Unfortunately, she couldn't do anything until she was released from the cell.

"I was right," she drawled, flicking a disdainful glance down to the guard's potbelly. "You should cut back on the ale. It's rotting your brain along with your body."

Her words had the desired effect. The guard took an impulsive step forward, his face twisted into a furious expression.

"We will never forget his scent," he rasped. "Or what he took from us."

Took from them? Sofie paused, her thoughts racing. She'd known that Ryshi hadn't been fully honest when he'd claimed to have entered the labyrinth merely to test his skills. Not even a reckless, fortune-hunting jinn would willingly enter a maze that no other creature had survived.

Now she had the opportunity to discover what he was hiding from her, and Sofie couldn't resist the temptation.

Not that she was going to ask outright. It was the one certain way to make sure she didn't get an answer. Instead, she wrinkled her nose in distaste.

"Why would anyone take anything from this place?"

"We have several priceless artifacts."

"Really? A shiny rock you found in the mud?" she taunted. "Maybe a pretty feather?"

"It was a gift from our goddess."

"That does sound extraordinary." Sofie didn't have to pretend to be impressed. Ryshi wasn't lacking in courage. Or maybe he had a death wish. To steal a holy relic from a species was one certain way to get your head chopped off. "What did it do?"

The minotaur shuffled his large feet, as if embarrassed to answer the question. "I'm not sure. But it was important."

That was...disappointing. This guard wasn't included in the need-to-know group for stolen artifacts. She doubted he was included in any groups. Not with the foul smell that was threatening to gag Sofie. No wonder he'd been given dungeon duty. Anything to keep him at a distance.

She tucked away her curiosity, returning her attention to luring the male closer to the bars. Just a couple of more feet and she'd be able to grab him.

"And someone stole it?" she asked.

"Not *someone*. Your friend stole it."

"Trust me, I don't have any friends."

There was an edge of sincerity in her voice that made the guard furrow his brow in confusion.

"You were seen traveling together."

"Then why isn't he here?"

"He disappeared."

"And left me behind?" Sofie snorted. "Not much of a friend, is he?"

Sour frustration further tainted the already tainted air. "Tell me who you are and why you're here."

"No."

"You'll tell me or I'll make you tell me," the guard threatened, shuffling even closer.

Sofie held out her hand and wiggled her fingers in invitation. "Come on, bully boy. Let's dance."

On the point of charging the cell, the guard was abruptly halted as a deep voice cut through the air.

"Stop, Jorgan!"

As if gripped by an invisible hand, the guard was jerked backward, nearly hitting the wall opposite Sofie's cell. Sofie cursed, watching as a male minotaur stepped into view.

This one was larger than Jorgan with long black hair that was braided to fall between his impressive set of horns. His face was shaven and remarkably clean while his massive body was covered by a long leather coat and pants that were thick enough to provide protection. The biggest difference between the two minotaurs, however, was the glitter of intelligence in the second male's eyes.

He wouldn't be easily tricked or manipulated. Sofie cursed again as the male moved to tower over Jorgan.

"What the hell is wrong with you?"

Jorgan performed an awkward bow. "Commander Stavros."

"I should have known you couldn't be trusted with the prisoner."

Sofie wasn't surprised the leather-clad male was a commander. He carried himself with an unmistakable air of authority.

Jorgan hunched his shoulders, trying to pretend he wasn't intimidated, his expression peevish.

"She's here, isn't she?"

Stavros pointed a finger toward the cell. "With your spear. How did she get it?"

"That wasn't my fault."

The commander made a sound of fierce exasperation, waving his hand toward the other male.

"Go away."

Jorgan wasn't overly bright, but he had enough brains to realize that his best option was to flee before he was punished. Still hunched over, he scurried out of sight. Like a rat jumping from a sinking ship.

Sofie dismissed the coward from her mind as she studied her newest threat. And he was a threat, she grimly acknowledged. If she intended to try to overpower him she would have to do it quickly. The silver collar would soon have her too weakened to fight.

The question was, how could she convince him to open the cell door?

"Are you next in line to threaten me?" she drawled.

The male turned to study her with dark, piercing eyes. "I prefer action to words."

"Fine with me. I'm growing bored." Sofie yawned, stretching her arms over her head in a slow motion that emphasized the slender curves of her body. Some males were susceptible to their physical hungers. "Are we going to fight?"

Stavros arched his brows in appreciation, but he was clearly not going to give in to any rash impulses.

"You have to earn the right to fight me," he informed her with a faint smile.

"Earn the right?"

In answer, the commander lifted his hands to clap them together. A second later three more minotaurs crowded into the space in front of her cell. There were two males and one female. All of them were large, all of them were holding heavy spears, and all of them were eyeing Sofie with anticipation. As if hoping she would do something that would give them a reason to skewer her like a shish kebab.

Still smiling, Stavros moved to grab the door of her cell. With one hard jerk he had it swinging open. Sofie stiffened, not daring to move. She was no match for four fully armed minotaurs. Even when she was at her full strength.

"Come with me," he commanded.

Sofie considered her options. It didn't take long. She could do as the male demanded or she could get sliced into tiny bits. Not the most pleasant way to die.

Cautiously, she stepped out of the cell, not sure whether this was some sort of trap. When she wasn't stabbed or poked or diced, she reluctantly followed Stavros as he led her down a cramped corridor lined with cells on one side. They were all currently empty, but there was a lingering stench that revealed they'd been in use in the past. Mostly by minotaurs, although she caught the scent of orc and troll mixed in the muck.

They reached a heavy door and she watched as Stavros laid his hand on the wood. Slowly it swung open. She assumed the locks must react to his touch rather than keys. Yet another barrier to her freedom.

"Where are we going?" she asked as they climbed the steps carved into the thick stone, acutely conscious of the guards following a few inches behind her.

She sensed she was being herded. And that she wasn't going to like her destination.

"Despite Jorgan's unfortunate display of ignorance, we are not all stupid enough to believe we can force a vampire to give us the information we desire," the commander assured her.

Sofie frowned. It was doubtful he was talking about torture. They would have left her in the dungeon for that. Did they have some sort of creature who could read minds?

"How many times do I have to repeat myself?" She forced out the words in an effort to keep the minotaurs distracted as she glanced around. At this point her only hope was escape. "I don't have any information."

Stavros ignored her protest, taking a sharp right as they reached the top of the stairs. They'd left the subterranean area, but they were in the same stone structure as they moved down a long hallway that curved to the left.

"Eventually you'll talk," Stavros assured her.

"Doubtful," she muttered, suddenly aware of the thunderous shouts that echoed in the distance.

She'd suspected they were in the colosseum and now there was no doubt. The question was whether they were leading her to a new location, or if she was going to be kept in this formidable structure. It would be easier to escape if they traveled through the congested city. The more distractions the better.

"There's no doubt," Stavros argued. "And better yet, we can lure your partner from the shadows. He won't escape again."

Sofie didn't bother to argue. The minotaurs had obviously seen him before he'd turned to smoke. And she realized that she had another opportunity to discover exactly why Ryshi had been in the labyrinth. This male was in charge. He would know precisely what was stolen and why.

"Your friend, Jorgan—"

"He's not my friend," Stavros interrupted.

It was her turn to ignore his protest. "He said that the male you're searching for had stolen a valuable artifact."

The minotaur made a sound of disgust. "Jorgan doesn't know how to keep his mouth shut."

"If you explain what it is, perhaps I can tell you if I have seen it," she said, veiling her interest with the pretense of bargaining for her release.

Stavros narrowed his eyes. "So you admit that you're partners?"

"Reluctant partners," she said. "Tell me."

Surprisingly, the commander appeared quite willing to reveal the truth. "It's a small blue stone shaped like an egg."

"I think that's familiar," Sofie smoothly lied. "What does it do?"

"It allows you to speak with another minotaur over a great distance."

Sofie blinked, doubly confused. Why would a minotaur need to speak over a long distance? And why would Ryshi risk his life to steal it? Maybe it had other magic.

"An odd item for a such a reclusive species to consider valuable," she pointed out the obvious.

The scent of minotaur was suddenly thick in the air. Not the stench of an unwashed body, but the raw power of this beast. Her words had obviously touched a nerve.

"We didn't always live in a cloistered society." Stavros clenched his massive hands. "There was a time when we regularly traveled far and wide."

It wasn't that unusual. Several species of demons had entered a world, then left. The merfolk were just one example.

"Why did you stop?" she asked, genuinely curious.

His heavy boots slammed against the floor with enough force to send tiny tremors through the stone.

"Intolerance. Fear. Mainly arrogance."

Sofie studied the male's tense profile. There was something different about Stavros. It wasn't simply the power that vibrated around him, or the cunning intelligence in his eyes. He had an unmistakable air of leadership. So why was he in this shithole instead of the homeland?

It wasn't hard to guess.

"Is that an opinion shared by the other minotaurs?" she asked, already predicting his response.

"It's an opinion that got me sent here."

Sofie wanted to know more. Like whether he'd been overthrown as king. And why the new ruler had decided to hide behind the labyrinth. It was odd. She never had an interest in anyone. Well, except for Ryshi, who'd been haunting her thoughts since she'd first caught sight of him. But why would she care about the minotaurs?

Was it because they'd retreated from the world as she had?

Sofie slammed the mental door on her disturbing thoughts. The only thing that mattered was finding a way to escape.

"I could return the stone to you," she offered. "Perhaps your sins would be forgiven if you could offer your people the missing artifact. Release me and I'll—"

The commander came to a halt, his expression stoic. "I have other plans for you."

Sofie slowed and turned back with a frown, belatedly noticing the large wooden doors set in the wall. Her stomach clenched. Had they reached their destination?

"What if I'm not interested in your plans?"

"Tough."

He reached out and laid his hand against one of the doors. There was a loud creak of rusty hinges before it opened. The thick scent of minotaur rushed in with a humid blast of air and Sofie leaned forward to catch a glimpse of a vast oval amphitheater. They were standing at the edge of the arena where she assumed the gladiators would fight, although it was currently empty. The hard-packed dirt field was surrounded by long bleachers that soared toward the gray clouds overhead. The seats were packed with minotaurs who were busy drinking from large steins and shouting insults at one another.

As Sofie watched, two minotaurs lunged at each other, throwing punches and spilling ale. The scuffle swiftly encompassed the surrounding demons until a dozen or more were shoving and pushing. It was a ridiculous spectacle, but that wasn't what captured her attention.

There were hundreds of minotaurs jammed into the stadium, all of them shouting at the tops of their lungs, but the sound was oddly muffled. Since she was fairly sure she hadn't lost her hearing, that could only mean there was a layer of magic laid over the actual arena. To keep the fighters from fleeing the battle. Or more likely, to keep the spectators from jumping in and joining the contest.

Sofie clenched her hands. She'd clung to the hope that she could somehow escape from her captors. Now it appeared she was going to have to find some other way to survive.

She turned toward Stavros. "You expect me to fight?"

He shrugged. "You have options. You can tell me what I want to know, or you can fight," he informed her. "At the end of each battle you will either be dead or you will once again have the opportunity to give me the information. We'll continue as long as necessary."

Sofie made a sound of disgust. She was powerful. Far more powerful than any minotaur. And she didn't need weapons when she had her mind control and lethal fangs. But the silver had sapped her strength and made it impossible to use her hidden talent. She would be destroyed in the first battle.

Lifting her hand to touch the collar, she glared at her companion. It was a long shot, but she sensed that this male had a sense of honor. Why go to the bother of putting her in the arena if he wasn't hoping that he could force her to give him the information he wanted?

"You expect me to fight with this around my neck?"

"Of course not. We aren't animals." With a grimace the male glanced toward the minotaurs who were still tangled in a melee that had grown to include dozens of the creatures. He returned his attention to her with a wry smile. "Not entirely. Once you're in the ring I'll have it removed. I'll also give you back your weapon." He smiled as her eyes widened in shock. "You see? Minotaurs are always fair."

Sofie couldn't disguise her surge of hope. Not only would she be able to use her powers, but her dagger carried a deadly curse that would allow her to destroy her opponent with one stab. She assumed the minotaurs hadn't been able to sense the magic on the blade.

Unless this was a trap?

Only one way to find out.

"Get comfortable," she murmured, mentally preparing for the upcoming battles. "This could take a while."

Stavros appeared unconcerned by her warning. "I hope so."

"Why?"

"Eventually your companion is going to try to rescue you," he explained. "Then I'll finally have him trapped. He won't escape again, I promise you that." Stavros motioned toward the guards behind Sofie. "Prepare her for battle."

Chapter 14

Entering the large cave, Bertha had expected to find herself surrounded by barren rock and cloaked in darkness. That's what proper caves were supposed to be like. This one, however, seemed to glow with a yellowish light that revealed the lush vegetation that grew everywhere. Even the ceiling.

Flowers. Grass. Ferns. Moss. If it was green, then it was growing someplace in the cavern. Bertha stifled a sneeze as thick pollen tickled her nose. Once she was out of there, she intended to spend several months in a place where plants wouldn't grow.

Like the Arctic. Or a desert. Maybe Vegas...

Wiggling her nose, Bertha was suddenly conscious of the dry scent of scales that laced the pollen-ladened air.

"Why do I smell reptiles?" she asked.

Walking beside her, Hades nodded toward the thin male who was leading them toward the center of the cavern.

"Many of Gaia's servants can take the shape of a snake," he informed her in soft tones.

Snakes? Bertha was instantly intrigued. She'd never encountered a creature who could become any sort of reptile.

"Are they venomous?"

"Lethal," he assured her. "Even to demons."

Hmm. She was still intrigued, but her curiosity was mixed with a new sense of caution. She wasn't eager to be bitten by a venomous reptile. It seemed like a nasty way to die.

"You should probably try not to piss her off," she generously warned her companion.

Hades jerked his head toward her, his expression one of disbelief. "If anyone is going to piss her off, it's not going to be me."

Bertha blinked, baffled by his implication that she might cause trouble. "Are you suggesting that I'm annoying?"

"You do have a tendency to speak your mind," he said in dry tones.

Bertha remained baffled. "Why shouldn't I? I have a very fine mind."

"Agreed. But while I appreciate your frankness, there are some gods who prefer to have lesser beings treat them with a...fawning devotion."

The scent of granite cut through the heavy perfume of wildflowers. "Did you call me a lesser being?"

"To Gaia that's what you are."

"And to you?" The words were forced between clenched teeth.

"You already know I find you sheer perfection."

"Oh." The swelling anger abruptly drained away, like the air from a pricked balloon. It was replaced by a sappy, goofy sensation of pleasure. "You are getting very good at that."

"I'm trying." Flames danced in his eyes as he allowed his gaze to slide over her. Then the fire was quenched and his features were tightening with something that might have been apprehension. "We're approaching Gaia's private lair," he said, his jaw clenched. "Be careful."

She shrugged at the silly suggestion. "I'm always careful."

"You're *never* careful," he muttered, coming to a halt as the servant turned and pointed toward Bertha.

"On your knees," he hissed.

Bertha's lips parted to tell the male exactly what he could do with his command, only to snap shut when she caught sight of Hades's smoldering glare. He didn't have to speak to warn her that this wasn't the time or place to assert her independence. Not if she was going to get the help she needed from Gaia.

With stiff reluctance, she sank to her knees and bowed her head. Out of the corner of her eye she watched as the plants parted and an exquisite female appeared, a halo of golden light surrounding her.

At first it was hard to make out any distinguishing features through the blazing power, but Bertha thought she could see a mass of golden curls and moss-green eyes as well as a curvaceous form that was barely covered by a silver toga as she glided to stand directly in front of Hades.

"At last," she breathed, her glow reaching out to surround the male. "I have waited an eternity for this moment."

"Gaia." Hades offered a stiff nod. "As beautiful as ever."

The goddess chuckled, stretching her arms over her head and practically shoving her large boobs into Hades's face. "Of course I am. I just awakened from a most refreshing nap." Slowly she lowered her arms. "Would you like to know what I dreamed?"

Bertha ground her teeth together, belatedly realizing why Hades had been so confident that the goddess would agree to see him. Gaia obviously wanted a relationship with Hades. It was visible in the hunger that burned in her eyes and the potent desire that spiced the air.

The urge to leap to her feet and give the goddess a good headbutt trembled through Bertha. Hades was never ever going to belong to Gaia. Not if she had any say in the matter.

Thankfully, she managed to suppress the instinct. For one thing, Bertha had promised herself she would never fight over a male. Why bother when there were so many to choose from? And for another, Hades was a god. He didn't need her to fight his battles.

Remaining in her kneeling position, Bertha forced herself to take a deep, calming breath. It helped to concentrate on the stiffness in Hades's body and the way he leaned back, as if trying to put space between himself and the beautiful goddess. Whatever Gaia's interest in him, it wasn't reciprocated.

Or at least, that's what Bertha was going to tell herself.

"I'm certain your dreams are fascinating," he assured the goddess.

"More than fascinating, they were glorious." Gaia reached out to trail her fingers over Hades's platinum hair. "And you were a part of them."

"I'm honored."

"Yes, you are." Her fingers moved to cup his chin, tilting his face so her ravenous gaze could admire each perfect feature. "Do you wish to know what we were doing?"

With a calm expression, Hades stepped back to dislodge her hand. At the same time, the glow she'd wrapped around him started to dim. As if he was using his powers to push it away.

"Perhaps later."

Gaia's face hardened at the subtle rebuff. "Now."

"Okay." Hades quickly soothed the female's temper, although he kept his distance. "What were we doing?"

Gaia tossed her golden curls, the movement impossibly elegant. "Conquering worlds. I've told you over and over that it is our destiny." She pinched her lips. "I do not know why you have been so stubborn."

For a single second, Bertha was in complete agreement with the goddess. Hades was stubborn. Even more stubborn than a goblin. Still, Gaia had no right to criticize the god. That was Bertha's prerogative.

"The underworld offers enough headaches," Hades said, an edge of sincerity in his rich voice. "Why would I want more?"

"Power." The goddess narrowed her eyes. "To please me."

"I'm sure another of the gods would be interested in your offer," Hades assured her.

Gaia released a pulse of golden light that flared through the cavern. Bertha hastily squeezed her eyes shut, sensing the glow would blind her.

"I don't want another god," she heard Gaia complain. "I want you."

"I'm content where I am," Hades insisted.

"Content?" Bertha cautiously opened her eyes in time to see Gaia stomp her foot, as if she were a human child and not a goddess. "Such a small word. You are not small, Hades. You are fated for greatness. Just like me."

Hades shook his head. "That isn't why I'm here, Gaia."

With a flounce, Gaia turned away, almost stumbling over Bertha, as if she hadn't even noticed she was there.

"Who are you?" she snarled.

Hades was swiftly moving to stand between Bertha and the goddess. "My handmaiden," he said.

Handmaiden? Bertha grimaced, but wisely kept her mouth shut. Not because she was afraid. Okay, maybe she was a little afraid. She was, after all, in the presence of two gods. But if she was going to save Levet, she had to let Hades convince the goddess to offer her assistance.

A task that seemed more difficult by the minute as Gaia pointed an accusing finger at Bertha.

"Why is she in my lair?"

"She is seeking your assistance."

"My assistance?" The goddess released a sharp laugh that echoed through the cavern. "She's a gargoyle. I have no interest in her needs."

"She is important to me."

An unseen power pressed against Bertha. Was it the goddess?

"Important? This...creature?" Gaia spit out in disbelief. Hades nodded and the female made a sound of sheer outrage. "Why?"

Hades shrugged. "A mystery not even a god can comprehend."

"Hey," Bertha started to protest, only to snap her lips shut as Gaia forced her head to slam against the ground.

Be careful....

Hades's voice whispered through her mind and Bertha tried to relax her tense muscles. For now the goddess could do whatever she wanted.

And obviously what she wanted was Bertha flat on her face.

"You traveled to my private lair to request a favor for another female?" Gaia bit out in a hard voice.

There was a hissing sound from the bushes, as if the hidden servants were bracing for something awful to happen. Bertha didn't blame them. It felt as if there was a storm gathering above their heads.

"It concerns your minotaurs as well," Hades informed the goddess.

Bertha could sense that his words caught Gaia by surprise. Thankfully it meant that the pressure against her head eased enough for her to sit upright.

"What about them?" Gaia demanded.

"I believe they might be in danger."

"Ridiculous. They're fine. I checked on them before I left...." Gaia turned her head, staring at the thin male who'd led them into the cavern. "How long ago?"

"One thousand two hundred and ninety-six years ago and fourteen days," the servant said without hesitation.

Gaia jerked, as if the number hit her with a physical force. "So long?"

The servant bowed. "Yes, my goddess."

"I had no idea." A portion of the arrogance faded from Gaia's expression, replaced with genuine concern as she returned her interest to Hades. "What has happened to my people?"

"I can't say for certain," Hades admitted.

"Why not?"

"No one has seen or heard from them since you retreated to this lair."

A tremor shuddered beneath Bertha's knees. An earthquake? Or Gaia's reaction to the thought of her people in danger? Maybe she wasn't utterly selfish, Bertha reluctantly conceded.

Gaia hesitated before forcing herself to ask the question that was clearly troubling her. "They've been destroyed?"

Hades shook his head. "No, they live," he assured the goddess. "But they refuse to leave their homeland."

"Refuse?"

"They hide behind the labyrinth, never letting anyone in or out."

The goddess breathed a sigh of reliefl; then, closing her eyes, she tilted back her head and spread out her arms. The glow that surrounded her spread throughout the cavern, but it wasn't harsh or blinding. Just the opposite. It provided a soft warmth that the plants greedily absorbed and caused her servants to sigh in rapture. Even Bertha felt pleasure as it bathed her. It reminded her of the years she'd spent on a temple in Greece. During the day she was in her stone form, but the sun and sea had seeped deep into her soul. Paradise.

At last the goddess dropped her arms and clicked her tongue in exasperation.

"I have located them," she assured Hades. "Stubborn creatures. I gave them the labyrinth before I left. I intended it as a source of protection, not imprisonment. What is the matter with them?"

Hades appeared genuinely sympathetic. As if he had his own share of stupid creatures.

"Lesser beings often mistake our gifts. They are forever attempting to alter or change them to suit their own desires."

"Too true." Gaia shared a glance with Hades before turning her head to gaze down at Bertha with disdain. "I still don't understand what my people and their retreat from the world has to do with this gargoyle."

"They have kidnapped my nephew," Bertha said, ready to get to the purpose of their visit.

She wanted to be out of the cavern. It was giving her a rash.

The sudden sound of hissing from the hidden servants warned Bertha she'd made a mistake even before the goddess lifted her hand, as if intending to strike her.

"Do not speak in my presence."

Hades stepped forward, blocking the blow and at the same time distracting the goddess.

"For reasons I do not comprehend, the minotaurs have decided to elevate a gargoyle to the status of a god."

Gaia made a strangled sound. Whether it was because she was thwarted in her desire to punish Bertha or because of Hades's words was impossible to say.

"That gargoyle a god?" She continued to glare at Bertha. "Don't be ridiculous. She's pathetic."

"No, not this one," Hades took another step forward, expertly guiding the goddess away from Bertha. "It's her nephew. A gargoyle named Levet."

"I don't believe you."

"May I?" Hades held out his hand.

There was a brief pause before Gaia offered a grudging nod of her head. "Very well."

There was a tingle of familiar magic in the air. The searing heat assured Bertha that this time it belonged to Hades. Moments later a long spear formed, balanced on his open hand.

There was a shrill cry from a bird before a dozen servants with bald heads and heavy robes burst out of the bushes and charged toward Hades.

"Stop!"

They jerked to a halt, as if they'd slammed into an invisible wall. Only the servant who'd greeted them was left free to point at Hades in horror.

"He has a weapon."

"It can't harm me. It belongs to my minotaurs," she chided.

"Yes," Hades agreed. "They have a prophecy etched into the shaft."

Gaia heaved a weary sigh. "A seer, I suppose." Holding out her hand, she impatiently snapped her fingers. "Let me have it."

Bertha could see Hades's jaw clench. He wasn't accustomed to obeying orders. In fact, he no doubt crushed anyone stupid enough to try to tell him what to do. But this time he didn't punish the goddess. Instead, he swallowed his pride and obediently moved to show her the spear.

Bertha's heart twisted with regret. He wasn't doing this to please Gaia. He was doing it to please her.

"This is the gargoyle," he said, pointing at the shaft.

Gaia frowned, bending her head to study the etching. "You're sure that's a gargoyle? It looks like a fairy."

"He's quite unique," Hades assured her. "That's why we knew immediately who it was."

Gaia grabbed the spear from Hades, continuing to study the prophecy that had been carved into the wood.

"What is happening to the paradise I created?" she muttered.

"Your people seem to believe the gargoyle can solve their problems."

"Gargoyles." With a burst of temper, Gaia shattered the spear in her hand, tossing aside the splinters. "I'll deal with this."

"We would like to have the gargoyle back alive," Hades informed the goddess.

Gaia stilled, a smile slowly curving her lips. "You'll be in my debt."

Without thought to her own safety, Bertha jumped to her feet. It was one thing to have Hades endure being ordered around like a servant, but there was no way in hell she was going to let him be in debt to this...this...bitch.

"No, Hades!" she cried. They would find Levet without the help of the goddess.

"Hush." Gaia waved a dismissive hand in her direction, her avid gaze never wavering from Hades's face. "We're negotiating."

Chapter 15

Levet pressed a hand to his tummy. It was churning, and not in a good way. In fact, it was downright icky. He'd spent a very long time taking pride in his ability to be a knight in shining armor. He might be the smallest gargoyle, but he was the one who'd saved the world. More than once.

Now he just wanted to be Levet. A tiny gargoyle who wasn't expected to do anything beyond causing trouble and charming the females. The problem was convincing the stubborn, oversize bull that he wasn't a mythical savior.

Scrunching his snout, Levet jumped off the railing. There was only one way to get out of this place, he grimly decided. He had to go to the original source of this disaster.

The seer.

With a flap of his wings he landed on the wooden planks and headed for the open doorway. There was a heavy thud of boots, and suddenly his path was blocked by his companion, who'd moved with unexpected speed.

"What are you doing?"

Levet sniffed. "I need to have very firm words with that seer of yours."

"Why?"

"She clearly made a terrible mistake."

"There was no mistake."

Levet scowled. Why was the minotaur so big? He was taking up the entire doorway.

"Move, s'il vous plaît."

"No."

Levet lifted his hand, prepared to create a very large fireball that would singe the fur between the male's horns.

"I do not desire to harm you but—" His words were rudely cut off as the male reached down to grab him by the horn. "Hey."

"You are not leaving until you have performed your duty," the minotaur growled, plopping Levet back on the railing. "Now do it."

Levet waved his arms in the air. He'd never felt so frustrated. And that was saying something considering he'd spent his childhood trying to dodge a mother who wanted him dead.

"I'm telling you that the seer is defective."

"There is nothing wrong with the seer."

"Her visions are whack-a-beaver. I am no god." Levet reached up to wipe away any fingerprints that might be marring the gloss of his horn. "Not that I am not blessed with many fine qualities," he hastily added. He wanted to convince the male to send him home, but false modesty was worse than arrogance. So vulgar. "I am handsome, and talented and charming. But a god?" He flapped his wings in disbelief. "Fah."

The minotaur stared down at him, his eyes dark with an emotion that was difficult to read.

"I'll admit that it does seem…beyond belief." The words were forced between clenched teeth. "But I have no choice but to accept the truth."

Levet clicked his tongue. When he'd first arrived in the minotaur homeland his pride had been bloated by the thought of being the center of a prophecy. And even more bloated at being called a god. It'd taken the sight of that poor female being sucked into the hole to remind him that he'd known thousands of seers and oracles and fortune-tellers. It didn't matter if they were legit or scam artists, their predictions were always sketchy. And just like beauty, the truth of the prophecy was in the eyes of the beholder.

"Your seer has never been wrong?" Levet asked.

The male's eyes darted away, a sure sign he was about to tell a lie. "Of course not."

"Never?" Levet pressed.

The male's jaw tightened. "Interpretations of the vision can vary."

"Exactly. You admit that there have been mistakes."

"Not mistakes. Variations." The male stubbornly refused to admit the truth. "The seer sees what she sees, but—"

"Can you say that ten times fast?" Levet interrupted the tedious explanation.

The male flared his nostrils as his temper threatened to get the best of him. "Shut up and listen."

Levet folded his arms over his chest. "That's no way to speak to a god."

The air suddenly pulsed with the threat of violence, but with an obvious effort, the minotaur battled back his urge to pummel Levet into a gooey mess.

"The vision is given by the seer," he rasped. "It is up to us to interpret what it means."

"Uh-huh." Levet tilted his chin. He wasn't afraid of the male. He'd been pummeled before. And he was starting to suspect that this male was hiding something. "Who does the interpreting?"

"The prophecy is reviewed by a council of elders, but it is the leader who decides which variation is the proper foretelling."

"You?"

The male shrugged. "For now."

Levet was surprised by the answer. Reclusive tribes—or herds—rarely changed leaders. That was why the leader kept them isolated. To protect his position.

"Does that mean you can get voted off the island?" Levet asked.

The minotaur frowned. "I'm not sure what you mean."

"That crown is not permanent?"

"No, it can go to someone else."

"How?"

The male made a sound of impatience. "The council chooses our leader."

"Interesting." Levet was genuinely intrigued. The bovine species was surprisingly democratic. A rare quality among demons. "And they gave the crown to you?"

The minotaur waved his hand toward the heavy circlet set between his horns. "Obviously."

Levet sniffed his disdain. He had no respect for crowns or thrones or even royal bloodlines. He had been born a prince, but it didn't mean he would be a decent leader. In truth, he would probably be a disaster.

"So, if you had the crown, then you were the one to interpret the vision."

There was a tense pause. The male didn't want to answer the question.

"Eventually," he ground out at last.

Ah. Now Levet was beginning to understand the male's grim determination to believe that a miniature gargoyle with fairy wings was a god. Even after he'd watched Levet's mighty fireballs sizzle and poof into cinders.

"There was another interpretation, was there not?"

The minotaur squeezed his hands into tight fists. "The previous king had his own ideas."

"What happened to him?"

"He was banished."

Levet didn't know anything about the former leader, but he felt an immediate sympathy for him. Like him, Levet had been driven from his homeland. It was a fate he would not wish on any creature.

"What did he see in the vision?" Levet asked.

"What does it matter?" The minotaur abruptly spun away, pacing from one end of the balcony to the other as if his seething emotions were threatening to boil over. "He refused to accept that the goddess's gift of the labyrinth was intended to keep us shielded from the world," he burst out, the words sounding oddly defensive. "And that the vision given to the seer was proof of the danger, not a promise of salvation. We had no choice but to get rid of him and his treacherous beliefs."

Levet wrinkled his snout in disgust. This male had used the previous king's unpopular opinion to gain power. And now he was desperate to cling to his throne, despite all evidence that he'd made a terrible mistake.

"How difficult was it for you to sway the other minotaurs into believing he was wrong so that you could claim the crown?"

The male came to an abrupt halt, glaring at Levet. "It wasn't like that. I gave the people hope."

"And took the throne."

"He was wrong."

"*Non.*" Levet shook his head, belatedly realizing what had been nagging at him since he'd been kidnapped and forced into the minotaur homeland. From the beginning there'd been a sense of familiarity about it. He couldn't place why it might feel as if he'd been there before. Probably because the two places were so completely different. But now he realized that it wasn't the surroundings that were familiar, it was the choking sense of claustrophobia that hovered over the fortress. Just as it had once hovered over the merfolk castle. Inga had rid the palace of the rancid atmosphere when she'd become queen, but only after she'd killed the previous king and forced her people back into the world. "He was right."

The male stomped his foot, causing the balcony to shudder beneath the impact. Levet dug his claws into the railing to keep from falling.

"Impossible."

"It is always a mistake to seclude yourself in such a manner," Levet informed the stubborn fool. "The merfolk did the same thing to protect themselves from the dragon wars."

"We're not merfolk," the minotaur snapped.

"*Non,* but they were isolated in their castle beneath the ocean, allowing the rot to come from inside. It is inevitable."

"There is no rot."

"Are you jesting?" Levet waited. It was a legitimate question. He often did not comprehend what others considered funny. When the male continued to glare at him, Levet pointed a finger toward the gaping black hole in the sky. "What do you call that?"

"Clearly it is an attack from some unseen enemy."

"There is no scent of an invader, not even when the black mist appeared to take the sacrifice," Levet pointed out in reasonable tones. "Besides, why would they create an opening and not use it to enter?"

"The vision—"

"The vision reveals a darkness in the sky and a gargoyle who happens to look like *moi*," Levet interrupted. He'd seen the prophecy stitched into the tapestry. And like all prophecies, there were several details without any sort of context. Like having a fairy pick a yellow daffodil and a unicorn farting. Both could happen at the same time without having any connection to each other. Levet wrinkled his snout. Perhaps that wasn't the best metaphor. "My presence doesn't ensure an end to the threat of your homeland."

"You are our savior," the male snarled.

Levet glanced toward the sky, a shudder racing through his body. "I possess no magic that can heal that rot."

"Don't say that."

Levet turned back to send his companion a chiding frown. "You should have listened to your previous king. Your ambition is going to destroy your people."

The minotaur was shaking his head before Levet finished speaking. "I don't believe you."

Levet silently wondered if all minotaurs were so obstinate. Of course, it wouldn't be easy to admit that his decisions had condemned his people to certain death.

"It no longer matters what you believe. The damage has been done."

"No." The male abruptly stepped toward the edge of the balcony, waving his hand toward the minotaurs below. "You simply need the proper motivation."

Levet watched the creatures scurry back into the fortress, his heart dropping to the tips of his toes. The minotaurs had no one to blame but themselves for the terrifying darkness, but he didn't want to watch them being sacrificed in a futile attempt to change their destiny.

Still, he couldn't reveal his weakness. The only way to stop this useless game was to refuse to play.

"You can allow the darkness to suck up as many screaming minotaurs as you want…." Levet grimaced. "Although I wish you would not; it is a horrible thing to witness. But it does not give me the power that is needed to close the hole."

The male turned to face Levet. "I have a different motivation in mind."

"More ale? Dancing girls?" Levet guessed, his wings drooping when the minotaur reached into the back pocket of his leather pants. Was he reaching for a weapon? Probably. "Is it torture?" Levet heaved a deep sigh. "I hate torture."

"There's no need."

Surprisingly, the minotaur didn't pull out a dagger. Instead, it was a round silver hoop the size of an orange. At first it appeared to be empty inside, but as he held it toward Levet there was a strange shimmer, as if an image was being formed. Was it some sort of scrying device? Levet had never seen anything like it.

About to snatch the thing out of the male's hand so he could more closely inspect it, Levet felt his heart stutter to a halt as the image came into focus and he could see the large female attired in a bright lime muumuu lying unconscious on a grassy field.

"Inga," he breathed in horrified shock. There was no mistaking the red tufts of hair and the solid body that could walk through a brick wall. Not to mention the Tryshu clutched in her hand. The large trident was the symbol of authority among the merfolk and only the true king or queen could touch it. "Where is she? What have you done to her?"

"She is my insurance that you will fulfill your destiny," the minotaur informed him.

Levet's gaze remained locked on the image even as he promised himself he would skewer the minotaur and roast him over an open fire if something happened to his beloved. "Is she hurt?"

"No. She's simply asleep." There was a tense pause. "For now."

"Where?"

"In the labyrinth."

Levet forced himself to lift his gaze to study the minotaur's face. He needed to determine if the male was telling him the truth.

"How did she get there?"

"We created a gateway into the merfolk castle."

"Impossible." Levet shook his head.

Inga had opened the castle to visitors and encouraged her own people to travel and explore the world, but there were still thick layers of magic that protected the merfolk. Including spells to keep gateways from being formed without the approval of the guards. Not to mention that the Tryshu that Inga carried was capable of destroying entire cities. Perhaps the world itself if she was mad enough.

"The magic of the labyrinth came from our goddess. Nothing is impossible."

Levet scowled. Perhaps they had managed to open a gateway, but there was no way they could force Inga into the labyrinth.

"That doesn't explain how she got there."

"Actually, it was easier than we expected," the minotaur confessed, a lingering surprise in his voice. "We created the opening and expected to have to battle to capture her. Instead, she walked in. I assume she wanted to discover what it was and if it was a danger to her people."

"Sacrebleu. Of course she did."

Levet didn't doubt Inga had willingly walked straight into disaster. She had many fine qualities. She was kind and loyal and beautiful. At least to him. But she refused to accept that her position as queen meant that she should do everything in her power to keep herself safe. Instead, she regularly plunged headfirst into trouble in an effort to protect her people. And she had the audacity to call *him* reckless.

"Now will you help?" the male demanded.

Levet wanted to lie. He wanted to assure the male that if the labyrinth would release Inga, he would close the stupid hole and everything would be hockey dockey. Wait...that wasn't right. Okey dokey? Whatever. But as hard as he tried, the words wouldn't form.

Not only would the stubborn creature insist on Levet performing the miracle before he would release Inga, but he would be condemning an entire species to certain death.

He gave a sad shake of his head. "I cannot."

"Think carefully, gargoyle," the minotaur growled. "We're not the only ones who are in danger from the darkness."

Levet had no idea what he was talking about until he once again tilted the hoop and Levet could see a gaping darkness that was slowly consuming the green field where Inga was lying.

Snatching the hoop out of the male's hand, he stared at the image in horror. He didn't know what magic was keeping her asleep, but if she didn't wake then she would be sucked into oblivion.

"You must release her."

The minotaur grabbed back the hoop, shoving it into his pocket as he glared down at Levet.

"She doesn't have much longer and neither do we. Use your magic or we all die."

Levet squared his shoulders. He couldn't close the hole. That was the only thing he knew for certain. But he was betting that the darkness threaded through the labyrinth was connected. If he couldn't save Inga, then he damned well intended to be at her side when they died.

"Remember, your ambition is what destroyed your people," he warned the minotaur, his voice as cold as a vampire's.

The male flinched, uncertainty flickering in the depths of his eyes. "I did what was necessary."

"For your own power."

"That's not true...."

Levet held up his hand, silencing the protest. They both knew who was at fault. Even if the male was too lost in his pride to accept it.

"I might not be a seer, but it's obvious that you are the rot." Levet spread his wings and the minotaur took a hasty step backward. Almost as if he was afraid that Levet was going to punish him for his sins.

"What are you doing?" he demanded when Levet didn't strike him with a bolt of magic.

"The only creature I intend to save is Inga," Levet informed the male, sending him one last warning glare. "Return your true king before you destroy your homeland."

With that, Levet flapped his wings and launched himself toward the sky. He had no idea what was going to happen. Whether he was about to be incinerated or sucked into hell. It wouldn't be the first time. But the only way to reach Inga was through the darkness. And that was where he was going.

He was at the edge of the hole when the minotaur belatedly realized what he was about to do.

"No!"

Chapter 16

Ryshi struggled to stay in his smoke form. Unlike a pureblooded jinn, it wasn't his natural shape and remaining incorporeal took a concentrated effort. Thankfully, he was able to focus on searching the dome of magic for a weak spot without worrying about Sofie.

At first, he'd watched in horror when she'd been led into the arena to face a towering minotaur with a huge battle-ax slung over his shoulder. He knew she was powerful, but it was obvious even from a distance that she was weakened from her time in the dungeons. But even as he desperately considered the best way to create a distraction, he'd seen Sofie calmly walk forward. As she neared, the minotaur abruptly dropped his ax to the ground, not twitching so much as a muscle as she stuck him with her cursed dagger.

A second later he was on the ground, twitching in agony.

For the moment, Sofie could hold her own, Ryshi assured himself, but eventually the crowd would grow tired of the easy victories. Then they would overwhelm her with a dozen fighters.

Finding the weakest spot in the shield surrounding the arena, Ryshi quickly backtracked to take out the guards who might block their escape. There was no point in rescuing Sofie only to be captured before they were out of the colosseum. Once he was reasonably confident he'd cleared a path, he slid through the shield and floated toward Sofie, who was busy finishing off yet another minotaur.

Returning to his solid form, he studied the growing pile of bodies in the center of the arena.

"Impressive," he congratulated his companion over the noise of the booing crowd. They didn't seem to appreciate the sight of their fighters being dispatched without a proper battle.

"Ryshi." She spun to face him, her exquisite features tight with fury.

Ryshi arched his brows. He hadn't expected her to cartwheel in pleasure, but she didn't have to look like she wanted to stick that dagger in his heart.

"Did you miss me?"

"What are you doing here?"

"You didn't think I would abandon you, did you?"

"No." She glanced toward the dome above their heads. Several minotaurs had crawled onto the magical shield, banging it with their large fists. "But I did hope you wouldn't be reckless enough to walk into a trap."

"Oh ye of little faith," Ryshi chided. "I'm the greatest thief of all time. There is no trap I can't escape."

She made a sound of exasperation. "You didn't escape me."

"Maybe I didn't want to." He flashed a wicked smile even as he heard the sound of a male bellowing over the crowd.

"Guards. Capture him."

On that command, a dozen minotaurs stepped through the arched openings. All of them wearing thick armor and all of them carrying heavy spears.

"Now what?" Sofie demanded.

"Follow me." Waiting until the guards had committed to entering the arena, Ryshi turned and raced in the opposite direction. "There's a weak spot in the shield."

Ryshi felt a surge of satisfaction as he sensed Sofie just inches behind him. She might not be willing to admit that she trusted him, but her actions spoke louder than any words.

Moving with a speed the minotaurs couldn't match, they reached the wall that surrounded the arena. Ryshi ignored the heavy double doors and angled toward the small square cut in the thick stone that was covered with an iron grate. A few feet away, he leaped in the air so he could hit the grate with the bottom of his boots. His fey blood was allergic to iron. He didn't want to touch it with his bare skin.

Crashing into the metal, he felt it bend beneath the impact of his weight, and with an ear-piercing wrench, was knocked out of the brackets that anchored it to the stone. Ryshi soared through the hole, ripping through the thin layer of magic so Sofie could easily follow.

He heard her sound of surprise as they tumbled down a long ramp coated in moss and a slime that Ryshi was trying hard not to notice. The arena had to dispose of blood and gore and bodies between fights. Not all of the carnage made it to the tunnels below. And worse, the ramp ended several feet above the floor, leaving them plummeting through the darkness to hit the ground at a bone-jarring speed.

With an elegance only a vampire could achieve, Sofie rolled to her feet, her dagger held out as she turned in a slow circle. Her nose wrinkled in disgust as she took in the barren tunnel with the stained walls and trickle of brackish water that flowed down the center of the paved floor.

"The sewers?"

"It's no worse than any other area of this place," Ryshi said, taking the lead as he headed toward the distant light.

"True," she dryly agreed, wisely keeping a few feet between them. If they were attacked they would both need space to fight.

They walked in silence, both on full alert as they moved through the thick, pungent darkness. The roar of the crowd above them was muffled, but it echoed loud enough to remind them that they were still in danger.

As they came to a side tunnel, Sofie slowed as she caught sight of the lump sprawled in the muck. Ryshi didn't bother to glance at the guard he'd killed before entering the arena.

"I assume that's your handiwork," she said, quickly catching up to his swift pace.

Ryshi grimaced. He was usually more skillful in his kills. He liked to take pride in his work. Whether it was creating the Oasis, stealing rare artifacts, or ending the life of a demon.

"Sloppy, but I was in a hurry." He waited for her to walk beside him before he continued. "I didn't realize you would have such an easy time demolishing the gladiators."

She shrugged. "They shouldn't have given me back my dagger."

"It wasn't just the dagger," he murmured. "You are a very dangerous female, my love."

She jerked, as if shocked by his words, then hastily pretended that she was indifferent to the casual endearment.

"Do you have a plan beyond running away?"

"Not really."

"If the minotaurs are banished to this place, there has to be a gateway to the homeland, right?"

Ryshi nodded. He hadn't wanted to get to the true homeland when he was here before. Which meant that he had no idea where it was or how it worked.

"Unfortunately, this isn't part of the labyrinth," he reminded her, leaping over the second guard lying facedown at the edge of the tunnel. "There's no pattern to follow."

"And I suppose there's the risk that it doesn't open from this side."

Ryshi picked up his pace. The stench was making him queasy. "Once we're out of here we'll worry about what comes next."

Intent on the sullen glow of light that poured into the end of the tunnel, Ryshi was nearly skewered when an iron portcullis abruptly dropped from a hidden slot in the ceiling.

Stumbling back, he barely avoided landing in the filthy water. Before he could appreciate dodging the final humiliation, however, a male voice called out from behind them.

"Dead end, I'm afraid."

"Damn," Ryshi muttered in frustration.

He'd been so busy checking for guards he hadn't bothered to make sure there weren't any concealed traps. Not that he'd had adequate time to search, he ruefully acknowledged. His escape plan had been nothing more than a hope and a wish.

Turning slowly, he watched as the large minotaur strolled toward them, leading a herd of guards to effectively block any hope of escape.

"I've made improvements since your last visit," the male informed Ryshi.

"So I see, very clever," Ryshi drawled, glancing at the thick iron gate with a pretense of indifference.

Inside he was recalling Sofie's warning that the minotaurs had a festering grudge because he'd stolen their stupid stone. Or maybe they were pissed because he'd managed to enter and escape before they could kill him. Either way, they were clearly obsessed with him. That was never a good thing.

"There's a saying about fool me once..." The male's words trailed away as pounding footsteps echoed through the tunnel.

"Commander!" an approaching guard shouted. "You must return to the arena."

Muttering a curse, the large male turned to glare at his guard. "What's going on?"

"There's a riot brewing," the guard panted, his eyes wide. "The crowd isn't happy that the entertainment was interrupted."

The commander looked as if he wanted to punch his fist through something. Or someone.

"Then send out the next group of fighters, you idiot."

"I tried. They refuse to enter the arena."

"Why?"

The guard pointed toward Sofie. "They don't want to fight the leech."

Ryshi chuckled in appreciation. Sofie had terrified an entire tribe of minotaurs. "I wouldn't either," he murmured.

The commander ignored his taunting, turning toward one of the guards standing next to him.

"Where's her collar?"

The guard paled, as if terrified he was going to be punished for someone else's mistake.

"Buford has it."

"Go and get it," the commander growled. "Now!"

The ground shook as the large male clapped his hands together, and with a squeak of alarm the guard offered a deep bow.

"Yes, Commander."

Not bothering to watch the smaller male scurry away, the leader focused his attention on the remaining minotaurs.

"I'm going to deal with the crowd. I'm expecting you to escort our guests to the dungeons." He stabbed a finger toward Ryshi. "Don't talk to them, don't listen to them. Don't even look at them until they're locked in a cell." The male grimaced as a fine dust fell from the top of the tunnel. Obviously, the crowd was threatening to collapse the entire colosseum with their displeasure. "If either of them escapes I'm holding each of you responsible," he finished his warning between clenched teeth. "Got it?"

The guards hastily moved to surround Sofie and Ryshi, their spears pointed at them in a visible threat. Presumably reassured that his orders would be carried out, the commander marched back down the tunnel in a visibly foul mood.

Once he was out of sight, Ryshi heaved a dramatic sigh. The commander was too cunning to be manipulated. The others, however, might be easier.

"Harsh. Is he always so unreasonable?" he asked in tones that dripped with sympathy. As if the poor creatures were being unbearably abused.

In response, one of the guards behind him poked Ryshi in the back with the point of his spear.

"Move," he ordered.

Ryshi glared over his shoulder. The blade had cut deep enough to make him bleed. "Careful with that thing, moo-boy," he snarled. "Another poke and it will be lodged up your ass."

The guard narrowed his gaze, poking him again. The scent of amber swirled through the air, but before Ryshi could carry through on his threat— and he fully intended to shove the spear up the male's ass—Sofie was grabbing his arm and urging him to follow their captors down the tunnel.

With a grimace, Ryshi forced himself to concentrate on the female next to him. He'd been trying to provoke the minotaurs into doing something stupid; instead, they'd neatly turned the tables on him. Again.

He had to start thinking like a master thief and not a male obsessed with protecting his...

His mate.

There. He'd said it. Even if it was just in his own mind. Hopefully, accepting his natural instincts would allow him to leash them long enough to come up with a plan.

"Sorry about this," he muttered, glancing toward Sofie's tense profile. "I intended to dazzle you with my dramatic rescue. I didn't realize they'd made improvements to the place."

She glanced toward him, her expression more determined than accusing. Thank the goddess.

"They are still angry that you escaped with their holy artifact," she said.

"Holy?"

"That's what they claim."

Ryshi rolled his eyes. Only a group of demons who'd been secluded for endless years would imagine the stone he'd taken was somehow sacred.

"It has magic. Like thousands and thousands of other stones." He shook his head in disgust. "Nothing worth holding a grudge for so long."

Her lips twisted, as if silently reminding him that he risked his life to acquire that particular stone, but she didn't say the words out loud. Instead, she shrugged.

"What else do they have to do beyond fight and hold grudges?"

"Fair point."

Sofie's grim expression returned as they were herded through an opening that led to a side passage. This one was smaller, but it was thankfully sewer-free. Not that it smelled much better. The entire colosseum needed to be torched to the ground to get rid of the stench.

"The dungeons are close." Sofie spoke softly to keep the guards from overhearing her words. In fact, Ryshi wasn't sure that she wasn't speaking directly into his mind. "We need to escape before they can put the silver collar back on me."

"Yes," he agreed without hesitation. The sooner Sofie was away from the guards the better. "I'll create a distraction and you—"

"No."

Ryshi flinched. Had she lost faith in his ability to be a partner? He wouldn't blame her. He'd blundered badly. It didn't matter that it wasn't entirely his fault. Or that his usually sharp wits had been dulled by his tumultuous emotions for the female.

"I swear that I won't fail again."

She ignored his promise, a chill spreading through the passage. "I need you to take your jinn form and leave this area."

"Absolutely not," he hissed in outrage. "I'm not abandoning you again."

"Ryshi." She was shaking her head before he finished speaking. "I'm not asking you to abandon me. But I need you to leave this area."

He scowled. "Why?"

"Once you're out of the way I can use my powers to...incapacitate them."

He jerked in shock. There were six very large, very formidable demons surrounding her. Not even the Anasso could battle so many at one time.

"All of them?"

She gave a sharp nod, her expression oddly pained. As if she was bothered by the thought of unleashing her powers.

"Yes, but I can't keep you from being injured." She reached out to touch his arm. "You need to go."

Ryshi frowned. There was something troubling her. "Sofie."

She squeezed his arm, her expression hardening with a bleak resolution. "We're running out of time. If they put the silver collar back on me I'll be helpless." She held his wary gaze. "Trust me."

He did, of course. He trusted her with his life, his heart, his very soul. But forcing himself to change into smoke and leave her was the most difficult thing he'd ever had to do. Including demanding his sister leave his lair.

If something happened to her...

It would be the end of him. That simple.

Drifting toward the ceiling, Ryshi wedged himself through a small crack and into the opening above the passageway. In this form he was indestructible, no matter what Sofie might do. But he didn't want to take the risk of distracting her.

Once he was sure he'd disappeared from her view, he positioned himself next to the crack in the floor to watch as Sofie came to a sudden halt. The guard behind her lifted his spear, but she ignored his warning as she squeezed her eyes shut and spread her arms wide. Almost as if she was casting a spell.

What thundered through the air, however, wasn't magic. At least no magic that Ryshi had ever felt before. It was sheer, raw energy that exploded from her with the force of a nuclear bomb.

And just as destructive.

Bellowing in agony, the minotaurs dropped their weapons and clutched their heads with their hands, as if trying to keep their skulls from exploding. Even in his smoke form, Ryshi could feel the enormous power pressing against him.

In awe, Ryshi suddenly realized how easily she could have crushed his mind when she was holding him captive. So why hadn't she used it before?

Confused by her reluctance, Ryshi watched the minotaurs drop like dead flies, landing in an awkward circle around her. In silence, Sofie stared down at the carnage she'd created; then, with a low groan, her head flopped forward, and her knees started to buckle.

With lightning speed, Ryshi darted from the ceiling, turning into his solid form in time to scoop the unconscious female in his arms before she could hit the floor.

Then, cradling her against his chest, he sprinted down the passageway without looking back.

Chapter 17

Sofie struggled through the darkness clouding her mind with a sense of resignation. She'd spent the past millennium without once being unconscious. Now she'd been knocked out twice in just a few hours. Which only reinforced her opinion that leaving her mountain lair was a huge mistake.

Of course, her lair didn't have a rich scent of amber or the delicious warmth of a male wrapped tightly around her.

Being safe is all well and good, but waking in Ryshi's arms is worth any amount of danger.

The unnerving realization seared her mind, refusing to be banished. With a muttered curse, Sofie lifted her heavy lashes and struggled to sit up.

"Easy," Ryshi whispered, his arms tightening as if afraid she might do herself harm. "I've got you."

Sofie relaxed against his chest. It was too late to fight. This was where she wanted to be. And for now, she was too weak to convince herself it was wrong. Instead, she glanced around at the stone walls and ceiling that surrounded them.

It was a barren space, but thankfully there was no filth coating the rocks and no stench of rotting food. In fact, beyond Ryshi's enticing scent of amber, the only smell was that of rich earth and pine trees.

That had to mean they were out of the colosseum and far enough from the city to be out of the stink zone.

"Where are we?" she asked.

"A cave I found in the middle of the woods."

She tilted back her head to study the male who was seated cross-legged on the hard-packed earth with her cradled in his lap. Despite the hellish hours they'd spent in the labyrinth, not to mention the recent battle with the minotaurs, Ryshi managed to appear as if he'd just stepped out of his shisha parlor. The dark green tunic and trousers didn't have a wrinkle or a speck of dust to mar the satin material. Even the wide copper cuffs around his ankles and wrists glowed in the dim light that filled the cave.

With an effort, she forced her attention back to their surroundings. It was that or rip off her companion's clothes and devour him.

"I don't smell minotaurs," she said.

"As far as I can tell they haven't been in this area in centuries. I'm not sure why, but for now we're safe."

Sofie shook her head, not bothering to figure out why the minotaurs avoided the area. They wouldn't be around long enough for it to matter.

"We're not safe. They'll soon track us here."

"They won't track us."

Surprised by the absolute certainty in his voice, Sofie turned to study him in confusion.

"How can you be so sure?"

A wicked smile touched his lips. "You're not the only one with skills."

Sofie flinched, grimly refusing to consider her own supposed skills. "Tell me how you did it."

"Smoke leaves no trail."

She blinked. He'd carried her on a waft of mist? No way. She might look small, but she was a vampire. She weighed a lot more than a human female.

"You couldn't have carried me here in your smoke form," she protested.

He shrugged. "It's amazing what you can do when you are desperate."

She gazed into the liquid ebony of his eyes, abruptly realizing that he wasn't just talking about his ability to whisk her away from the tunnels beneath the colosseum.

A shudder raced through her. "True."

There was a brief silence before he brushed his fingers through the short strands of her hair.

"Does it hurt you?"

"Being carried in smoke?" She deliberately misinterpreted his question, hoping he would take the hint.

He didn't.

Of course.

"Releasing your powers," he clarified. "Does it cause you pain?"

"No."

His fingers traced the stubborn line of her jaw. "Sofie."

"Yes," she grudgingly conceded. "Yes, it causes pain."

"Physical pain?" She shook her head, but she refused to say more. Ryshi gently cupped her chin in his palm, his features softening as he gazed down at her. "Sofie, talk to me. Please."

"We need to find the way out of this place," she muttered, but she didn't make any effort to try to wriggle out of his arms.

Probably because she didn't want to leave them.

"I have set alarms around the cave. If someone approaches, we'll have plenty of time to flee," he told her. "For now, you need to rest and recover your strength. Tell me why your powers hurt you."

She glanced away, giving one more shot at ending the unwelcome conversation. "I don't talk about my past. Not with anyone."

His thumb traced her lower lip, the light caress sizzling through her like a lightning bolt.

"I'm not anyone."

He was right. She tried to deny the truth. Even when her heart had already decided that if they survived—and that was yet to be determined—she wanted to have this male in her life.

He deserved to know what she'd done. Even if it meant revealing that she was a monster.

"As far as I know I'm the only vampire who possesses the talent," she said, her gaze locked on the wall across the narrow space.

She felt him lean down to brush his lips over the scar in the middle of her forehead.

"Smart. Beautiful and utterly unique." His lips brushed her skin as he spoke. "No wonder my jinn soul craves you."

Sofie cherished the feel of his lips and the strength of his arms that surrounded her. It stirred her desire, of course. She wanted him with a desperation that was becoming impossible to resist. But more importantly, it offered her the courage to dredge up the memories she'd buried in the depths of her mountain.

"Being unique isn't necessarily a good thing."

"Why not?"

"Because we had no idea what my powers could ultimately do."

His fingers stroked through her hair, offering her comfort. "We?"

"The clan who took me in after I wakened as a vampire."

"They weren't pleased with your gift?"

A wry smile twisted her lips. She'd still been trying to figure out what she was and how to survive when a clan had passed by the abandoned fortress where she was hiding. They hadn't been eager to offer her a place in the clan, but when she revealed the trick she'd accidentally discovered to control her prey, they'd realized she could offer them an advantage.

"In the beginning," she said, the words a low whisper. "It came in handy when we wished to capture an enemy. Or to control one of our own clansmen who the chief wanted to punish."

"A little more than handy," he said dryly.

It had been. And she'd been rewarded for her skills with riches and treasures beyond her wildest dreams.

"For centuries I was treated as a favorite of the chief."

Ryshi stiffened, as if outraged by her words. "His mate?"

"No, he had a mate," she swiftly assured him. "I was a secret weapon that allowed him to gather power."

She felt his muscles ease. "Were you happy?"

"At the time. I was surrounded by my family and secure in the knowledge that my gift made me special. It felt as if nothing could destroy my future."

"But something did?"

Sofie watched the ice crawl over the floor and up the sides of the cave. She couldn't completely control her emotions. Not when she was ripping open a wound that had never fully healed.

"We were traveling through Siberia when we were attacked by a tribe of orcs." She had to force the words past her stiff lips.

"That was bold of them."

Sofie didn't blame Ryshi for his surprise. A pureblooded orc could match strength in a battle with a lone vampire. And a tribe would certainly overwhelm one. But no demon would be stupid enough to attack an entire clan, even if they outnumbered them.

"I discovered later that the orcs had been held as prisoners by the local vampire clan. The bastards had ruthlessly starved and tortured the poor creatures so they were feral when they released them to annihilate any intruders."

"Seriously?" Ryshi made a sound of disgust. Most fey creatures possessed a deep hatred for creatures who enslaved other demons. Usually because they were the ones being enslaved. "I don't know whether to be impressed or horrified."

"Horrified," she promptly assured him.

"What happened?"

Sofie closed her eyes, reluctantly allowing the images to flood her mind.

It had been a cold night. Bone-chillingly cold. And the moon had reflected off the snow and ice with a blinding light. They'd been on their way to the Ural Mountains, where they'd heard a tribe of goblins had dug a mine that was filled with emeralds. Sofie's clan chief was determined to gain control of the mine and increase his enormous wealth.

Oddly, Sofie had been uneasy as they'd traveled through the shallow valley. She'd sensed they were being watched and warned the others they needed to turn back. They refused to listen, all of them anxious to get their hands on the piles of emeralds the chief had promised them.

It wasn't until they reached the center of the valley that the orcs appeared from the illusions that had hidden their presence, pouring down the side of the mountain and surrounding them before they could escape.

"We walked into an ambush." The words came out in a harsh rush. She needed to get them out before she lost her courage. "The orcs were trampling us in a mad frenzy. I thought if I could grasp their minds and contain them long enough, my people could escape. I...panicked."

He tightened his arms until he would have crushed her if she'd been a human.

"The heat of the battle affects every demon," he reassured her. "We all do things we later regret."

"Not like this. I released my powers and they exploded. Like a nuclear bomb." She shook her head, the horror spreading through her like a black hole that threatened to suck her under. "I didn't control them, I crushed them."

"All of them?"

In her mind she could vividly see the pile of orc bodies that surrounded her. They had lain in the snow, staring sightlessly at the starry sky with expressions of wretched agony twisting their features.

Their death had been swift, but acutely painful.

She nodded. "All of them."

"It must have been a shock, but it was a battle," he reminded her. "Things happen."

He was right. It had been a shock. She'd hoped to slow down one or two of the orcs. Anything to give them the opportunity to escape. To destroy a dozen of them at one time had been sickening. Even if it had been in a battle.

Things had gotten worse when she'd turned back to discover how many of her clan had managed to escape.

The ice coating the cave thickened as her emotions threatened to engulf her.

"It wasn't just the orcs that I destroyed."

There was a long silence, as if Ryshi wasn't sure he wanted to ask the question.

"The vampires?"

Sofie forced herself to meet his searching gaze. He needed to fully understand what it would mean to accept her into his life.

"I remember gathering my power, but not releasing it," she told him. "It was like it suddenly transformed into something beyond my control. I think I tried to stop it once I realized something was wrong, but there was nothing I could do. It exploded out of me, and it wasn't until the darkness receded that I realized the orcs were lying dead on the snow. And my clan…"

The words refused to form. As if by not saying them she could change the past. Sofie swallowed an agonized laugh. Nothing could rewrite history. The goddess knew she'd tried everything.

"Dead?" Ryshi asked in sympathy.

"Worse." She burrowed against his body, seeking his strength as the memories battered against her. "They had become mindless zombies. Like those created by human wizards. They remained standing exactly where they'd been when I released my power, but their minds had been destroyed."

He pressed his lips against the top of her head, his hands stroking down her back in a comforting motion.

"What happened to you?"

"I was desperately trying to wake them when I was captured by the vampires who'd sent the orcs to attack us."

"Did they take you prisoner?"

"No." At the time she'd barely noticed the leeches who'd seized her with a silver net. Not until she found herself being held down as the chief was using a flaming hot knife on her forehead. "They were too afraid of me. They carved this into my forehead and covered it in salt."

Ryshi hissed as she reached up to touch the scar that was still rough beneath her fingertips.

"Damn."

She shrugged. The mark didn't bother her. It was a reminder that she had to control her powers or suffer the consequences.

"Then they bound me to a pole," she continued, wanting to be done with the grim story. "They planned to have me watch my family being consumed by the sun before the dawn reached me and I was turned into ash."

"How did you survive?"

"Styx. He found me just seconds before it was too late."

This time her smile was genuine. At first she'd assumed the massive shadow approaching her was the grim reaper. The thought hadn't brought fear. She'd just witnessed her clan being consumed by the approaching sunlight and she'd been deeply relieved at the knowledge her suffering was about to end. Instead, he'd cut through the silver bands that held her to the post and tossed her over his broad shoulder.

Ryshi brushed his lips over her cheek. "Thank the goddess."

"I wasn't thankful at the time," she told him in dry tones. "I wanted the sun to end my agony."

"Don't say that," Ryshi breathed in genuine horror.

"It's true." Sofie had fought and clawed as Styx had carried her into a nearby cave. She'd been desperate to join her clan. If the male hadn't been so big and stubborn, she wouldn't be alive. "I'm not sure I ever forgave him for rescuing me."

Ryshi's hands continued to stroke up and down her back, his cheek resting on the top of her head.

"And you punish yourself for surviving by imprisoning yourself in a mountain."

She clicked her tongue at the ridiculous accusation. "I'm hardly imprisoned."

"You live there alone and you never leave unless you're forced. What else would you call it?"

"I went there to learn to control my powers," she told him. It was true. She'd devoted centuries to discovering the best way to keep the deadly skill contained.

"And to punish yourself," he insisted.

She shrugged. She didn't call it punishment. It was common sense to avoid any conflicts that might force her into a battle.

"I'd done enough damage. I swore I'd never let myself get into a position where I would need to create such carnage again."

"It's not your fault."

She tilted back her head, meeting the liquid darkness of his gaze. "I doubt the minotaurs would agree with you."

"I'm not talking about the minotaurs, although they fully intended to kill both of us. Did you blame me for killing the guards to try to clear a path for our escape?"

Sofie stubbornly shook her head. "It's not the same. I destroyed my family."

"Because you couldn't fully control your powers," he insisted. "You didn't intend to harm them. You were trying to save them."

"It doesn't change the outcome."

He made a sound of impatience. It was the same sound Styx made when he was trying to reason with her. It had to be a male thing.

"You can't blame yourself forever."

A part of her yearned to believe him. Being with Ryshi reminded her how empty her life had become. And the delight of sharing her nights with someone who challenged her and made her laugh. She even enjoyed his company when he was being annoying.

But what if she accidentally hurt him? Or he realized that she truly was a monster?

She couldn't bear it.

A sudden burst of panic raced through her.

"What I can't do forever is lie here waiting for the minotaurs to find us." Struggling out of his arms, Sofie forced herself to her feet, determined to protect Ryshi. "We need..."

Her grand gesture to shield the male she was certain was her fated mate was ruined as she took a step toward the nearby opening and promptly collapsed.

Obviously, she was weaker than she realized.

More annoyed than frightened, Sofie plunged forward. Inches from smacking her head on the hard floor, however, strong arms wrapped around her and she found herself being gently turned and stretched out on her back.

Kneeling beside her, Ryshi brushed his fingers over her cheek. "I'm starting to make a habit of this."

Sofie gazed into his exquisite face, the fight draining out of her.

She didn't want to push this male away. She didn't want to return to her lonely lair beneath the mountain. Not without Ryshi.

Reaching up, she grasped the end of his braid, tugging on the leather strap to release the silky mane. It tumbled free in a shimmer of copper fire, framing the stark beauty of his male features. Sofie felt her fangs lengthen as she battled back the intense urge to reach up and tangle her fingers in the glossy strands.

"There's only one way for me to recover my strength," she told him, her voice thick with the emotions she worked so hard to keep leashed.

The dark eyes glowed with a pagan heat. "Tell me."

"I need to feed."

Chapter 18

Ryshi sensed the change in the atmosphere. He wasn't sure what had happened. It wasn't anything he'd said. Or a special way that he'd touched her. It was as if she'd simply decided that she couldn't fight fate.

Or maybe she was just too tired to fight, he wryly acknowledged.

Whatever the cause, he could feel the wariness ease as a fierce hunger pulsed through the air.

Trying to leash his flare of excitement, Ryshi gazed down at her pale features, lingering on the scar in the center of her forehead. He'd known the story behind the wound would be bad. It took a painful effort to mark a vampire. Fire, sun, or salt.

But not even in his wildest imagination could he have guessed that she'd not only destroyed an entire tribe of orcs, but her own clan as well. His gaze swept down to her body, which appeared ridiculously fragile beneath the pink sweater and jeans.

"The sooner you feed the better," he assured her, not surprised when the crystal blue of her eyes darkened with a surge of fear.

"Ryshi."

Ryshi smiled. This female had spent endless years convincing herself that she couldn't risk being around people. Especially those who might have some special meaning for her. It wouldn't be easy for her to let down her barriers.

It didn't bother Ryshi. In fact, as long as he was certain she'd accepted that he was destined to be her mate, he didn't mind convincing her that he trusted her. And that she could trust him.

With her heart. Her soul. And her body.

Heat flowed through his veins, setting off sparks of hunger as he leaned over her.

"Before you start telling me all the reasons this is a bad idea, let me tell you why it's the *best* idea," he insisted.

"Do I have a choice?"

"No." He grabbed the long strands of his hair and swept them aside to expose his neck. "I will be feeding you for the rest of eternity. We might as well start now."

She arched a brow at his arrogant tone, but he could see the tips of her fangs between her lips and catch the scent of chamomile that swirled through the air. She was starved for the taste of him.

"You made that decision all on your own?" she demanded.

"Fate made that decision."

He watched a shiver race through her body, but there was still a hint of fear shimmering in the depths of her eyes.

"You aren't thinking clearly."

"I don't need to think." He cupped her pale cheek in his palm, silently willing her to accept the inevitable. "Everything inside me—my very essence—yearns to be with you. For an eternity."

"I'm a recluse who lives in a mountain," she reminded him.

Ryshi shrugged. He didn't mind the thought of sharing an isolated lair with this female. In fact, nothing had ever been more tempting.

"I'm half imp."

"Precisely. You would hate the darkness."

"My fey blood means I can create portals." He skimmed his fingers down the stubborn line of her jaw. "Traveling between your lair and the Oasis would be as easy as stepping from one room to another."

"What about your sister?"

He flinched as she struck a direct hit. It was the only shadow in their future together. Well, the only shadow unless you counted the fact that they were currently trapped with a group of minotaurs who wanted them dead.

"My sister will be found," he said, the words a solemn promise before his lips twisted into a rueful smile. "Any other barriers you want to put between us?"

She paused, then she offered the true reason for her hesitation. "You've seen what I can do."

Ryshi understood how important his answer was going to be to their future. Sofie had convinced herself that she not only had to punish herself for what had happened in the past, but that she had to isolate herself to protect others. But even as he sought to find words of sympathy to ease her fears, he decided on blunt honesty.

"I've never felt prouder in my life," he told her, remembering the moment she'd defeated the minotaurs. He was not a demon who celebrated death but watching Sofie overcome an impossible situation was amazing. "You're marvelous." He bent his head to press a light kiss on her mouth. "There's something extraordinarily satisfying about knowing my mate can kick anyone's ass."

"I'm a deadly weapon," she insisted, as if he'd somehow forgotten.

He nipped her lower lip. "True, but you don't need special powers to be deadly. I watched you in the arena. You were cutting your way through those gladiators like a lava sprite through ice."

She grabbed his face in her hands, gazing up at him with a troubled expression. "I massacred my clan."

"An accident."

"An accident that could happen again."

"You held my mind with yours." He pulled her hands away from his face, turning them over to place a lingering kiss in each palm. "I trust you."

"Ryshi."

His name came out as a soft plea, but Ryshi could sense she was on the brink of capitulation. She knew that they were destined to be together, but she'd needed to be reassured that she could trust herself.

"You said that you secluded yourself to learn to control your powers," he reminded her in gentle tones, leaning down to grab her shoes and tug them off.

She made a strangled sound of excitement. "Nothing is perfect."

"Exactly," he readily agreed, straightening to send her a teasing glance. "Except for me, of course. See?"

Grabbing the hem of his silk tunic, he pulled it over his head and allowed it to drop on the floor. He wasn't entirely sure what her reaction would be. Oh, he could sense her desire. It pulsed through the air with an icy insistence. Not to mention the fact that her fangs were fully extended. A sure sign she hungered for his blood.

Or she wanted to rip out his throat.

Maybe both.

But he didn't expect her to reach up and stroke her hand over the bare skin of his chest.

"You're right. You are perfect," she approved in low tones.

A scalding pleasure blasted through him, a groan of need wrenched from his throat.

"I've made my share of mistakes," he growled. "But this isn't one of them. I've belonged to you since the moment you grasped my mind."

Her fingers traced the muscles that clenched beneath her light touch. "I knew I was in trouble when I couldn't erase you from my dreams."

"Ah. I like the thought of featuring in your fantasies."

"I said dreams, not fantasies," she corrected him.

His lips twitched as he gazed down at her. "Is there a difference?"

"Dreams are desires you crave to fulfill. Fantasies are fleeting whims that fade into nothing."

"Ah." He leaned forward, burying his face in the curve of her neck. "Then what do you call a dream that comes true?"

"A miracle."

She scored her nails down his chest, sending pulses of excitement darting through him. Ryshi shivered. It wasn't just the pricks of painful pleasure that were setting him on fire. It was her soft words that smashed into him with shattering force.

Yes. She was right.

It was a miracle.

One he'd waited his entire life to experience. And if the past had taught him nothing else, it was to grasp what he desired and never let go.

Slipping his hands under the hem of her sweater, Ryshi tugged it over her head and tossed it aside. His mouth watered at the sight of her pale, flawless skin and the soft mounds of her breasts crested with pink nipples. He wanted to taste her from head to toe and all the yummy places in between.

"A miracle, indeed," he breathed.

The silver that rimmed her astonishing blue eyes shimmered in the shadows. As if they were lit by an inner fire.

"And what of your jinn desire to roam?"

With reverent care, Ryshi cupped her breasts in his palms, his heart thundering with a fierce craving.

"My only desire is to be with you, Sofie." His thumbs stroked her nipples into hard buds. Sofie quivered, the sweet scent of chamomile perfuming the air to wrap around Ryshi like an embrace.

Suddenly he understood the meaning of *magnetic attraction*. No matter how far he might travel from this female, he would always be compelled to return to her side. Like a lodestone calling him home.

And nothing had ever made him happier.

Sofie, however, didn't appear nearly so certain. Her expression was wary, as if afraid to accept that their destinies had been decided.

"Easy to say now," she insisted. "You'll soon get bored."

Ryshi wanted to laugh at her ridiculous accusation. What male could ever become bored with such a fascinating creature? Thankfully, he had enough experience with females to keep his amusement to himself. She was wary, on edge, and seeking an excuse to push him away. He wasn't going to give it to her.

"When I roam you will be at my side. It's time for you to return to the world."

Skimming his hands down her narrow waist, Ryshi efficiently slid off Sofie's jeans. He blinked in astonishment when he revealed a surprising triangle of red silk.

The fragile undies were a tantalizing glimpse into Sofie's romantic heart. She might pretend to be a cold, callous hermit, just as he pretended to be a reckless thief with no concern for the future.

They both yearned for more.

"I don't know if I'm ready to return to the world," she protested.

"We'll take it at your pace," he assured her, rising to his feet to shed the remainder of his clothing.

He paused as he stood over her, gazing down at her slender form. He'd never seen anything more beautiful. She was sheer perfection from the short strands of her golden hair down the graceful strength in her slender body to the tips of her tiny toes.

With a sense of awe, he sank to his knees beside her. She was a rare masterpiece that was his to protect. His chest seemed to tighten, as if the emotions inside him were too big to contain.

Bending forward, Ryshi brushed his lips along the curve of her neck before nuzzling a path down to the hollow at the base of her throat. Sofie growled in appreciation, her hands reaching up to thread her fingers in his hair. Then, with a sharp tug, she guided him toward her breasts.

"Teach me what pleases you," he murmured in approval, releasing tendrils of smoke to caress her body as his lips captured the tip of her nipple.

"Yes." She arched her back off the hard ground. "Like that."

Ryshi chuckled, using his tongue and smoke to tease her to a fever pitch even as his fingers trailed down her body to trace the waistband of her undies.

"Are these your favorite?" he asked, moving his lips to pleasure her neglected nipple.

"Why?" she panted.

"I want to know how angry you're going to be when I do this."

Grasping the fragile material, he ripped them off her body. Satisfaction shuddered through him as she hissed with anticipation.

"They used to be my favorite." Her complaint was ruined by the desire smoldering in her eyes.

"I'll have them replaced," he promised. "Every color of the rainbow."

"So generous."

He grasped her legs, gently tugging them apart. "Not generous," he corrected. "It's entirely selfish since I intend to rip them off you on a nightly basis."

Her eyes glowed with an unexpected burst of amusement. "Generous and ambitious."

"Only two of my many fine qualities."

Her lips parted, but before she could speak her words were lost on a tiny cry of need as Ryshi settled between her thighs and found her sweet spot with his tongue. The taste of her exploded on his tongue, and Ryshi groaned. Glorious female power and intoxicating sexual temptation. It was more addictive than the finest nectar and he knew in that moment he would never have enough of this female. Not even with an eternity together.

Eternity.

The world whispered through his mind, and with a last lingering lick, Ryshi kissed his way up her naked body.

He desperately wanted to be buried deep inside her. Already his erection was hard and aching for release.

But first...

"Drink, Sofie," he urged, angling his neck to give her full access.

She tensed, her fingers grasping his hair to tug hard enough to lift his head up to view her somber expression.

"If I take your blood, I'll be bound to you," she warned in a husky voice.

Ryshi shrugged. He didn't know the intimate details of a mating, but he did know that once they shared blood their union would be indestructible.

"We're already bound together. The blood merely makes it official."

"You're sure?" she pressed.

"It's the one thing that I have ever been sure of," he assured her, once again offering his neck.

This time, Sofie didn't hesitate. Like a snake, she struck with blinding speed, sinking her fully extended fangs deep into his throat.

Ryshi jerked, his hands grasping her hips as the pain that was on the right side of bliss seared him.

Who knew the feel of her fangs could create an erotic tidal wave that threatened to overwhelm him? Or that each suck of his blood could make his erection twitch in response?

It was glorious.

Moaning in approval, Ryshi positioned himself between her legs and with one steady thrust buried himself in her body. They moaned in unison, both savoring the intense satisfaction as they at last surrendered to their desire.

For a joyous moment, Ryshi held himself rigid, etching this memory into his brain. Becoming Sofie's mate was the reason he'd been created. And nothing would ever be the same again.

As if impatient with his determination to treat this momentous occasion with the respect it deserved, Sofie wrapped her legs around his waist. Her new position allowed him to sink even deeper and with a muttered curse, Ryshi gave into the driving hunger.

Surging in and out of her, Ryshi was only vaguely aware of Sofie removing her fangs from his neck and gently licking closed the tiny wounds. He was far too focused on the delicious pressure clenching his muscles as they moved together with a desperate urgency.

It wasn't until Sofie used her fingernail to slash through the skin of her upper breast that he understood they still needed to complete the mating.

Ryshi didn't hesitate. He'd never wanted anything more than to be this female's eternal companion. Lowering his head, he lapped the tiny droplets of blood that formed on her skin.

He'd expected to feel...something.

A mating was a rare and wondrous gift that only happened once in a demon's life. The creation of the union would obviously cause a reaction.

But nothing could have prepared him for the shocking awareness that blasted through him. It wasn't the small glimpse into Sofie's mind that he'd experienced when she used her powers. This was an all-encompassing sensation of becoming utterly and completely entwined with Sofie.

They weren't a couple. They were one. One heart and one soul forever merged.

The realization that he'd been unmade and re-formed into a new being might have terrified him if his climax hadn't chosen that moment to explode through him. Shattering pleasure scorched away any thought beyond the shudders of bliss that raced through him.

"Sofie," he rasped, burying his face in the curve of her neck as he felt her convulse around him.

At the same time, she released a burst of ice that collided with the smoke dancing over his body.

The combination created a mist that filled the cave and surrounded them in a cocoon of pure magic.

Chapter 19

Sophie snuggled close to Ryshi on the hard ground, shivering as the male traced the mating mark that scrolled beneath the skin of her inner arm. The intricate crimson tattoo had appeared the moment they'd shared their blood, and precisely matched the one on Ryshi's arm.

"This is amazing," Ryshi murmured, turning his head to press a light kiss on her temple. "You are amazing."

Sofie savored the feel of his warm lips brushing her skin. She was still absorbing the sensations that had blasted through her when she'd sunk her fangs into his neck. Not only the taste of him, more addictive than the finest nectar, or the gloriously intimate feel of him nestled in the center of her unbeating heart. But the stunning power that flowed through her like lava, replenishing her strength and allowing her to share the ephemeral magic that was unique to Ryshi.

"We are bound together now," she said, her tone edged with satisfaction.

"Thank the goddess."

Sofie reached out to sweep her fingers through the long strands of his hair. She loved the satiny feel of it brushing over her skin.

"It's time for you to trust me."

His brows formed a straight line as he gazed down at her. "I trust you with my life."

"But not your secrets."

He flinched, as if he'd hoped to avoid this particular discussion. "The secrets aren't just mine," he told her.

"Agreed." She held his gaze. "They're *our* secrets now."

"True."

With a smooth motion Ryshi sat upright, gathering his clothes to begin pulling them on. Sofie followed his lead, stretching out to collect her jeans and sweater. It wasn't a rebuff. She could sense through their bond that Ryshi wasn't angered by the question. He needed a few seconds to gather his thoughts.

Once they were both dressed, Ryshi tugged her back into his arms and leaned against the stone wall of the cavern.

"I told you about my sister."

"You said that she disappeared."

"Yes." An echo of frustration pulsed through Sofie, as if she was the one who'd dedicated her life to locating the missing jinn. "I searched for what seemed to be forever with no indication if she was alive or dead."

"Your mother couldn't help you?"

His lips twisted as he recalled his meeting with the female who'd given birth to him.

"She wasn't interested enough to try. She had already found a new mate and was pregnant with their child."

Sofie tilted her head to study him with a narrowed gaze. Jinn were elusive, mystical creatures. There was going to be a steep learning curve to discover more about her extended family.

"How many mates can a jinn have?"

He shrugged. "As far as I know there is no limit. Many of them have large harems filled with mates and their offspring."

Sofie made no effort to halt the layer of ice that crawled over the floor. This was something that needed to be clarified right quick and in a hurry.

"And you?"

He released a burst of magic. Expecting the delicious smoke that created erotic pleasure as it crawled over her skin, Sofie blinked in surprise when the ice shattered and a small green plant sprouted from a crack in the stone, swiftly growing until a tiny flower with white petals and a yellow center burst open.

Chamomile. The perfume brushed over her like a soft caress.

"I'm half fey," he reminded her in husky tones. "Once they mate it's for eternity. Besides, what I feel for you isn't about fate or destiny."

Tilting back her head, Sofie allowed herself to become lost in his eyes. "It's not?"

He cupped her face in his hands. "They call me a thief, but you're the one who stole my heart."

Sofie wrinkled her nose at the cheesy compliment. "You're straying back into that creep zone again."

Ryshi laughed, the rich scent of amber washing over her. "Okay. I'll say it in plain words. I love you." He stroked his thumb over her lips, the gesture as tender as a kiss. "And it has nothing to do with the mating. I love your strength and intelligence and your unexpected humor." His voice held a sincerity that was unmistakable. "I love spending time in your company and knowing you have my back in a fight."

Sofie melted. Or at least that's what it felt like as she gazed into the bottomless black eyes.

"I love you too."

He studied her, as if waiting for her to say more. At last he clicked his tongue in chastisement.

"And?"

"And what?"

"What do you love about me?"

Sofie wrinkled her nose. She wasn't into all this mushy, kissy-kiss stuff. Well, she enjoyed the kissing part. A lot. And, truthfully, she was starting to relish hearing Ryshi tell her how wonderful she was and how much he adored her....

So maybe she was into mushy stuff after all, she ruefully acknowledged.

Not that she was going to allow his skillful seduction to distract her from the original direction of the conversation.

"I love your charm, even when it annoys me," she told him. "And your cunning. It's rare for any creature to outsmart Styx. Not and survive."

He sucked in a startled breath, as if she'd managed to blindside him. "I don't know what you're talking about."

She arched a brow. She'd suspected the truth from the moment he'd revealed his terror of being trapped in the labyrinth.

"There's no way you meekly allowed yourself to be imprisoned in that dungeon," she said dryly. "You were sneaking out, weren't you?"

His lips parted, as if he intended to deny her accusation, then realized that the mating had ensured she would know he was lying and heaved a sigh.

"Perhaps," he conceded. "Although I would prefer you not share that suspicion. At least not with the Anasso."

"But most of all, I love your devotion to your sister," she continued. Despite her loyalty to her Anasso, she had no intention of sharing Ryshi's talent with anyone. Not even Styx. "She obviously disrupted your life, but you are determined to find her. Even if it meant coming to this place. Am I right?"

"I did say you were smart." His lips twisted. "Or maybe I'm not as clever as I thought I was. Hard to believe."

She reached up to press her fingers against his lips. He was a master at dancing around a subject.

"Talk to me, Ryshi," she commanded.

"You're right," he grudgingly conceded.

"Of course I am."

His lips twitched at her teasing, but his eyes smoldered with a raw regret. "After Zena disappeared, I searched for years to locate her. I traveled through dimensions and paid outrageous sums to various trackers to discover her trail. Finally, I was forced to accept that I needed more than my skills to locate her. Or to determine if she was dead."

Sofie resisted the urge to wrap him in her arms. Comforting him would soon ignite the passions that still ran white-hot between them. A delicious means of healing his pain that would have to wait until they'd managed to escape this place.

"Why would you risk coming to the labyrinth?"

"I have contacts among demons who deal in rare artifacts. They whispered of a stone that would allow the user to speak with another demon no matter how great the distance."

Sofie nodded. Stavros had told her the truth when she'd asked about the missing object. He might currently be her enemy, but he was an honorable demon.

"You obviously found the stone," she said, returning her attention to Ryshi's story.

"I did. I even managed to escape from this place with it."

"Did you locate your sister?"

"No, but I managed to contact her."

"Then you know she's alive." Sofie felt a surge of relief. She'd been concerned that he was going to reveal that his sister was dead. If that had happened, Ryshi would never, ever forgive himself.

"Yes."

"Then why couldn't you locate her?"

"Because she didn't know where she was."

"I don't understand."

"After she left the Oasis, she traveled to various harems in the hopes of locating her father."

Sofie didn't fully understand the young jinn's need to locate her father. She had no idea who'd sired her, or who she'd been before she'd been turned into a vampire. But then again, she'd found a group of vampires that had become her family. And even after they'd been destroyed, she'd always known that Styx would welcome her into his clan.

Maybe every creature craved the feeling of belonging to somebody.

"Did she find him?" she asked.

"No. She eventually gave up and was on her way back to the Oasis." His jaw tightened, curls of smoke dancing over his body. A sure sign he was struggling to contain his temper. "But before she could return to me, she was captured."

"Who could capture a pureblooded jinn?"

"A vampire."

Sofie snapped her brows together, genuinely confused. Vampires were at the top of the food chain, but a jinn possessed the sort of powerful magic that made most leeches avoid them. And even if they were stupid enough to try to capture one, the jinn could turn to smoke and escape.

"How?"

Ryshi struggled to contain his fury. "All she could remember was being in a large cavern when a vampire appeared. She said that she turned into her jinn form to flee, but he possessed a magical container that he trapped her in."

Sofie studied his hard features. "A genie in a bottle? I thought that was a myth."

"Most myths have some truth at the heart of them."

There was an edge in his voice that warned he didn't like giving away the secrets of the jinn. Not even to his mate. She didn't blame him. Every species was careful to disguise their weaknesses.

It was all about survival.

"So where is the container?" she asked, not pressing for a more detailed explanation of what was involved in sucking a jinn into a bottle and how it was sealed to contain them.

They had an eternity to learn more about each other.

"She doesn't know."

Sofie shoved herself out of Ryshi's arms, turning to face him as the truth hit her like a lightning bolt. She'd known that his excuse of searching for rare items had been a lie.

"That's why you've been searching the lairs of vampires. You're looking for the container."

"Yes."

A surge of satisfaction raced through Sofie at finally knowing Ryshi's motivation for creeping in and out of lairs despite the danger. Now she could concentrate on helping him locate his missing sister.

"Did she tell you anything about the vampire?"

"He was big."

She rolled her eyes. "Not helpful."

Ryshi furrowed his brow, as if dredging through his memories for what Zena told him.

"She did say something about long greasy hair and crazy eyes," he finally said with a shrug. "But I assumed she was exaggerating because she was infuriated at being trapped."

Sofie's spine stiffened. She didn't think it was an exaggeration. In fact, she was betting she knew exactly who had captured Zena.

"The Anasso," she muttered.

Ryshi sent her a puzzled glance. "I've seen Styx. He might be an arrogant pain in the ass, but he's never greasy and his eyes are spooky, not crazy."

A shiver inched down her spine. After Styx had rescued her, he'd taken her back to his clan, which had been traveling through Siberia. She'd assumed that Styx was the chief, considering he had enough power to make the earth quake beneath his steps. Instead, she'd found herself being introduced to a male who had created the position of Anasso, King of the Vampires.

At the time, she'd been reluctant to get too close to the male. Certainly he was powerful and he had claimed the loyalty of those around him, but there'd been a sour scent in the air. As if there was something rotting beneath the surface.

Just like the darkness they'd seen in the labyrinth.

Though the Anasso's mind had steadily deteriorated over the years, unfortunately he hadn't lost his strength. Which meant that he'd created widespread chaos and devastation.

"I'm talking about the former Anasso," she told Ryshi.

"I never crossed paths with him."

"He went insane drinking tainted blood at the end...." She shook her head in disgust. She didn't have the words to describe the pathetic creature the once proud vampire had become. "He was horrifying."

"Greasy with crazy eyes?" Ryshi asked, a cautious hope easing his tense expression.

"Yes," Sofie assured him. "Plus he spent the last few years of his life in a series of caverns just south of Chicago."

Ryshi released his breath on a low hiss. "That would explain why I felt drawn to that area."

Sofie nodded. She'd only visited the caverns a couple of times, but she had been told that they stretched for miles along the banks of the Mississippi river with endless places to hide treasure. It wouldn't be surprising if the container holding Zena captive was still buried among the previous Anasso's belongings.

"We should search the caverns. The container was probably left behind when Styx moved into his lair in Chicago."

He paused, a strange smile touching his lips. "We?"

"Of course. We're partners, remember?"

His eyes blazed with pleasure, his smoke swirling through the air to wrap around her.

"I like the sound of that."

"Me too." Unable to resist the caress of his magic, Sofie started to lean forward only to halt as the floor shuddered beneath them. "Ryshi."

"I sense it."

Grabbing her hand, Ryshi leaped to his feet and pulled her close as they watched a hole begin to form in the middle of the floor.

Sofie muttered a curse. She'd been on guard for any hint of the minotaurs, but she hadn't considered being trapped by the strange darkness.

"We need to get out of here."

Together they skirted the edge of the rapidly expanding hole, trying to reach the entrance before the entire floor disappeared. They might have escaped if a mist hadn't suddenly poured out of the hole, wrapping around their ankles and dragging them into the black pit before they realized their danger.

Holding tightly to each other, they tumbled through the endless void that consumed them.

Chapter 20

Levet fell out of the sky like a rock being tossed over the edge of a cliff. Landing on his head, he bounced twice before coming to a halt next to a babbling stream.

"Ouch."

Grimacing in pain, Levet forced himself to his feet, rubbing his bruised horns. He'd been assured that his skull was the thickest part of his body, but it hadn't kept his brain from being scrambled by the bone-shattering impact. He could already feel a headache forming. Grumbling in annoyance and imagining the pleasure of giving the stupid minotaur a huge, putrid abscess on the tip of his snout, Levet was distracted as he caught sight of the large figure sprawled on the grass. With a soft cry, he scurried forward to lean over the female who'd stolen his heart.

"Inga!" Her eyes remained closed, and her body didn't so much as twitch beneath the green muumuu that spread around her like a tidal wave of lime. "*Non!*" Leaning forward, he yelled directly into her ear. "Inga! Can you hear me?"

There was a grunt, followed by a cough before Inga slowly lifted her lashes to reveal her stunning blue eyes. Mermaid blue.

"How could I not hear you?" she grumbled. "Why are you shouting in my ear?"

"Oh." Levet's wings fluttered in relief. "You are awake."

"Who could sleep through that racket?"

"I thought you were dead."

"Why would I be dead?" Inga struggled to sit upright, gripping her massive trident in one hand while she used the other one to scrub through her red hair. When she was done, the thick tufts stuck straight out, giving her a crimson halo. "Wait. Where am I?"

"In the minotaur labyrinth," Levet explained.

Inga swung her head around to stare at him in disbelief. "Are you serious?"

"Why would I jest?"

"The labyrinth." She shook her head, genuinely baffled. "How did I get here?"

"What do you last recall?" Levet demanded.

She took a minute to search through her memories. "I was at the castle. I'd been sitting in the throne room waiting for you to contact me."

Levet sucked in a shocked breath at her low words. "But I did contact you—or at least I tried to. Over and over." He pressed his hands against his stomach, which clenched with anxiety. "I thought you were ignoring *moi*."

She blinked, blatantly confused by his words. "Why would I ignore you?"

"I feared you had grown tired of waiting for me to return."

"I will always wait for you."

Levet's breath released on a shaky sigh at her soft words. He'd been worried. Desperately worried that Inga had decided he was too much trouble. It happened with females more often than he cared to admit. But until that moment he'd hadn't understood the sheer depth of his terror.

If she'd truly decided to be done with him, Levet wasn't entirely certain he would have the desire to go on.

"I sensed your annoyance when I revealed I was leaving with Troy to search for the missing vampire," he reminded her. "And then I was sucked into the netherworld with no way to contact you. It would be understandable if you were tired of waiting."

"It wasn't annoyance," she corrected him. "It was fear. I'm always concerned you will be hurt, but I also know that it's your destiny to rush into danger." She heaved a resigned sigh. "It's who you are. Just like I will always be awkward and clumsy and—"

"Beautiful," Levet interrupted.

Inga snorted. "Never that."

"Hush," Levet said in stern tones. This female would never comprehend just how wondrous she was. Even though she'd gone from a slave to the Queen of the Merfolk. Of course, her humble nature was part of her charm. "You are beautiful and loyal and terrifyingly powerful," he informed her. "Absolute perfection."

She blushed so hot her skin turned as red as her hair. Levet doubted there would ever come a day when she could accept compliments with grace. And that was just fine with him.

"I still don't understand what I'm doing here." Inga hurriedly changed the conversation.

"You were recalling your last memories, were you not?"

"Oh. Right." She pursed her lips, returning to her recollections. "I was in the throne room, and I heard screaming in the hallway. I went out to see what happened."

"You should have stayed in the throne room."

Inga made a sound of disgust. "As if you would have."

"You are a queen." With a sigh, Levet moved to grab the dented crown off the ground. He doubted Inga would realize that she'd lost it. Or care. She'd never wanted the duties that came with being royalty. Unfortunately for her, the Tryshu that she was holding in her hand decided who was going to sit on the throne. And the powerful weapon had chosen Inga. "I, on the other hand, am not important."

"You're important to me," she retorted without hesitation. Levet blinked, for once in his very long life completely speechless. "Anyway," Inga hurriedly continued, her blush still staining her cheeks. "I went out and discovered a black hole had formed in the wall."

Levet shook his head, his pleasure at her words forgotten as a stab of frustration pierced his heart.

"Where were the guards?"

"Rimm arrived at the same time I did," she said, referring to the captain of her guards. A merman who'd done everything in his power to convince Inga to allow him to deal with security in the castle. "He was organizing the guards when I decided I should be the one to check it out."

"Why must you be so stubborn?"

Her mouth dropped open in disbelief. "Me? You think I'm stubborn?"

"*Oui.* You." Levet pointed an accusing claw in her face. "Exploring strange holes that appear in the wall is the duty of your warriors, not you."

Inga jutted her chin to a defiant angle. "I'm not going to ask my people to do anything that I wouldn't do myself."

"See? Stubborn." Levet held up his hands in defeat. "What is the point of being the queen?"

"To lead."

"Bah."

Rolling her eyes in resignation, Inga heaved herself to her feet and glanced around the open meadow. In the distance there were a few trees and more empty fields, but they currently seemed to be alone in this section of the labyrinth. Levet didn't know if that was a good or bad thing.

"How could the minotaurs create a gateway into my castle?" Inga asked. "The shields should have prevented it from forming."

"The magic belongs to a goddess."

Inga widened her eyes. "A goddess opened the gateway?"

"Her servants."

"Oh. Why?"

Levet waved his hands in an airy motion. "Because they believe I am a god."

Inga blinked, looking as if she was certain that she'd misunderstood him. "Excuse me?"

Levet tried and failed to look modest. After all, it wasn't as if he was mistaken for a god every day.

"It is a very long and boring story," he said, hoping to avoid revealing the details. Inga wasn't going to be pleased when she discovered there'd been strippers involved. "But a seer had a vision that I would arrive and halt the darkness that is consuming their homeland."

"You?"

Levet scowled at the shock in her voice. "Why are you surprised? I am a powerful demon with many skills."

"Agreed, but you don't have a connection to the minotaurs, do you?"

Ah, her surprise was caused by his lack of a relationship to the bull-folk, not disbelief that he could be a god.

"*Non*, not that I know of."

"Then why you?"

"I am not certain." Levet shrugged, repeating the words that the minotaur had used to explain the prophecy. "The seer sees what she sees. Which is a lot of sees…"

"Hmm." Inga didn't appear to be satisfied with his answer, but she didn't press. Instead, she once again glanced around the grassy field. "Then why me?"

"The minotaurs had been spying on me. I do not know for how long." Levet shivered in outrage. It was creepy to think they'd been watching him to discover his various weaknesses. "They realized that you were important to me and that I would do whatever they asked to keep you safe."

Inga made a strangled sound, as if someone had punched her in the belly. "I'm important to you?"

Levet tilted his head, baffled by the ridiculous question. "How could you ever doubt it?"

"I..." Her words died on her lips as Inga tilted back her head. "What is that?"

"Nothing." Levet's tail twitched with impatience as he stepped toward the towering female. For what felt like forever he'd been waiting for Inga to admit that she cared about him. And every time some disaster arrived to interrupt them. "Tell me what you were about to say."

Inga's nose wrinkled, her expression distracted. "I smell vampire."

"*Non*, there is no one here but us."

"I smell vampire," Inga insisted. "And..." She sniffed again, her brow furrowed. "Is that fey?"

With a sigh that came from the tippy tip of his toes, Levet closed his eyes and sucked in a deep breath. A second later he opened them to send Inga a resigned glance.

"Fey and jinn. A mongrel." His wings drooped. "Why must stupid creatures be forever interrupting us?"

"We can finish this conversation when we've returned to the castle," Inga assured him.

Levet clicked his tongue. "That is what we promise, but something always interferes. Always."

On cue, the sky above them opened and two demons landed on the ground next to Levet. One was a tall, slender male with copper hair and the other was a blond vampire with amazing blue eyes rimmed with silver and a witch's mark carved into the center of her forehead.

Odd.

It was even odder when the female straightened and narrowed her gaze as she caught sight of him. Almost as if she recognized him.

"At last," she growled. "We have been searching for you."

"*Moi*?" Levet took a strategic step backward. That couldn't be a good thing. "Did the minotaurs send you?"

She frowned at the question. "Of course not. Styx sent me."

"Oh. Really?" Levet scrunched his snout. "Why would that oversize leech care where I am?"

"I don't think he does care," she bluntly admitted. "But there's a very large gargoyle perched in his garden that he wants to get rid of."

Levet was momentarily confused. Was his mother trying to hunt him down? She'd always wanted him dead, but she'd never gone to the effort of leaving the comfort of her lair. Then he abruptly realized that there was one gargoyle who might be looking for him who didn't desire to kill him.

"I hope it is Aunt Bertha," he murmured, reaching up to scratch his stunted horn. "Although I do not understand why she would be in Styx's garden. She detests leeches—"

"Save the chitchat," the male sharply interrupted. "We need to get out of here."

"Rude." Levet sniffed, sending the male an annoyed glare. At any other time he might have been curious why a jinn mongrel would be helping the leeches, and how they'd gotten into the labyrinth, but right now he wasn't in the mood to deal with the male's pissy attitude.

"This place is about to collapse." The jinn glanced up at the hole they'd been dumped out of before pointing a finger at Levet. "I don't want to be here when it does. Get us out of here."

Levet widened his eyes. It was utterly unfair that everyone expected him to save the day. He was not Superman, although he would look very fine in a pair of pantyhose and a cape.

He was just a tiny gargoyle.

"Why would you assume I can rescue you?" he demanded. "I was kidnapped and forced here against my will. *You* do something."

The two males glared at each other, neither willing to be the one to back down. At last he heard Inga mutter something about *balls* and *brains* beneath her breath.

"I can get us out," the ogress announced in a loud voice.

The jinn glanced toward the towering female. "Who are you?"

"Inga. The Queen of the Merfolk," Levet said.

The jinn released a low whistle. "That's the Tryshu?"

"It is." Levet puffed out his chest as he spread his arms. "Stand back and watch in astonishment."

Chapter 21

Ryshi had heard stories of the mighty Tryshu. There wasn't a jinn who didn't salivate at the dream of getting their hands on the weapon. Not only was it one of a kind, which made it precious to any collector, but it was infused with the magic of the ancient merfolk. Plus, the rumors claimed that it possessed unimaginable power.

Unfortunately, only the true leader of the merfolk could touch the massive trident.

Hurrying to stand next to Sofie, he wrapped his arm around her shoulders. "You should brace yourself."

She sent him a worried glance. "What's going to happen?"

"I have no idea." He grimaced, glancing toward their companions. He'd never seen anything like them. The queen, a towering ogress with tufts of red hair, wearing a dress that would make the fashion police scream in horror, and an undersized gargoyle with fairy wings and an attitude that was in serious need of adjustment. "And I'm guessing the odd couple are just as clueless."

"Hey, be quiet." Levet waved his arms in their direction, his commanding tone rubbing against Ryshi's raw nerves. "The queen needs to concentrate."

"No, I don't," Inga muttered, hefting the Tryshu in one hand as she pointed it toward a spot in the center of the open field.

Ryshi felt a tingle of magic radiating from the queen and caught the scent of an ocean breeze before a blinding ball of light exploded from the tip of the Tryshu. The power sizzled through the air, smacking into the magic that guarded the labyrinth. There was a weird screeching sound, as if the illusion was being ripped in two, then an epic explosion that sent them flying backward to land on the thankfully soft grass.

"Damn." Sofie jumped upright, absently brushing the grass from her jeans as she watched the distant trees shatter and collapse, like a sandcastle being destroyed by the rising tide. As they disappeared, Ryshi could see a rolling wheat field and an apple orchard. "What happened?"

Ryshi spread his feet as the ground continued to roll and quake beneath their feet. "I'm just spitballing here, but it's possible that she just destroyed the barriers that guard the labyrinth."

Sofie arched her brows, casting an admiring glance toward the ogress. "The Queen of the Merfolk isn't playing. I like her."

"Me too," Ryshi acknowledged. "She's certainly an original."

The gargoyle, however, remained annoying as ever as he flapped his ridiculous wings. "Oh no."

"Is something wrong?" Inga asked.

Levet nodded toward the impressive fortress that was built on a towering hilltop.

"This is the place I recently left. The minotaur homeland."

Ryshi swallowed a curse, watching as a drawbridge was lowered on the side of the fortress and a herd of armor-clad minotaurs poured out.

"We're about to have company," he warned.

A layer of ice suddenly coated the ground around them as Sofie stepped forward. "I can deal with them."

Ryshi moved to grab her hands, forcing her to turn and meet his worried gaze. There was no way in hell he was going to let her use her powers. Not when they caused her pain.

"No, Sofie."

Her expression was hard with determination. "Take the gargoyle and return to Styx."

He made a sound of disgust. "I'd rather stay here and have my mind fried. I just met the rodent and I already want to squash him."

"Hey. I am a gargoyle, not a rodent," Levet protested, holding up his fists as if challenging Ryshi to a boxing match. "And I dare you to try to squash me."

Inga clicked her tongue. "Not now, Levet."

The gargoyle pouted, but he readily lowered his hands. "He is very rude. Almost as rude as a leech." The gray gaze shifted to Sofie. "No offense."

Ryshi rolled his eyes. "Why on earth would Styx want him back?"

Sofie ignored the petty squabbling, squeezing Ryshi's fingers in a bone-breaking grip.

"You need to get out of here."

"I'm not leaving you."

She sent him a frown of frustration as the sound of pounding footsteps echoed through the air and the scent of damp fur made Ryshi's nose wrinkle in distaste.

"There's no need. I can deal with them." Inga interrupted their battle of wills, an unmistakable anticipation shimmering in her blue eyes.

She was clearly pissed at being trapped in the labyrinth and eager to have some revenge.

She was in the process of lifting the Tryshu when there was a warning tingle of magic before a female appeared as if being created out of thin air. At first it was impossible to make out anything beyond the glowing halo that surrounded her, but at last Ryshi could see golden hair and soft curves that were hidden by a silver toga.

"Halt!" the mysterious female commanded, lifting her hands.

Magic thundered through the air and Ryshi found himself frozen in place.

"I can't move," Sofie rasped, her features tense as if she was straining to free herself.

"Just relax," he warned.

"Do you recognize her?"

"Gaia," Ryshi said, watching as the goddess turned toward the minotaurs, bringing them to a halt with a sharp gesture of her hand. Then, wiggling her fingers, she lifted the largest minotaur off the ground, floating him forward before dumping him on the grass in front of her. "And she doesn't look happy."

The male pressed his horns to the ground, nearly losing the crown he had stuck on his head.

"Blessed Mother," he rasped.

"What's the meaning of this?" Gaia demanded.

The male cautiously lifted his head, staring at the goddess with a wary expression. "The meaning of what, Mother?"

"That." Gaia pointed toward the large opening in the sky.

"A perversion." The minotaur turned his head to glare toward Levet, who was blessedly silent for once. "We captured the gargoyle to close the hole, but he escaped."

Gaia appeared genuinely confused. "How could a gargoyle repair my magic?"

"The seer—"

"Sees the future, not the truth," the goddess sharply interrupted.

The male licked his lips, as if realizing things weren't going his way. "We were lost without you, Mother."

"Where is Stavros?"

"He..." There was more lip licking. And a drop of sweat trickled down the male's forehead.

Gaia's power pulsed through the air. "Tell me."

"He was banished."

"Why?"

"He insisted we open our homeland to invaders." A pleading whine entered the male's voice, his arrogance starting to crack beneath Gaia's fierce glare. "I had to protect your people."

"Protect." Gaia glanced around, a hint of disgust twisting her impossibly beautiful features. "You have imprisoned them."

"No."

"Look at them." She waved a hand toward the herd, who huddled together in fear. "You've taken the paradise I created and jealously guarded it until it began to decay."

"You promised us that the labyrinth was created to keep out the unworthy," the male desperately reminded her.

"Yes, the unworthy. Not every creature who seeks the peace of our lands is unworthy. How can new seeds spread and grow if they are hidden in the darkness?"

"We were safe."

"You smothered yourself until you began to fade from the inside out." The goddess tilted back her head, gazing at the hole in the sky. "My magic is dying a slow, painful death."

"Mother, please listen...."

The male's pleading words died on his lips as Gaia turned away and concentrated on a spot behind the minotaurs. Seconds later, the illusion once again shattered, this time revealing the filthy city where the minotaurs who had been banished were trapped.

Shouts of alarm could be heard as the minotaurs poured out of the colosseum to discover what was happening. No surprise that Commander Stavros was in the lead. He was the sort of demon who would take charge of any situation.

A smile of pleasure curved Gaia's lips. "Stavros, come to me," she commanded.

"No, he's a traitor...argh." The groveling male at the goddess's feet was suddenly flying through the air, landing in the orchard with an audible thud.

Gaia watched Stavros striding toward her before she turned her attention to Levet.

"Your relative has bartered for your freedom," she said. "Take your friends and go." The moss-green eyes narrowed. "And never return to this place."

Ryshi snorted. "I'm going to guess he's heard that before."

Levet parted his lips, but before he could further annoy Ryshi, power rushed over them, as vast as the breaking of a dam. It was like nothing Ryshi had ever felt. Warm and lush and scented with clover. A golden glow surrounded them, lifting them off their feet.

Then everything faded to black.

* * * *

Sofie couldn't sense the magic of the goddess, but she knew they were being transported away from the minotaur homeland. Thankfully, she easily recognized her surroundings as they were dumped out of the darkness onto yet another green patch of grass.

This one happened to be in Styx's garden.

Rising to her feet, she grasped her dagger and turned in a slow circle. There was no smell of minotaur or the weird stench of the labyrinth. There wasn't even the smell of gargoyle. Obviously, Inga and Levet had been sent to another location.

Which was fine with Sofie.

She was ready for some alone time with her new mate.

Turning to make sure that Ryshi was unharmed, Sofie muttered a low curse and moved to stand in front of him. A vampire was approaching.

"Finally," a male voice drawled as Styx stepped into the garden, his six-foot-plus frame covered in leather and his long black hair pulled into a tight braid. "I was beginning to fear you couldn't escape the labyrinth."

Sofie grimaced. Right now she didn't want to think about her time stuck in the maze. It was going to give her nightmares for years to come.

"I'm not sure we could have without the help of a goddess," she admitted.

Styx scowled. "A goddess? What goddess?"

"It's a long story."

Easily sensing her reluctance to discuss her adventure, Styx glanced around, as if looking for something. Or someone.

"What about the gargoyle?"

Sofie shrugged. "He was with us, along with the Queen of the Merfolk. I'm assuming they were returned to her castle. The goddess was definitely eager to get us all out of her homeland."

"What was Inga doing in the labyrinth?" Styx held up his hand, a shudder racing through his large body. "Never mind. It doesn't matter. As long as Levet isn't here and his relatives stay the hell out of my garden, I don't care where they are or what they're doing."

"No shit," Ryshi muttered, obviously sympathizing with the Anasso's distaste for the tiny gargoyle.

Styx narrowed his eyes, turning his attention to Ryshi. "As for you—"

"He's mine," Sofie interrupted, stepping until she fully blocked her companion.

"Excuse me?" The lights inside the mansion flickered as Styx's temper flared, but before the male vampire could punish Sofie for her defiance, his nostrils flared and his eyes narrowed. "Ah. You've mated the jinn. Interesting."

It was more than interesting, Sofie silently acknowledged. It was earth shattering. But only if she could convince her king not to toss him back into the dungeons.

"He saved my life," she said. "More than once."

Styx arched a brow. "You believe his debt is paid?"

"I don't believe he had a debt in the first place."

Styx stilled, as if shocked by her words. "Explain."

Sofie glanced toward Ryshi, who had wisely kept his lips shut. "Do you trust me?" She waited for his hesitant nod before returning her gaze to her king. "The previous Anasso trapped his sister in a magical container. That's what he's been searching for."

Styx made a strangled sound, glaring at Ryshi. "Why didn't you come to me and tell me what had happened?"

Ryshi folded his arms over his chest. "I had no idea if you were the vampire responsible for trapping her."

Styx snorted. "I have a pureblooded Were as my mate. Darcy would chop off my tender bits if I had a female trapped in a container."

That was true. Sofie had met Darcy and didn't doubt for a second the tiny female would punish anyone stupid enough to capture and imprison a helpless victim.

"We need to find her," Sofie said. "I assume the container must be hidden in the old caverns?"

Styx shook his head. "Actually, I emptied out the last of his belongings from the caverns a few weeks ago."

Ryshi lunged forward, almost as if he intended to grab Styx by the shoulders and give him a shake.

"What did you do with them?"

Styx hissed in warning, pulling back his lips to reveal his enormous fangs. As if the sword strapped across his back wasn't scary enough.

"Easy, thief."

Sofie carefully sheathed her dagger, trying to ease the sudden tension throbbing in the air.

"Please, Styx," she said in soft tones. "It's important."

Styx continued to glare at Ryshi, but he answered Sofie's question.

"I dumped most of the stuff in an empty cell in the dungeon."

Chapter 22

Ryshi held the plain wooden box in the palm of his hand, outrage still burning in the pit of his stomach.

"I can't believe it," he growled, kneeling next to the pile of objects that had been scattered in the center of the cell just two down from the one he'd been locked in for the past decade. "She was right next to me while I spent my days searching from one vampire lair to another."

Sofie kneeled next to him, her expression impossible to read. "You're sure that's the right container?"

Ryshi studied the polished box. He'd dug through the various artifacts, ignoring the rare and sometimes dangerous treasures until his fingers had brushed over the seemingly worthless box. He'd felt a tingle of recognition, but it wasn't until he'd broken through the spell that he was certain.

"Positive," he told his companion. "Now that I removed the disguise spell, I can sense her presence inside."

Sofie nodded. "Now what?"

"Now I release her."

Ryshi felt an odd flutter of nerves as he rose to his feet. He wasn't sure how his sister would react. Would she blame him for abandoning her? Maybe even want to punish him?

There was only one way to find out.

Grasping the top of the box, he broke the seal holding the lid closed and pulled it open.

Less than a heartbeat later, a curl of smoke rose out of the box, twirling faster and faster until a tall female with flowing black hair and eyes as dark as a midnight sky formed. She was wearing a sheer gown that revealed her soft curves and she had copper bands around her wrists and ankles.

Blinking as she tried to get her bearings, Zena gasped as she caught sight of Ryshi.

"Brother!" Throwing herself into Ryshi's arms, she gave a cry of relief. "I knew you would come for me."

Ryshi hugged her in a tight grip, allowing her familiar scent to heal the guilt that had haunted him.

"Always," he swore in a rough voice.

For a long moment they simply clung to one another, both relishing this long-overdue reunion. Then, blindsiding Ryshi, Zena shoved her hands against his chest, making him stumble backward.

"What took you so long?" Her dark eyes flashed with anger and her expression was accusing. "I've been in there forever."

Ryshi heaved a sigh. Well, some things never changed. "The same Zena, I see." His lips twitched with rueful amusement. "I missed you."

Zena's anger melted as swiftly as it had appeared. "I missed you too." About to put her arms back around Ryshi, Zena froze as she caught sight of Sofie. "Leech."

There was a blur of motion as Zena launched herself toward his mate, and with a burst of magic, Ryshi was shifting into his smoke form to wrap around his sister in a strangling grasp. Dammit. Why hadn't he realized that Zena would strike out at any vampire? She'd been trapped for years because of one of them.

"No!" He used his mental connection to communicate with the female struggling to break out of his hold. "Zena, stop this."

Zena narrowed her gaze. "You would protect that creature?"

"She's my mate."

"Who cares?" Zena was a typical jinn. She had no comprehension of what it might mean to be eternally bound to another. "I want my revenge."

"I won't let that happen," he warned. "Not even if I have to return you to that container."

Zena froze in shock at his threat. "You choose that...female over your own sister?"

Ryshi released his hold, shifting back to his solid form. Then, deliberately stepping next to Sofie, he placed a protective arm around her shoulders. He needed Zena to realize the price of hurting Sofie.

"She's my mate," he said out loud. He wanted Sofie to hear his words. "I will always choose her first."

The sweet scent of chamomile swirled through the cell, but Ryshi never took his gaze from his sister. Zena wasn't helpless. She could create enormous destruction if she decided to punish him.

Instead, she stomped her foot like a thwarted teenage human. "You haven't changed at all."

He met her glare for glare. "Neither have you."

"Are all jinn this immature?" Sofie asked in dry tones.

"Shut up, you," Zena hissed.

"Zena." Ryshi shook his head. "Sofie's right. You're acting like a spoiled brat and I'm reacting like an overbearing father." He paused, a wry smile tugging at his lips as he recalled their endless petty squabbles. He'd promised himself if they were ever reunited he wouldn't let that happen again, but here they were, repeating the same old pattern. "I spent years searching for you after you disappeared. I regretted telling you to leave the moment you walked out the door. I'm sorry."

Zena blinked, a portion of her outrage fading at his apology. "I'm…I'm sorry too. I didn't mean to cause so much trouble."

He removed his arm from around Sofie's shoulders and stepped forward to gently take Zena's hands in his.

"We both made mistakes. Agreed?"

"Agreed," she reluctantly admitted. "Although you made more mistakes than me."

Ryshi rolled his eyes. That was as good as he was going to get from the stubborn female.

"And you will always have a home at the Oasis."

Zena glared over his shoulder at Sofie. "With her?"

"Yes."

There was a short pause before Zena heaved a resigned sigh, clearly sensing she wasn't going to win that particular argument.

"Fine." With a shiver she glanced around the barren cell. "I just want to get out of here."

"Return to the Oasis. I'll contact the staff to have your room prepared." With a last squeeze of her fingers, he returned to stand at Sofie's side, gazing down at her pale, perfect face.

"What about you?" Zena demanded.

"I'll join you later."

Zena narrowed her eyes. "How much later?"

He dropped a kiss on the top of Sofie's head. "Probably much later."

The young jinn looked as if she was considering another tantrum; then, catching the warning in Ryshi's eyes, she instead tossed her hair and sent him a smile of pure challenge.

"Good. I haven't had a decent party in years."

Blowing a kiss in his direction, Zena shifted into her smoke form and drifted out of the cell. Ryshi waited until her presence had faded from the dungeons before he sent his mate a small grimace.

"I apologize for my sister," he murmured, turning to wrap her in his arms. "I guess that being locked away for years did nothing to tame her volatile temperament."

Sofie reached up to thread her fingers through his hair. "She's certainly going to keep our lives interesting."

Leaning down, Ryshi brushed his lips over her mouth. "Hiding in your mountain lair is sounding better and better."

Sofie allowed her fangs to lengthen, her eyes smoldering with a hunger that pulsed through Ryshi.

"As long as we're together."

"Together." Ryshi swept her in his arms, heading for the open door of the cell. "Forever."

Epilogue

Levet was on his way to the throne room when a golden-haired female attired in a sparkling gown appeared from one of the side corridors. Although she wasn't in her gargoyle form, he easily recognized his aunt Bertha.

"Ah. There you are." His relative sent him a chiding glance. "I have been searching for you everywhere."

Levet ignored the chastisement. He'd been returned to the merfolk castle beneath the ocean by the goddess, and because he had no desire to leave Inga's side, he'd stayed there. It wasn't as if he'd been hiding.

Besides, he was much more interested in how his relative had managed to catch him by surprise.

"How did you get in here?" he asked.

Bertha shrugged. "Hades opened a portal for me."

Levet clicked his tongue. "Inga is going to have to put up some sort of god-repellent around the castle. They keep opening gateways."

Bertha blinked. "Is that possible?"

"I do not know." Levet was instantly intrigued by the thought. Possessing a god-repellent spell would certainly be worth exploring. "Perhaps I should check in Jagr's library," he said, speaking more to himself than his aunt.

"Later," Bertha suggested.

"*Oui*. Later." Levet's wings drooped. "I promised Inga that I would not take off each time a new thought entered my head."

"Good luck with that," Bertha breathed.

"It is very hard," Levet agreed. He couldn't count on how many occasions he'd been prepared to flit away from the castle only to force himself to stay. "But Inga is worth the effort."

Bertha sent him a stern glance. "Yes, she is."

Levet tilted his head to the side. Over the past few weeks he'd heard a number of fantastic tales of how he'd managed to be rescued from the minotaurs. Most of them included the female standing in front of him.

"I am happy you have popped in," he said. "I was told that you attacked the King of Vampires and forced him to send his warriors to rescue me. And that you bartered with Gaia to ensure my safe return."

She waved a dismissive hand. "Something like that. I was worried about you."

Levet's heart warmed. "Thank you."

Bertha looked confused. "For what?"

"For caring." The words were simple, but there was nothing simple in the emotions that surged through Levet.

He'd spent his life being detested by his mother, mocked by other demons, and even enslaved because he was different. To have someone risk themselves to rescue him...

It meant more than he could express.

"We're family." Bertha reached out to brush her fingers lightly over the top of his wing. "We have to stick together."

"True." Levet nodded. He would do anything to protect Bertha. "Do you wish to see Inga?"

Bertha shook her head. "Not on this visit. I just came to tell you that I won't be around for a while."

Levet studied her rigid expression. "Is it time for your hibernation?"

"No. I'm going to spend some time in the netherworld."

Levet flapped his wings, his eyes narrowing. "Is Hades forcing you to go with him?"

Bertha made a sound of disbelief. "Don't be ridiculous. No male forces me to do anything I don't want to do."

Okay. That was true. He'd once seen Bertha rip a drunken troll in two when he tried to touch her wing.

"Then why?"

She turned her head to study the marble statue of Poseidon. As if she was embarrassed to reveal the truth.

"I've decided to get to know him better," she muttered. "Plus, I want to be close in case some brazen goddess tries to take advantage of him."

Levet was brave. In fact, he was the bravest demon he'd ever known. But he wasn't stupid. He wasn't going to press for answers his aunt obviously didn't want to share.

"Um...very well. I will miss you."

She turned back to send him a grateful smile. "As I will miss you. Take care of yourself, Levet." She leaned down until they were eye to eye. "And never stop listening to your heart. It's what makes you special."

Giving him a pat between the horns, Bertha straightened and turned to leave.

"Be careful," Levet called out.

She glanced over her shoulder, sending him a small smile. "Not a chance in hell."